HANK

Returning home has never been so dangerous...

Returning to her hometown was never part of the plan for Daisy Hughes. But after the sudden death of the grandparents who raised her, Daisy finds herself inheriting her family's farm in Bell Ridge, Texas. When she begins to receive anonymous threats demanding she sell her land, it becomes clear that not everyone is happy with her return.

If Daisy doesn't figure out who wants her out of Bell Ridge, and fast, her home won't be the only thing she loses.

Clarence County Sheriff Hank Porter is perfectly content going through life on his own. He's closed off, more than a little rough around the edges, and distant, but that suits him just fine. After his ex left him with no warning five years ago, Hank hasn't had any desire to explore a relationship with anyone else. That is, until Daisy Hughes goes flying past his radar gun one afternoon with tears in her eyes.

Struggling to move on from his past, Hank does everything in his power to stay away from Daisy. But as the danger surrounding her escalates, it becomes clear that he needs to step in and help. He can't stay away and let her be hurt...or worse. While the chemistry between them grows, Hank and Daisy must race against time to uncover the sinister force trying to destroy her life.

Will Hank and Daisy discover in time that in the heart of Clarence County, love is the ultimate lifeline?

HANK

MEN OF CLARENCE COUNTY

BOOK ONE

TILLY H. COLSON

GOLDFINCH & KEYS PRESS

For anyone who has ever felt inherently unworthy of love because of those who walked away, may this book serve as a reminder: your value isn't defined by those who left. Here's to resilient souls, discovering their own strength and love from within.

Author's Note

While Hank and Daisy's story is full of heartfelt happiness, there are also tough topics tackled within the pages of this romantic suspense.

These topics include: parental abandonment, stalking, assault with weapons, attempted sexual assault, mentions of past sexual assault, loss of parental figures, and kidnapping.

Please read with caution and above all else, remember your own mental health is important.

ONE YEAR AGO...

"Daniel, you're on highway traffic today." His deputy was about to argue, but Hank Porter didn't have the time. He held up his hand as if to stop the unspoken complaint. "It's that slowdown initiative the state is pushing. Got a problem with it? Take it up with MacDonough. He swapped shifts with Jones here, who can only be on desk duty right now. I've got just enough people to cover the shift assignments."

The coffee in his cup was cold. He couldn't even remember how long it'd been since he poured it, but it didn't matter. He drained the liquid from his mug and continued on with the daily briefing. The never-ending dull ache in his left knee made him wince as he shifted his weight to his other leg. The fact that he'd had to cut back on his morning run because of the old injury was probably making him seem even more aggravated than normal, but Hank didn't care. He had a job to do, and as Sheriff of Clarence County, his only concern was keeping the people who lived there safe. Got a gripe about the work assignments for the day? Too damn bad.

He dismissed the deputies and headed back to his office. After two hours spent looking over reports and swearing more times than he'd like to admit at the ancient computer he was working on, Hank was itching for anything to do outside of the office. Maybe he'd just take a walk around town and make sure the pie at the Main Street Diner was still as good as he remembered it being. Being sheriff required a certain amount of mingling with the public, and if he could sneak in a piece of pie while he was out fulfilling his duties, well, that was just a bonus.

His phone rang just as he finished logging out of his computer.

"Hank." The deputy's voice was an octave higher than normal, anxiety pushing through.

"Dan, what's going on?"

"Chelle's in labor. I guess she's been having contractions for the past couple of hours, but her water just broke, so the baby is definitely coming."

"Congrats, man. Listen, go get Michelle to the hospital and don't worry about anything else. I'll take over your assignment."

"Thanks, Hank. Sorry to do this to you on a day when we're short."

"Don't sweat it. Not like you could control it, anyway. Just take care of your wife."

"Will do."

A pain constricted his chest. At thirty-five, Hank had always imagined he'd have a wife and a couple of kids by now, but apparently fate had different plans for him. No, he'd been engaged four years ago, and thought they'd been happy and in love. That was until one day when he came home from work and found all of her things gone, just a simple note left on the kitchen table. He swore to never be in a situation where he'd be vulnerable to feeling that sort of heartache again, and so he gave up his dream of a family and a white picket fence.

Shaking the painful memories from his mind, Hank

grabbed his keys off the desk and his hat from the coat rack just inside his office door before strolling to the front desk.

"Hey Jonesy. Michelle went into labor, so I'm heading out to take over writing tickets for Dan."

"Got it, boss." The deputy took a sip of coffee. "You in on the baby pool?"

"Yeah, but I'm already out of the running. I guessed she'd go two days over." He shrugged. "Never thought she'd go a month early."

The deputy nodded in agreement. "I hope they're both okay."

"They will be. I'll stop by the hospital later to see if I can get an update." He tapped his fist twice on the desk and put his hat on as he strolled out of the building, ready to put the fear of the speed-limit gods into the residents of Clarence County.

———

"Daisy, I needed those focus group analytics done and on my desk three hours ago." This day could not get any worse. Daisy Hughes was trying her hardest to help her boss prepare for a big ad pitch that would happen later in the week, but the team fell behind and was now facing another late night in the office if she didn't get things back on track, and fast.

"I know, Shay, I'm sorry! I'm trying to finish printing the report now. I promise it'll be on your desk in the next hour."

"It better be! I don't need Ned screaming at me again." She rolled her eyes and walked towards her office, letting the door close a little too loudly. Emotions were high, Daisy understood, but her boss could be a real pain in the ass sometimes.

Daisy had worked at AdVantage Advertising Group for three years, one year as an intern during her senior year of college, and the previous two as an administrative assistant. AdVantage was an extremely competitive advertising firm in the heart of Dallas. Cutthroat might be a better way to describe it. But even after she received glowing reviews during her time as an intern, the only job she could secure after graduation had been as an assistant to Shay, who herself was a lower-level member of the company.

She'd been heartbroken when her degree and previous experience didn't land her a job actually designing advertisements, but after a good cry and lots of encouragement from her grandparents, she forced herself to walk into work each day with a smile on her face. Throughout the past two years, she organized meetings, took notes, fetched coffees and salads from different shops around the city, dropped off Shay's dry cleaning, and dreamed about the day when someone would finally look at her portfolio and help her move up in the company.

The printer stopped making its loud, electronic, back-and-forth noise, sending Daisy to her feet. As she scooped the paperwork off the printer, exhaustion hit her bones. With two large cups of coffee already circulating through her veins that morning, guilt churned in her stomach. Her penchant for living off of the hot, caffeinated beverage was nothing new, and she needed the fuel after only getting a few hours of sleep the night before. Her Grandma Pat had made her promise to take better care of herself so she wouldn't burn out before she'd even turned twenty-five. That wasn't happening. Maybe one day soon she'd learn to better balance life and work, but she knew that was a fat chance, seeing as how she wanted to move up in the company even more than she wanted the next cup of hot coffee.

Just as she was typing the password back into her computer, Daisy heard her cell phone ring. Shit! How had she forgotten to turn it to silent mode before getting to the office that morning? A bright red flush washed over her face as multiple people in the office turned in her direction. Shay wouldn't hesitate to reprimand her in front of everyone if she knew. Just another mark against this exhausting day.

Daisy made a mental note to treat herself to a bubble bath in the insanely small tub in her apartment and boatloads of wine when she finally made it home from work.

The phone in her hand rang again. Damn telemarketers about to get her in trouble at work. She'd known it wouldn't be her grandparents. They only called on the weekends. And that effectively left no one else. She was too busy for friendships and definitely way too busy for relationships.

Looking down at the phone before shutting it off, her breath crashed in and out of her chest as she read the caller ID: Clarence County Sheriff.

Her grandparents lived in Bell Ridge, Texas, and Bell Ridge was home to the Clarence County Sheriff's Department. What on earth were they doing calling her?

"Hello?" she answered quietly as she raced out of the busy office and into the hallway. She wouldn't be able to focus until she knew why the sheriff's department was trying to contact her.

"Is this Daisy Hughes?" A gruff voice on the other end of the phone asked.

"Yes, speaking."

"Ms. Hughes, I'm Deputy Carl Morris from the Clarence County Sheriff's Department. I'm calling about your grandparents, Pat and Joe Wilkins."

"Yes, what's going on? Are they okay?"

"I'm sorry ma'am. There was an accident on their farm this morning. They've been taken to St. Clare's Hospital in Bell Ridge."

The hallway narrowed, and the floor tilted beneath her wobbly legs. Pushing her back against the wall for some stability, she took in a deep breath and pushed through the initial wave of worry.

"Oh, my God. Are they okay? What happened?"

"I'm sorry ma'am. I don't have any more details than that."

"Okay, thank you, deputy. I'm on my way."

With shaking hands, Daisy ended the phone call. She needed to get back to her desk. She needed to gather up her things and get to her car as quickly as possible.

"Hey, I just dropped more files off on your desk. I need them organized and then filed away under the Wilmont project." Daisy heard Shay's voice, but it sounded like it was coming through a tunnel from a mile away. "Are you okay? You're really pale."

"My...grandparents. I have to go."

"What's going on?"

Snapping out of her daze, Daisy ran to her desk.

"Hey, what's going on?"

"Shay, I have a family emergency. I'm not sure when I'll be back. I'm so sorry, but just ask Jessica to file the reports. She knows how it's done."

Shay's toes tapped as she stood in front of Daisy's desk, effectively blocking her from leaving. "You cannot leave until your work for the day is done. There are only a few more hours, plus the small amount of overtime you'll have to put in so we are prepared for the presentation on time. You can leave after that. I'm sure everything will be okay."

She could not be serious. Daisy waited for her to give some clarification, to tell her she had misunderstood, but it never came. Shay just stood staring at her.

"I'm not staying here another second, Shay. My grandparents are in the hospital. I couldn't get the sheriff's deputy to tell me any information on the phone, and I now have a three-hour drive ahead of me to get to them. Get out of my way."

The words forced their way through her clenched teeth as she fought back tears.

"This will have to go on your annual review, Daisy. Don't expect anyone to look at your portfolio when you refuse to make work a priority."

The blood in her veins felt like it was about to boil. There wasn't time to have it out with Shay right now, but when she got back, she'd share exactly what was on her mind about continuing to work for AdVantage.

Daisy pulled her purse over her shoulder, held her head up high, and ran towards the elevators. Once out of the building, her heart pumped harder than it ever had before, propelling her towards her car. She wanted so badly to fall apart as she slid into the driver's seat, but there would be time for that later. Plugging her phone into her car's console, she set up the GPS to take her the fastest route home.

In a heartbeat, she was nearly three hours into her drive, her head aching from worry. She'd run through the same scenarios and same questions a thousand times since receiving the phone call. What injuries had they sustained? Would they pull through? Would she make it in time to say goodbye if not? Oh, the tears came even harder at the realization that she may not get to tell them thank you for all they'd done for her in her life.

Tears streamed down her face, quickly swept away by the breeze from her open windows. Traveling ten miles an hour over the speed limit, Daisy knew she could easily be pulled over for speeding, but she didn't care. She needed to get home. Back to Bell Ridge.

It had been nearly five years since she'd been home for any extended amount of time. A holiday here or there, a weekend back now and then to check in, sure. Her life was busy. First college, then her internship, and once she landed a job away from home, forget it. She couldn't take time off if she wanted to rise to the top of the company, as evidenced by Shay's insistence that she work instead of taking time off to check on her grandparents. Making it in advertising was all she ever dreamed of. Escape small town life. Run from the heartache and memories.

Now, at the thought of losing her grandparents, all that time away didn't seem worth it. Sure, it was a childish notion, but she just assumed they would always be around. What sort of accident had happened that both of them ended up in the hospital?

Daisy's Grandma Pat and Grandpa Joe were not just her grandparents. They had raised her since she was six years old, and her heart crushed in her chest all over again as she thought of all the beautiful memories she had with them. She needed to make it back in time to tell them thank you. How had she never gotten around to saying it? It wrecked her to know she always thought there would be more time, but that may no longer be the case.

How could she have been so naïve? Everyone knows you say what you want to say when you see the people you love because you never know when the last time will be. But it had seemed like such a heavy task, such a monumental thing to say thank you for.

They gave her safety and love. They made her feel wanted when her parents had just walked away. She needed to say it all, to feel the warmth of her Grandma Pat's hug, and hear a few of Grandpa Joe's wise words. What if she didn't get to, though...

No! She was going to make it. Daisy knew in her heart that they would hold on, they would wait. Now traveling fifteen miles an hour over the speed limit, she pressed her foot even harder onto the accelerator. She crossed into Clarence County without an issue and flew down the highway towards the hospital.

"Ten more minutes, you guys," she said. "I'll be there in just ten more minutes."

Flashing lights hit her rear-view mirror and a curse burst out from between her lips. Pulling over to the side of the highway, she prayed whoever this deputy was, he'd be lenient and let her go on her way, quickly.

"Ma'am." A gruff voice jolted her from her thoughts. "Do you know why I pulled you over today?"

Daisy took a deep breath and mustered up the courage to look up at the deputy. Except it wasn't a deputy. It was the sheriff himself.

She had heard from her grandparents about the new sheriff...Hank something, wasn't it? Grandma Pat had described him in great detail, and Daisy could see for herself that her grandma wasn't lying. What had she said?

"Daisy! He's drop dead gorgeous. Muscles on muscles and lord, is he tall! The finest man to grace Clarence County in a long time, that's for sure!"

She had heard her grandpa huff in the background, which got a quick response from Pat.

"Oh hush now, you old geezer. You know he's got nothing on you."

That had made both Daisy and her grandparents laugh.

"I heard he just got out of a relationship, so I've been chatting with him at church and telling him all about you! You'll have to come visit us soon so we can introduce you to him."

God, all she wanted was to hear them laugh one more time, to visit home and have them all in her business about dating and falling in love.

"Ma'am? Do you know why I pulled you over today?"

Daisy cleared her voice and wiped her eyes, gathering the strength to look up at the man.

"Yes, I'm sorry. I know I was going over the speed limit." Her voice wavered, but she kept her eyes clear of tears.

"Is everything okay?"

She knew he'd be able to tell that she'd been crying, and maybe that would help her explain her irrationally fast driving.

"No, Sheriff. I'm sorry. It's not." And then the tears flowed even faster.

"What's going on?"

"My grandparents were in an accident at their farm. I'm trying to get to St. Clare's before...b-before... well, before they..." and then she was lost to the tears again.

"Farm accident?" She watched understanding wash over him. "Pat and Joe Wilkins are your grandparents?"

"Y-yes. I'm Daisy Hughes. I'm their granddaughter. Do you know what happened? Or how they're doing?"

"I'm sorry, I don't. I didn't respond to the call."

Daisy nodded. She'd hoped he would have heard something that could help put her nerves at ease.

"Alright Daisy, are you okay to continue driving? If so, I'll escort you over to the hospital. Not twenty miles an hour over the speed limit, but fast enough. If not, we can leave your car here and you can hop into my vehicle."

She steeled her shoulders, breathing in deeply before answering.

"I t-think I'm okay to drive. No, I know I am. Thank you so much, Sheriff."

The sheriff did just as he promised to and escorted Daisy all the way to St. Clare's Hospital in the heart of Bell Ridge. Parking her car in the emergency room lot, she ran towards the sliding doors, waving at the sheriff before he could even get out of his vehicle. Her feet pounded across the tile floors until she reached the receptionist.

"I'm Daisy Hughes, my grandparents are here... Pat and Joe Wilkins. I'm their next of kin."

"One moment." The receptionist said coolly as she typed

the names into her computer. Her eyes went wide and the look on her face changed to one filled with compassion.

"They're up in the ICU, honey. Take the elevators to your left up to the fourth floor. A nurse there will be able to help you."

"Thank you." Daisy took off running. Her body moved in a blur, her eyes focused on nothing but her next step.

As the elevator counted up from the ground floor, she held her breath. ONE, TWO, THREE, and finally FOUR illuminated on the level indicator. The doors opened, and Daisy hesitated for a moment. No matter what, this next step would give her the knowledge of what was going to happen to the two people she loved most in this world. The smell of antiseptic hit her nose as she stepped into the hallway, the elevator doors closing behind her.

———

He had no reason to stay. Not really. Hank had originally told himself he needed to stay to check in on Deputy O'Connor and his wife, but within a few minutes of being there, he'd learned they welcomed their son into the world with no complications. Now, there were piles of paperwork he'd need to muddle through back at the station, and there would be questions about what happened today at the Wilkins' farm. But seeing their granddaughter's heartbreak, he just needed to know how everything turned out. He couldn't leave without knowing.

Not to mention, she was stunning. It had actually almost knocked the wind right out of him when he bent down to look into her eyes. They were sparkling like the star filled sky on a clear spring night, and he wasn't expecting her gaze to stir something so primal within him. He hadn't felt anything like that for a woman since before his fiancé walked out of his life.

Lord, why was he thinking about Anna? She hadn't wanted to give him an explanation for her leaving back then, and all it did was make Hank think he wasn't capable of having someone love him. It had shattered him in such a uniquely human way, but he'd never been able to put all the pieces back together. He'd dedicated himself to his work and protecting the citizens of Clarence County. And that's what he had to tell himself now. Daisy was just another citizen, or rather, her grandparents were, and he wanted to help her because of that. Certainly not because her rose-colored lips and faint blush had called to something within his own heart he lost a long time ago.

Feeling the roughness of his late-day stubble as his hand brushed over his face, Hank glanced at his watch. Almost eight. Visiting hours for the ICU were strict, and although they could allow for special cases, he knew most likely she would come down soon for the evening. He'd wait just a few more minutes to see. Sipping the same cup of coffee he'd been nursing over the past hour, Hank heard the elevator ding, alerting him to someone arriving back on ground level.

Looking from the seat he'd taken up for most of the evening in the small, empty waiting area near the gift shop, Hank swung his head around to see who had arrived.

Out stepped the beautiful blonde woman he'd met earlier that day. Her face was puffy, dark circles pooled under her eyes, and she looked dead on her feet.

"Daisy?" Hank gently said her name as he stood, watching her walk down the hall, tears silently streaming down her face.

She walked right towards him, but he might as well have been a ghost. She didn't see him at all. Reaching out to touch her arm, Hank called out her name again. But it was his touch that she stopped moving to.

Looking down, he realized just how much he towered over her. Her legs buckled beneath her and she collapsed down towards the ground, shuddered sobs piercing the surrounding air. Hank caught her, easily sweeping her body up in his arms, walking to the quiet lounge. He set her down in a chair, making sure she was steady enough that she would not tumble out when he moved. She needed something to drink or eat. It looked like she was seconds away from shock. When he sat down, her head fell forward into her hands and sobs wracked her body. A desire to wrap her up in his arms felt like it punched him in the stomach, but he knew better. Hank settled on just sitting beside her, hoping his presence was enough support.

"I-I'm so sorry," she finally said after a long moment passed between them.

"No need to apologize."

"N-no, I need to. I-I should have been able to keep it together. I d-don't even know you." She may not know him right now, but there was something in the way the emerald green flecks in her blue eyes sparkled that made him want to spill every bit of information about himself, so they were never strangers again.

"I'm Hank. Hank Porter."

"Did you stay to give me a ticket?" She sniffled, trying to smile.

"No, sunshine. I didn't." His voice held steady, much to his surprise. Her cries had shifted something within him that he wasn't comfortable with.

Hank cleared his throat. "How are your grandparents?"

"They, um." He watched her pause, apparently trying her hardest to force down what he imagined were the burning emotions in her chest. "My grandpa passed away before I got here. I got to go in and say goodbye to him. But my grandma held on for me. I've just been there, holding her hand, and saying goodbye. She passed a little while ago."

Hank watched Daisy's hand fly to her heart just as a sob

escaped her throat. More tears fell, and he sat there, this time silently placing a hand on her shoulder.

"I'm so sorry, Daisy." Her breath came in jagged pulls, and he watched her turn a shade of pale he didn't know was possible.

"I c-can't breathe." Panic filled her eyes as she grabbed at the shirt that covered her chest.

"Here. Lean over your knees and just take slow, deep breaths." Hank pushed gently against her back until her head was in line with her legs. "Slow, Daisy. Nice and slow. It's going to all be okay."

"I d-don't think it will." More tears. More tugging in Hank's heart.

When her breathing finally evened out, Daisy sat back in the chair and closed her eyes. "I'm sorry. I haven't had a panic attack in such a long time. I just...this doesn't seem real. It's probably silly of me to say that. My grandparents were in their eighties. I just wasn't ready for this day."

"It doesn't seem silly at all. I think you're having a perfectly normal reaction to what's happened." Hank watched a small smile form on her lips and his heart skipped a beat. What the hell was wrong with him, thinking about how attractive she looked when she smiled? She just lost two members of her family.

"D-did you stay this whole time?" Daisy asked, pulling him from his self-hatred.

"I wanted to make sure you were okay." He looked deep into her blue eyes. "Daisy, is there anyone coming to be with you? Or is there anyone you'd want me to call for you?"

Sitting up, she winced as if pained by his question.

"No. I have a cousin in Miami I'll call, but besides her, there's no one."

She really had no one to support her through this? No

close family? No boyfriend? It didn't feel right she would be left to deal with something so tragic all on her own.

"Are you feeling okay now? Maybe we should get you home." He stood and extended his hand out to her.

"Oh, yes, you're right. I s-should go to their house. Thank you, Hank—Sheriff. For staying and being here for me. You didn't have to do that, but I appreciate it."

"Well, I'm not going anywhere just yet. Come on, I'll give you a lift out there. I'll have one of my deputies drop off your car in the morning."

"I can't possibly ask that of you."

"You're not. I'm offering. And to be honest, Daisy, I want to know that you get out there safe and sound. You're not in the best condition to be driving."

She seemed to think over what he'd just said. A soft sigh filled the space between them before she nodded in agreement.

"You're right. I don't really feel like I'm in my body right now."

"Then it's settled."

The mechanical noises coming from Hank's vehicle filled the silence between them as he drove towards her family's farm. Daisy hadn't said a word to him since leaving the hospital, but that was okay. He was happy to sit in the silence, stealing the occasional glance to make sure she was okay.

"She wouldn't have wanted to be here without him, so in a way, I'm glad they went together. I just wish I had more time with them," she offered quietly into the silence as she continued to stare out the window.

"How long were they married?"

"Almost sixty years. I always teased them about making it to fairy tale years. You know? I think every little girl dreams of being the princess who finds her Prince Charming and lives to see their golden anniversary. They were actually together since they were both eighteen, but they didn't get married for a few years."

"That's really amazing. You don't see too much of that commitment around anymore."

"You really don't." Daisy sighed, her fingers twisting in her lap. "Did you know them? My grandma told me about you once, when you first took over as sheriff." He watched her cheeks flush and wondered what Pat had said to her about him. "I thought maybe you knew them, too."

"Oh yes, I knew them. They greeted me every Sunday in church. Pat brought me a pie every once in a while and bragged about the amazing granddaughter she had who worked in a big, fancy advertisement firm in the city." Before he could think, Hank reached out, using the pad of his thumb to wipe away the tear that had just escaped from Daisy's eye. The blush deepened on her cheeks and he brought his hand back to the steering wheel.

He spent the next twenty minutes sharing stories with Daisy, his heart soaring when he heard her laugh for the first time. The worry in her eyes faded as she took in just how loved her grandparents were in the community. Finally, he pulled his truck into her grandparent's driveway and parked in front of their porch.

Before she could protest, he was outside the vehicle, opening her door for her.

"Thank you for everything, Hank. It was so kind of you to wait at the hospital and to drive me home. I know it's probably all just a part of your job description, but I truly appreciate it."

"It was nothing. Our community lost two people who were very loved. If there is anything I can do, let me know."

She took in a big, shaky breath and lifted her eyes towards his. Placing a hand on his chest, he felt her resolve falter.

"Thank you. For the help this afternoon, for being here just now."

"You're welcome. Are you going to be okay?" He brushed his hand once more on her face, this time tracing the flush in her cheeks.

"I will be, eventually."

She stood on her tiptoes and kissed his cheek. He watched her pull away, embarrassment flaring in her eyes. Before she could land back down on the earth flat footed, Hank moved his arm around her back and pulled her into a kiss.

His mouth pressed against hers, feeling the soft, warm skin of her lips brush against his. For a second, he hesitated, but she kissed him back, this time nothing shy or unsure in her movement. His world exploded as his body burned for more. More contact. More closeness. More touch.

He was such an ass. Her grandparents were gone, and he knew she just wanted to replace the pain with something warmer than the ache of saying goodbye forever. He was taking advantage of the situation, of her grief.

This never should have happened. As fast as it started, everything stopped. Hank straightened and cleared his throat.

"I'm so sorry, Hank. I shouldn't have done that. I'll just be running inside now to hide for the rest of forever."

He couldn't help but smile as he tucked a wayward strand of hair back behind her ear.

"I should be the one apologizing. I kissed you."

"Well, um, in that case, I totally forgive you. Thank you again for your kindness today."

"Of course." Looking her over once more, Hank sighed and placed his hat back on his head.

"Goodnight, Sheriff."

"Goodnight, sunshine."

ONE

The air was crisp, and Daisy wrapped the checkered blanket tightly around her body as she sat on her front porch. As a child, she would sit on the porch swing with her grandparents, sipping hot cocoa and listening to them talk about the town's happenings.

She loved those mornings, and sitting there now, in the same spot her Grandma Pat would sit, made her feel closer to them. It hadn't been an obvious decision to give up her career to return full time to Bell Ridge. There were hopes and dreams that she left behind when she resigned from her job and packed up her sparse apartment nearly a year ago. But when she stepped back out onto her grandparent's land, onto her land, she'd known it was the right choice. The only choice.

She would have been out of her mind to not accept the inheritance of the precious farmhouse and land where all her treasured childhood memories were built. Daisy could recall hours and hours spent in the old-fashioned kitchen, making jams and jellies and baked goods with her grandmother. In fact, Daisy's brownies, now famous around town as her favorite thank you gift, were perfected with her grandpa as the official taste tester. Of course, he'd given his stamp of approval to every batch and variation she made.

There had been an overwhelming amount of grief to process through at the loss of her grandparents. They'd stepped up and taken care of her for nearly all of her life. That was even true in their deaths, and she never truly thanked them for that sacrifice. On top of everything, she never imagined they would leave their home and land to her, but they knew it was her home, too. Despite the option to sell the property and split the proceeds, Daisy and her cousin, Grace, agreed that Daisy should have the house and land with no financial obligations towards Grace.

Over the last several months, Daisy had been working hard to learn the ropes of taking care of a hobby farm. Her land included fields that needed to be planted, fruiting trees that needed to be pruned, and a small smattering of random animals that needed tending to. There had been many nights where she'd collapsed into bed, tears threatening to run wild down her face at the overwhelming amount of things she needed to take care of.

Her chest tightened with emotion as she stood, walking back into the house. It was time to grab her harvests from the root cellar and head to the farmer's market in Bell Ridge. Saturday was easily her favorite day of the week, not only because she usually sold out of her produce and could replenish her budget, but also because she got to catch up with her friends. It wasn't at all because of a sexy sheriff who patrolled the market. At least, that's what she tried to convince herself as her heart rate skyrocketed.

———

"Those are some real pretty flowers you've got this morning, Daisy," June Callum called out from across the market.

"Thanks, Mrs. Callum. Save some strawberry jam for me today, okay? I'll be over to pick it up after the market closes."

"Of course, sweetheart. Just make sure you wait until Aaron gets back here. He'll be thrilled to see you."

Aaron Callum, June's youngest son, was just a few years older than Daisy. As soon as Daisy had returned to town, the woman started playing matchmaker between the two. Aaron was handsome, but honestly, she just couldn't see him as anything more than a friend. She really couldn't see any man as more than a friend since she'd shared that searing kiss with a certain handsome sheriff.

"You are too much, Mrs. Callum." she replied, before turning back to her booth to appear busy.

This was Daisy's first season doing the farmer's market, and she had never felt so poorly prepared for anything in her life. Despite growing up on her grandparent's farm, her time in the city made her forget almost everything her Grandma Pat taught her about farming.

Daisy rushed to the market that morning, arriving thirty minutes late and forgetting her boxes of ripe strawberries. That week was going to be one of the best for strawberry sales. They had been perfectly ripe and sun kissed. Oh well. She'd just have to bake some pies this week and sell those at the farmer's market the following Saturday.

The farmer's market really was a beautiful sight to see. All her neighbors and other farmers in the area would set up booths with their produce, and as a kid she enjoyed stopping to chat with everyone as she checked off the items her grandparents were looking for that particular week.

She still vividly remembered the steam rising from the coffee cups on the vendors' tables during chilly fall mornings.

Looking at her booth now, she admired all the hard work that had gone into each precious flower and vegetable in front of her. Revitalizing her grandparent's farm had been difficult;

she'd known it would be. But Daisy underestimated it by about ten miles. The barn was falling down, and no one had tilled or cleared the fields in years. There also wasn't adequate shelter for the animals she planned to introduce to the land.

The grief of losing her grandparents threatened to bubble to the surface as she looked over her table of goods. Even with the missing strawberries, she felt proud of all she could accomplish each week. Maybe her grandparents were proud of her too, wherever they ended up on the other side of life.

"Hey, Daisy." Samuel Cooper, whose own family ranch was a few miles down the road from Daisy's, called from the booth next to her. Pulled from her memories, she turned towards the handsome farmer. "Looks like your hens are enjoying the new food."

"Hey Sam!" Daisy replied with a big smile. Her neighbor wasn't just a six foot tall, muscular and tanned rancher worthy of any woman's fantasies. He was absolutely one of the nicest people she knew. Sometimes, Daisy felt so overwhelmed that tears would stream down her face, and all it would take is one call to Sam, and just a bit of his knowledge and advice, for her to get right back up and start working again.

"You know, as soon as I tried that new blend you suggested, the girls started giving me twice the eggs. I really appreciate the help." Daisy walked to the back of her truck and pulled out a brown paper bag. "I baked up a little something to say thanks." She handed the bag over to Sam, who smiled as he looked inside.

"Are these your triple chocolate brownies?" She could see the excitement written all over his face.

"You know it."

"God, I hate my sweet tooth. These will be gone before the market is over," he laughed. "Thanks, Daisy."

"You better not be giving all your brownies to Sam!" Daisy

turned to see her friend Emma hustling down the street, coffee cups in hand.

"I wouldn't dream of it." She walked back to her booth. "I've got a container for you in the truck. Oh hey, is one of those for me?" Daisy looked at Emma's hands, a travel cup of coffee in each.

"You know it. My signature caramel macchiato. The secret is making the caramel from scratch."

"Oh, you are an angel!"

Local shoppers began filtering through the booths as the clock rolled to eight, so Daisy turned her attention to them while she and Emma chatted. She was nervous and excited at the same time about introducing some of her pickled products to the market. Her grandmother's pickle recipe had made a perfect base for her trial run with green beans, garlic, and even some jalapenos. If people were willing to pay a premium for a jar, it would go a long way towards helping to monetize the farm. She was woefully unprepared for how difficult a task that would be. Those pickled products could be a nice money maker for the farm, or they could be a failure. At least she could say she tried.

Boisterous laughs came closer to her booth, and she immediately recognized who they belonged to. Caleb Davis and Jackson Boone were a few years older than her, but Jackson had grown up in Bell Ridge and been a staple in her life for nearly a decade. Jackson even dated her cousin, Grace, the summer before he shipped off to boot camp. That's where he met Caleb. When they got out of the Army, Jackson convinced Caleb to come back to Bell Ridge with him and join the fire department.

"Hey guys!"

"Hey, Daisy. Wow! The booth looks amazing today." Caleb grabbed a jar of her pickled jalapenos and smiled. "Have you made this before? I definitely want to try these!"

"I think you'll like them. They turned out better than I thought they were going to. I'm not one for too much spice, though. I'm a bit of a baby."

"We'll remember to not put you down as a potential judge for our five-alarm chili cook off," Jackson joked.

"I'm more than happy to enter as a contestant, but yeah, I don't think I could handle the heat of tasting more than my own."

The guys continued to look over her other offerings.

"Jackson, your mom was telling me you were just in Miami. Did you look up Grace while you were there?"

He smiled, but she could swear his face also flushed a bit. Jackson and Grace had been in love as kids, but something had happened between them and their relationship suddenly ended. Her cousin kept the details to herself, only revealing that her heart was shattered, and she had no desire to discuss it further. Daisy respected her wish and didn't push.

"No."

"There's a story there. You're not fooling anyone, Jackson," Emma chirped.

"Emma! Leave him alone. If he wanted to share, he would have. It's none of our business."

"When a very handsome guy friend of mine blushes at the mention of a woman's name, yeah, I want the details."

"Well, sorry to disappoint, but there aren't any details to share." His gaze remained on the basket of blackberries in his hand.

Emma sized Jackson up and Daisy prayed she would just leave it be. It was clearly not something he wanted to talk about. She hadn't meant to touch a nerve, and Emma had clearly made things even more uncomfortable for him. She needed to switch the topic all together before she let her awkwardness run wild.

"How are your parents settling in?" she asked Caleb. His

mom and dad had moved to Bell Ridge to be closer to their son after their retirement. It was such a sweet thought to Daisy.

"They love it here. I need to get them to come down to the market one weekend, but they are homebodies. I'm hoping they'll get involved in the community and break out of their shells a bit."

"Well, you'll have to take them a couple jars of my pickled goods and some veggies as a welcome gift. Here, I'll grab a basket and put it together before you go. Maybe that will convince them to come by next week and say hello."

"That's really kind of you, Daisy."

"It's nothing. But you do have to buy that jar of jalapenos."

Caleb let out a hearty laugh. "I wouldn't dream of not buying it."

"Good."

The guys, along with Emma, said goodbye to Daisy a few minutes later, and she fell into her normal market groove, bustling along to the steady flow of customers. Her breath hitched in her throat when she noticed a familiar face looking at her. Actually, staring at her would be more appropriate. And his gaze made her legs feel like jelly. Could he make other parts of her body feel that way?

She felt heat rise in her cheeks, sure he had just read her mind as a small quizzical look fluttered across his brows. Sheriff Hank Porter was one of the most delicious men Daisy had ever had the pleasure of looking at. He was tall, towering above her petite five foot three frame. And those muscles. She'd let him rescue her any day. She had an undeniable attraction to men who were protective, and Hank had shown his gentle nature on the worst day of her life. The romance books she read had nothing on the never-ending loop playing in her mind of his supportive hand on her shoulder as she cried. God, how many times since then had she prayed for him to hold her, just to not feel so lonely when she was sad? And that kiss. It had tipped her world right off its axis.

That night had apparently been an anomaly though, because the next time she saw him, the sheriff had been so closed off. She hadn't seen a single ounce of that tender compassion from the grumpy man since. Even though their paths crossed often, he barely said more than three words to her at a time. But she saw him watching, always keeping an eye on her.

Daisy never understood how someone so good looking could be so oblivious to all the women in town drooling all over him, but Hank was just that. Or, at least, he pretended to be. And he certainly never acted like he knew her deep, dark thoughts about him. If he did, she'd probably die from embarrassment right at his feet.

Oh shit. He was walking towards her now, still with that questioning look on his face.

"Hey Sheriff, how's it going today?" Daisy tried to sound aloof and not like she had just been imagining watching him change out of the weekend clothes he was currently sporting and back into his uniform. God, that black T-shirt fit him in all the right ways, hugging every damn muscle on his arms and chest.

"Good." One-word answer, so typical. She worked overtime to not roll her eyes.

"Are you off duty today? I can't remember seeing you out of your uniform before." His raised eyebrow and slight turn up of his lips had her blushing at how poorly she had phrased that.

"I just meant here at the market." She cleared her throat, hoping he wouldn't notice the blush rising in her cheeks. "Do you have today off?"

"Yes." The one-word answer had her grinding her molars together.

"Okay. Well, I hope it's a nice day off for you."

Daisy stood looking at Hank, her smile slowly falling as the seconds passed by. He looked as if he was going to turn away, but much to her surprise, he took three steps closer. He was close enough now that she could smell his...what was it? Aftershave? Cologne? Whatever it was, it was glorious. Masculine, woodsy, it seared into her thoughts and turned them from the family friendly farmer's market to her bedroom after dark.

"I know the anniversary is coming up soon. I just wanted to say I am truly sorry about your grandparents and I hope you're doing okay." She watched his piercing gaze shift as she registered what he had said.

"Oh, um, thank you." Her palms began to sweat. It was still so hard for her to talk about them. But with Hank, he was there when she'd lost everything, and then she'd lost him too. Not that she'd had him for more than a single kiss, but it still felt like a loss to her. She suddenly felt very exposed. "It's been hard being here without them."

"I can imagine. Good luck with the market today." He walked away, leaving her wondering what in the world that was actually all about.

———

God, she was beautiful. He'd thought about her every damn day since they'd shared that kiss. It'd been stupid of him to stick around the hospital that night, waiting for her to come out with news about her grandparents. He'd known the accident had been bad, though, and figured she didn't have anyone else around. When Daisy crumbled to the ground in front of him, scooping her up and comforting her while she cried hadn't been the only thing he wanted to do with her. And for that, he was a bastard. He was nearly ten years older than her. He had no business thinking anything about her other than making sure she was safe, just like every other citizen in Clarence County.

Watching her laugh with Jackson and Caleb had stirred something up in his chest. He wanted her to laugh with him. To catch up about things that had happened over the week and have her pure happiness fill his heart. But all he could manage was to bring up the one subject that made her look like she was about to burst into tears.

Hank shoved his hands into his pockets and made his way back toward his friend, who was busy looking at him with a stupid ass grin on his face.

"Uh, what was that all about?" Dr. Jacob Rahni had been the first friend he'd made when he moved to Bell Ridge. His ex had wanted to live near her parents and Hank thought he was giving her a grand gesture, but apparently all it did was give her the strength to leave him.

"What do you mean?"

"What I mean is, I think that was the first time I've ever seen you go out of your way to talk to anyone in town."

Hank glared at Jake, who genuinely looked shocked.

"I talk to you all the time."

"Yeah, but we're friends. And it took me a long fucking time to chip away at your grumpy exterior and wiggle my way into your heart."

He tried to stifle his laugh.

"I'll just let you keep thinking you're in my heart."

"Oh, no thinking necessary. I know I'm there. Stop trying to distract me with talks of your undying love for our friendship. What's going on with you and Daisy?"

Well, if that wasn't the million dollar question. What was going on? Nothing really, aside from the fact that he found himself thinking back every time he saw her to that red-hot kiss they'd shared when he'd taken advantage of her pain. And then, after a few minutes of sitting in that lustful heat, he'd feel the overwhelming hate and guilt for what he'd done wash over him, reminding him why he needed to stay away.

"Nothing. I just know she's thinking of her grandparents. The anniversary of their accident is coming up soon, and it was hard for her, losing them. Just figured I'd say something."

"Maybe that icy heart of yours is melting. I didn't know if that would ever happen."

"Yeah, yeah. It was one friendly comment. Don't start making wedding plans for us."

Why had he said that? Now he was going to have to figure out a way to get the image of Daisy in a white dress out of his mind.

"Too late. I've already got the venue booked, and how do you feel about going out of the country for a honeymoon?"

"I'd rather shoot myself in my foot."

"Noted."

"Alright, are you ready to get out of here?"

"No way, I've got wingman work to do! You go toddle off somewhere so I can go sing your praises to a beautiful woman."

Hank froze.

"Don't you dare," he growled.

"Fine, fine." Jake held his hands up innocently. "I'll just get my weekly stock of vegetables and be on my merry way."

"Good. If you need me, I'll be at the end of the block. I should check in with the deputies who are patrolling the market anyway."

Two

The past week had flown by. Sam kept his word and came over to help her make a repair to the chicken coop and the leak in her kitchen sink. She'd gone into town to hang out one night with Emma and her boyfriend, Steve. And her cold storage was full of yummy harvests from her garden that she knew would sell like hotcakes at the market in a few hours. It was going to be a good day.

She truly believed that until she saw another one of those damn notes taped to her door. It didn't surprise her, not really. After all, she'd been getting the notes about once a month since she moved back to Bell Ridge. They contained nothing original, just your unfriendly neighborhood notion that she should sell her farm and go back to the city.

At first, she'd been terrified, but the thought of bringing it to Hank or one of his deputies just seemed like a waste of time. There wasn't a threat in the note. Whoever was toying with her made sure to just phrase their message as a matter of fact. They felt she should leave. And after a while, she just stopped paying attention to them. Whoever it was could have their opinion. She was staying.

Daisy tucked the note into the pocket of her apron and headed back towards the barn to check in on her sweet cow, Maisie. It hadn't been a simple decision to add Maisie to her farm, but she was enjoying taking care of the sweet, soon-to-be-a-mama cow. She was looking forward to the calf joining them in the upcoming weeks, and really wanted to try her hand at making homemade butter and cheese once the calf was old enough to share Maisie's milk.

As much as she wanted to stay with Maisie and continue daydreaming about all her homesteading plans, Daisy needed to gather up the eggs from her chicken coop. The girls had a mean habit of pecking at her if they weren't fed and properly distracted before she attempted to get the eggs. It had caused her to be late more than once.

Lost in her own thoughts about the market and all the things she needed to remember to bring that week, she missed the feathers scattered across her yard. That was until she walked through something slick. Blood. Oh God, there was so much blood. But where was it coming from?

That's when it registered. The feathers. The blood. Her chickens! Three of them laid still, right next to the coop, and as she walked closer, the breakfast in her stomach threatened to come up.

Had she forgotten to close the coop for the night? Her eyes frantically searched the area around the coop for any sign of what had happened. Maybe a predator had been able to get to them? It wasn't unheard of for the area, but she was always so careful to make sure she secured the hens in their coop each night.

Then she saw it, the ax laying next to her hen, Gerty. Her heart shattered. Why would anyone want to hurt her hens?

While she should have been gathering eggs and getting

ready to head to the market, Daisy took the time to clean up the mess. Her face was puffy from all the tears she cried, and frustration was simmering just below the sadness.

She needed to talk to Sam. He'd recently had some trouble with local kids on his ranch. Maybe it was the same group of kids who did this. Luckily, she'd see him at the market.

Another half hour passed before she could finally start her truck up and get out on the road to the market. If she wasn't in and setting up soon, they wouldn't allow her vehicle to enter. She would probably have to carry everything in by hand, as they roped off Main Street after a certain point in the morning. Luckily, her booth was near the end of the street and shuffling things in by hand wouldn't be too bad.

Finally, she was on her way to town. Her mind wandered to Hank. She probably should run what had happened by him, especially when it happened on the same day she'd gotten another one of those notes. But what if she was just overreacting? She could handle a couple of kids acting out. Getting authorities involved might not be the best path to go down. She'd talk to Sam like she originally planned and see what he had to say. There would be time to talk to Hank, or a deputy, if anything else weird or upsetting happened.

Her mind snapped back when the truck sped up erratically, forcing her to grip the steering wheel tighter.

"Oh, shit," she whispered, pressing the brakes to the floor. But the truck didn't slow. And with every second, Daisy's panic grew.

Downshift and try to get the truck in neutral, Daisy. If anything ever happens with your brakes, pump 'em, downshift, and try to keep it on the road.

Hearing her grandpa's voice in her head from all the driving lessons he'd given her when she was sixteen, she took a deep breath and in the next instance, downshifted the truck, while still trying to get any response from her brakes. Nothing happened.

The road was about to curve around the Miller's farm, and she realized she was still driving too fast. Right as she hit the curve, the wheels caught the edge of the narrow road. Her truck bucked up onto its side and slammed into the ground, skidding into the ditch. Everything in Daisy's world happened in slow motion until the snap of her neck and the cracking of her head against the window slammed her into darkness.

THREE

"Hey, got any plans for the weekend?" Sam caught Hank right as he was walking towards Daisy's empty booth.

"Eh, you know, just the usual. Catching up on some chores around the house. I need to look at my hot water heater, too. It's only a couple of years old, but the damn thing just started acting up on me. Life of a homeowner, though, am I right?"

"Yep! It never ends."

"Is Daisy not here this week?" Hank asked as he pointed towards her empty spot.

"She was supposed to be here, not sure what happened. I talked to her a few days ago and I know she was excited to see how well her cut flowers would sell this week." Sam shrugged his shoulders, not seeming too concerned about her absence, but Hank felt a pit growing in his stomach. Daisy had been at the market every week, albeit sometimes running a little late. Those mornings were some of Hank's favorites. He'd see her hustling to get everything unloaded from her truck and into the booth while her cheeks burned bright red from the rush.

"It isn't like Daisy to miss the market. I tried to call her cell when I saw she wasn't here about a half hour ago, but she didn't answer," Sam continued. "I know she's been having trouble with her truck. Maybe she couldn't get it started this morning? I'll stop out after I pack everything up here and check on her on my way back to the farm."

"No, I'll head out now and check. Thanks, Sam," Hank said gruffly, turning and heading to his own truck.

"Sure thing, Hank. Let me know she's okay."

He tried to control his pace back to his truck, but his intuition screamed for him to move faster. Something in his belly was telling him that this wasn't just normal car problems, and he trusted his gut. The realization put him even more on edge.

By the time he was on the outskirts of Bell Ridge, Hank was driving faster than he should have been. He just needed to make sure that everything was okay. If something happened while she tried to fix whatever was going on with the truck, she could be injured with no help around. His mind was racing, thinking about what he would find when he finally made it out to her farm. She was probably fine and would be confused when he showed up. Would she be able to tell how deeply he cared about her?

No. This was something he would do for anyone in town. He took a deep breath to settle his nerves. While he might check on anyone, sure, he probably wouldn't be imagining every worst-case scenario possible. And he certainly wouldn't be worried about never getting the chance to tell them how he really felt.

As he pulled onto the road that led up to Daisy's farmhouse, he saw exactly what he was terrified of. Off the road, on its side in the ditch, was Daisy's truck. Produce was scattered all around on the ground, but he couldn't see her anywhere. Parking his truck a few feet from hers, Hank ran towards the ditch.

"Daisy!" he yelled, frantic to get to her.

As Hank pulled the driver's side door open, he saw her body laying limp against the taut seatbelt. Jumping into action, he dialed for emergency services while feeling for a pulse. Luckily, it was there when he searched, strong and regular. Just as he gave the directions to the dispatcher and placed his phone back into his pocket, Daisy stirred.

"Hey there sunshine, take it easy. Try not to move too much. I already called for an ambulance, so you just sit tight until they arrive."

"Hank? I-I don't know what happened."

"Shhh, it's okay. Doesn't matter right now, we'll get it figured out. I just need to make sure you're okay. Anything hurt?"

"My shoulder. I think it might be dislocated. And my head." She winced as she moved her uninjured arm towards her head.

A car door slamming shut registered in the back of his mind, but he was too busy watching blood slowly drip down the side of Daisy's face to acknowledge whoever it was. Shit, that cut would definitely need stitches.

"Holy shit. What happened?" Hank turned to see Aaron Callum running over. "Is she okay?"

Sirens sounded loudly in the distance, and Hank let out a sigh of relief.

"We need to do something, don't we? To get her out of there. She looks pretty banged up."

Hank stood up tall and stepped towards Aaron. "You need to step back. I've got this handled, and you saying things like that isn't helpful. Now, go back to your car and flag down the ambulance when it gets here."

"Yeah, no. Sorry. Of course." What a bumbling idiot. At least he'd listened to Hank's directions.

"Hank?" Daisy called out.

"I'm right here, sunshine."

All the color had drained from her face. "Can you help me get out?" Her breathing sounded erratic and labored. His mind jumped back to the night at the hospital, when she'd mentioned her history of panic attacks. "I don't do so well when I feel trapped somewhere."

"I don't want to move you until the rescue guys get here, just in case there is an injury I can't see. I'm sorry, Daisy. Just focus on me. I can hear the ambulance coming now. It won't be too much longer."

"I tried to stop, Hank. Honestly, I tried. My foot was almost to the floor on the brakes and nothing happened. I-I couldn't stop."

"It's okay. We'll figure out what happened. I promise." He watched her eyes grow wide. Had he seen fear just flicker behind the tears?

"What's wrong?"

"Do you smell gas? Or is that just in my banged up head?"

Hank's eyes focused as he checked under the truck.

"Definitely not in your head, Daisy. Change of plans. I've got to get you out of here. I'll try to be gentle."

It was all about risk versus benefit now. With leaking fuel, Hank couldn't take the chance that the fumes would hurt Daisy or possibly ignite, causing her to be trapped inside a burning inferno.

"Okay."

He didn't like how timid she sounded. She kept her left arm tucked into her side, inhaling sharply as Hank maneuvered his arms around her body.

"I'm so sorry. Just one more second and I'll stop moving you around," he whispered into her ear as he lifted her. Her only response was to place her head onto his chest, and fist her hand into his shirt.

He walked to a safe distance from the crash and then sat down, leaving Daisy in his lap.

"Daisy?" His finger tipped her chin up towards his eyes. Her eyes remained closed, her breathing still strained.

"I'm okay."

Aaron jogged towards them. "What's going on?"

"You need to back up."

"She's my friend, Hank. I just want to make sure she's okay."

"Do you have medical training?"

Aaron's eyes shot fire at Hank. He didn't care. Daisy was his only priority. "No."

"Then all you can do right now is maintain a safe distance from her truck, which is currently leaking fuel. The ambulance shouldn't be too far away. Now go back to your car like I asked and help flag them down."

Fuck. He didn't care if he came off like an asshole. The last thing he needed was for someone else to get injured and complicate the situation. Daisy was the priority. Looking down at her laying across his lap, his emotions flared at seeing how fragile she was in that moment. Her eyes had drifted closed while he was barking at Aaron, a new pang of fear spearing him through the stomach.

"Daisy, let's keep those beautiful blue eyes open, honey."

"Am I your honey?" she asked sleepily, fluttering her eyelashes at him as she tried her best to open her eyes.

"Well, you sure are always sweet as honey to me, even when I don't deserve it."

"Mmm."

Hank stayed with her laying in his lap while Aaron flagged down the fire engine and ambulance. Recognizing the crew, the relief of knowing Daisy would be in excellent hands washed over him.

"Hank." She stirred a bit, groaning.

"I'm right here, sunshine."

"I think I'm going to be sick."

"That's okay, if you need to be."

"I-I don't want to be sick on you. Can you help me?"

She shifted her body with his help and tears fell from her eyes as her body rolled through violent spasms.

"Okay, you're okay, Daisy. Just try to breathe." Hank rubbed tiny circles into her back.

"Hey, Sheriff. Daisy."

Hank looked up at the firefighters surrounding him. "Caleb. Tom. Jackson."

"You know, Daisy, if you wanted to hang out with us today, you didn't have to go through all this trouble." Jackson bent down and examined the gash on her forehead.

"You know me. I love the drama." He was pretty sure nothing could be further from the truth, but the fact she was joking helped ease the worry in his chest.

"Daisy, can you tell us what happened? Where are you hurt?" Caleb asked.

"The brakes went out on the truck. My head and shoulder got the worst of it, I think. But my chest and stomach hurt, too." Their eyes all roamed over Daisy's body and Hank had to stop his hands from forming fists. Their evaluation of her was medically necessary, he reminded himself.

"I think Daisy has a concussion. I didn't want to move her from the truck, but we started smelling gas, so I thought it was the safest option."

"Erica! Noah!" Jackson called over to the paramedics. "Hank, that was smart. Do you think you can lift Daisy onto the gurney?"

"I'll help." Caleb reached out for Daisy's legs, but Hank moved them closer to his body. He knew she'd have to be put on the gurney at some point, but she just felt so damn good in his arms. Plus, feeling her breathe against him kept his nerves in check. If he could feel her breathing, he knew she was okay.

When the paramedics arrived next to him with the stretcher, he stood in one graceful movement, never even jostling Daisy.

"Okay, Daisy, looks like we're headed to the hospital."

"I'll go with her." Aaron walked up to the ambulance, nodding at Hank.

"No. I'll be right behind." Hank was more than capable of making sure Daisy was okay, and he sure as hell wasn't about to let this creep near her.

"For fuck's sake. I'm her friend. I'm going to make sure she's okay." He ran his hand through his greasy hair and Hank fought to push down his anger.

He was about to confront the prick, but Daisy interrupted before he could speak.

"Aaron, it's okay. I want Hank to be there."

His heart clenched in his chest. He needed to take a deep breath. Daisy wasn't his to feel possessive over, no matter how much he wished she was.

———

Daisy's scream pierced through the air as the doctor manipulated her arm to place her shoulder back into the socket. Christ, the noise had Hank's stomach rolling. He knew she had been administered some form of pain medication, but the resetting had still caused her so much pain she'd cried. He was stuck in a small waiting room, pacing nervously while she got scans and had her shoulder fixed. The anticipation of hearing if she was alright almost crushed him.

"Sheriff Porter?" A nurse with gray hair and kind eyes called his name, snapping him out of his mind and into the present.

"Yes." He cleared his throat. "How's Daisy? Is she going to be okay?"

"We're just getting ready to close the wound on her forehead. She's been asking for you."

"She has?"

"Yes." The nurse gave him a knowing smile. "You can come with me, if you'd like. I'll bring you to her room."

"Yes, thank you."

When he walked into her room, the invisible band around his chest squeezed tighter. Seeing her lying there in the hospital bed, eyes closed and skin still so pale, made him feel sick. Of course, things could have been so much worse. He needed to remind himself that Daisy would be okay. She had to be.

The nurse gestured to a plastic chair in the corner of the room, and Hank sat down quietly. He would wait for the doctor to finish up with the stitches before getting up to talk with her. Just as the doctor was leaving the room, Jake walked in, nodding to Hank with a slight smirk before he began speaking to Daisy.

FOUR

"You were an absolute champ with getting that shoulder reset, Daisy. I know you probably don't feel that way, but I've seen grown men pass out when I've popped their shoulders back in before. How is the pain level now?" Jake asked.

She was lucky Jake had been working in the ER and immediately jumped in to take over her care when she arrived at the hospital. It had been nice to have a friendly face there when she was feeling vulnerable. Of course, Hank had been there too. But she hadn't seen him since she came back from all her tests. And that was okay. He probably needed to get back to whatever he was doing. She knew he didn't want to stay; he didn't care.

"So good. The meds are making me feel a bit loopy, though." She smiled and laughed, closing her eyes against the dim light of the room. Her head was definitely feeling the effects of her concussion. "You're really handsome, Jake. Are you seeing anyone?"

The corner of the room growled at her.

"You do seem pretty loopy there, Daisy," he chuckled.

"But loopy is better than in pain. I'll write you a prescription to help manage the pain over the next few days, too. You were lucky that the shoulder was just a dislocation and there wasn't a break, but I still suspect you're going to be pretty sore for the next few weeks."

Daisy grimaced in agreement. She tried to open her eyes, but lord, the room was dancing around her. How much morphine had they given her? She didn't enjoy feeling out of control, but maybe just this once, she would lean into the blissful release of feeling nothing.

"That didn't answer my question, handsome."

Another growl. Was there an animal in her room? She opened her eyes just wide enough to see Jake smiling at her.

"No, I'm not seeing anyone right now. Or at least, not seriously."

"Interesting."

"Are you hitting on me?" His smile reached all the way to his eyes, which were now darting between her and the snarling animal in the corner of her room. Maybe she didn't want to know what was over there. Best to just close her eyes again and rest. "Because I have to warn you, I'm not allowed to fraternize with my patients."

She could feel her face turn red.

"You're a catch, Jake, but doctors aren't really my thing. Now, law enforcement..."

"Daisy." Jake's laugh interrupted her train of thought. "As much as I'm enjoying this conversation, we need to talk about your injuries."

"Go for it, Dr. Handsome."

"Well, it's mostly good news. You've got some bruising across your chest and abdomen from the seat belt, but no internal bleeding. Those will clear up over the next week and you'll be sore. You've also suffered a mild concussion, which is a little trickier. You might experience some light sensitivity and nausea, even some dizziness and, of course, headaches as you heal. I know you want to get back to the farm, but I think it's best if you stay here, at least for a day, so that we can monitor you."

"I can't stay."

"Daisy."

Fine. She was going to have to get pushy with the handsome doctor and insist on her discharge. Although Daisy wasn't known for her backbone, she could stand up for herself with Jake and insist on her discharge. She could advocate for herself.

"Maisie."

Okay, maybe she could advocate for her cow.

"Who's Maisie?"

"I can't leave her alone at home."

"Daisy, who's Maisie?"

"My cow."

That got another chuckle from Jake and a sound, something like a disgruntled sigh, from the corner of her room. Why was the corner so mad at her?

She finally grew curious enough and opened her eyes again, moving them towards the opinionated corner. Oh shit. Hank was sitting there, arms folded across his chest. Clearly, he hadn't left.

"Daisy, I think you've got it backwards. You're more important, and if you have complications, your cow won't be able to help you."

"I'll take it easy. No help." Daisy winced as a pain ricocheted through her head, forcing her to lay as still as possible against the flat pillows of her hospital bed.

"I don't think you understand," Jake interjected. "Someone needs to be with you, at least overnight, but it would be best to have someone stay for a few days. With a concussion, you need to make sure it doesn't develop into something more serious. Having someone around to check in on you every few hours will give us the best chance of finding something wrong at the start, and not when it reaches a crisis point. Plus, you'll need to be in a restrictive sling for at least a week, and then limit your activities with the arm for another three to five weeks. That means no farm activities this week. You just need to rest and recover. I'm okay releasing you, but you need to either go stay with someone or have someone stay with you. Do you have any local family that can help?"

Daisy felt heat flush in her face, aware that Hank was now all but staring at her, waiting for her answer. She shouldn't feel embarrassed by the question, but she was. Her grandparents had been her only family. She wasn't sure where her parents were, or if they were even alive. No aunts or uncles, and only one cousin that she saw every few years.

"I have a cousin in Miami," she said. " But I don't think she'd be interested in coming up here. Her life is very busy, and very glamorous."

"Friends?"

Daisy giggled. She wasn't sure why the idea of her having friends was funny, but it was at that moment. Sure, she had Emma, but her apartment was above the diner and she was already living with Steve. No way Daisy could stay there, and no way Emma could stay on the farm when she had the diner to run. She was not about to crash with Caleb or Jackson, who probably had shifts to work over the next few days, anyway. And both Sam and Aaron lived with their moms. No, she couldn't be a burden to any of her friends.

"Okay, well, I think it's best that you stay here then, at least for the next twenty-four hours. We can reassess after that." Jake stood up from the short stool he was sitting on and rolled it to the corner of the room.

"Why don't you stay with me?" Hank offered, causing her to jump slightly at the booming timber of his voice. When she forced open an eye, she flushed, watching him stand with his arms crossed over his body like some pissed off Adonis. Maybe her concussion was messing with her vision, or the medicine was making her see things, because it almost looked like he was truly worried about her.

Daisy stared at him in disbelief. Feeling her mouth gape slightly open, she giggled some more.

"No," she whispered once she finally got herself under control.

"No?"

"I need to be out at the farm."

"Okay, well, how about I come stay out at the farm? I'm off duty tomorrow and that means I'm available to check on you during the next twenty-four hours. You can boss me around and teach me about the chores you need to take care of."

The idea of bossing Hank around was appealing, but she could barely stand the tension between them when they saw each other for two minutes at the market. How would she survive knowing he was in her house? She could already smell the familiar cedar musk that delighted her whenever he was near, and imagining that scent filling her house was almost too much to bear.

"What about cedar?" he asked, stepping closer to her bed.

Had she really said that out loud? The medicine was clearly going to get her in trouble. Why was she being forced to have a conversation when it was clearly best for her to not say anything?

"Uh, nothing. I appreciate the offer, but no. Thank you, though."

"Why? I know I didn't grow up on a farm, but I'm sure I'm up for the tasks."

Was he insulted that she'd turned his offer down? She was

giving him an out, which is exactly what she thought he wanted.

"Hank, you don't exactly like me. Wouldn't it be uncomfortable?"

"You don't know how I feel about anything, Daisy," he grumbled. "I'll be fine."

The pain in her head was overwhelming, especially after she nodded gently. Maybe things for him were more gray and less black and white than she'd originally thought. One night of having him stay at her house wouldn't be terrible. Even though it was early afternoon, she really just wanted to get home, crawl into bed, and sleep until the weekend was over.

"Well, okay. If you're sure. I would really like to be out at the farm. Thank you, Hank, I'll take you up on your offer. As long as Jake thinks that's an okay idea."

"Yeah, that'll be fine, Daisy. I'll get your discharge papers ready. Hank, why don't I go over some things to look for with you while we let Daisy rest for a minute?"

———

Hank closed the door to Daisy's hospital room as quietly as possible. When Jake turned and punched him in the shoulder, he had to stop himself from forming a fist and punching his friend square in the jaw. He'd have no problem messing up the handsome doctor's face.

"What the hell was that for?" Hank asked, moving the fisted hand over to massage his shoulder.

"What's going on here? Did something happen between you and Daisy in the past week and you just forgot to tell me?" Jake's words seared into Hank.

How he wished. If they were involved, Hank would have picked Daisy up for the market today in his truck. She would have been safe, and she sure as hell wouldn't be laying in a hospital bed recovering from a concussion and a dislocated shoulder.

"No. It's not like that. She needs someone, and I'm available."

"You know I can read you, right? I know you aren't saying everything. If I have to watch you fumble all over yourself at one more farmer's market just to say two words to her and run away like you do every other week, I might lose my mind."

"I'm going to ask Dr. Grantham to schedule you for every Saturday shift for the next year. Officially, as the sheriff. I'll tell him it's some undercover project you're helping me with and then you won't have to worry about me and my fumbling."

"Alright, easy there, tiger. It's just, I haven't seen you this worried about someone before. I know we don't talk about Anna, but I have the feeling you weren't even this worked up over her when she left."

"Daisy is not Anna." Hank grimaced at being forced to say his ex's name.

"Man, don't I know it. Look, you're my friend. And I just wanted to say, if there is something between you and Daisy, I think that's great. I just want to see you happy."

"Mmm. Well, it's not like that. I'm just trying to help. You saw how uncomfortable she was when you asked if she had anyone she could call to come for help, and she had to say no."

"Yeah, but it's not like you to feel any sort of obligation towards a random person."

"Drop it."

"Okay, but I'm here, man. If you ever want to talk."

"All I want to talk about is what I need to look for with Daisy's concussion and any restrictions I need to know about for her shoulder."

FIVE

“Gosh,” Daisy raised her hand to her head and closed her eyes, “has this road always been so bumpy?”

"Sorry," Hank replied. "I'll try to take it a little slower."

Silence filled the truck again. It'd been nice. Most of the ride was quiet, and Daisy fought to remind herself that anything she was feeling compelled to say was probably because she was under the influence of pain relieving medication. Spilling her heart to the man she'd been drooling over for the last year wasn't actually the best course of action.

But he'd been so willing to step up for her. He'd growled at the idea of another man being with her while she was recovering. Literally growled. She had thought that was only something that happened in her favorite romance novels, not anything that a living, breathing, real life man in uniform would ever do. And lord, if that sound hadn't made her feel bliss beyond anything the numbing medication they had administered her could.

"I don't understand, Hank." Oops. Why had her mouth just betrayed her mind? Now was not the time to have an extra boost of medicated courage for this awkward conversation while she sat in his truck.

"About what?"

"I'm the one with the concussion, right?"

"Yes." She saw him flinch and wondered if he was thinking about finding her in her truck earlier that morning.

"Well, why are you the one acting so weird, then?"

He laughed. A big, loud, genuine, from the belly laugh. Her mouth flew open. Surely she was hallucinating. Maybe she even needed to go back to the hospital.

"I think I'm dead, Hank. Or dying. Did you just laugh? I didn't even know you could do that."

"Why do you think I'm acting weird?"

"Because you haven't said more than two words to me at a time since...well...the night I came back to Bell Ridge. And now you've volunteered to come stay with me and wake me up every few hours to make sure I'm okay and look after my farm for me. I just don't understand why."

"You need help. I'm available." He sounded sincere, but Daisy still pushed.

"Why didn't you ever talk to me? After, you know."

His silence was deafening. She wished she could open the door and roll out of the truck, even at full speed, to get away from her embarrassment.

"Hank?"

"I shouldn't have kissed you that night, Daisy. You were vulnerable and hurting, and it wasn't my proudest moment. I guess, in a way, I'm hoping I can make up for it now."

"Oh."

"Oh?"

"Well, it's just that I kissed you back. I liked it. I enjoyed feeling connected to you. I liked the warmth that flooded my body when you touched me. I've spent the last year thinking there must have been something wrong with me that after it happened, you didn't so much as look at me for months."

She watched his eyes widen, looking deep into hers before turning back towards the road. Was that desire she's just seen in his eye? No, no, the medications were definitely throwing off her ability to read people.

"I'm sorry, Daisy. I took advantage of the situation and that wasn't fair to you. You had just lost Pat and Joe, and I didn't want to intrude on your grief. You wouldn't even look at me at their memorial. I thought you regretted what we shared that night. Or you felt like I took advantage of your vulnerability. Hell, I felt like I did. But that was my mistake, and now I'd like the opportunity to help you out and make up for it."

Her throat was suddenly dry as she watched the chords in his jaw clench while he waited for an answer. How was she going to survive the next few hours with this handsome man in her home?

"I mean, I'm pretty sure if I said no right now, you'd turn your truck around and drive me back to the hospital. So, the lesser of two evils, I guess." That answer got her an eyebrow raise from the sheriff, but no reply. And just like that, they fell back into silence.

"Don't you need to get stuff from your house?" Daisy asked as they pulled onto the road that would lead them to her farm.

"I asked someone to drop some stuff off for me."

"Oh. Who?"

"Are you hungry? When we get to your house, should I make something to eat?"

Daisy immediately noticed his deflection, but was too tired to press him on it. Maybe it was a secret girlfriend. She'd never seen him out and about with anyone, and surely Emma would have filled her in on any gossip about him dating.

She'd made the mistake of telling Emma about their kiss during the very first girls' night they'd had together. Daisy blamed the alcohol, but she'd really only had one glass of wine and had been desperate to share the story with someone. Squeezing her eyes shut, she finally admitted to herself that even if he was seeing someone, it clearly was none of her business.

"You can for yourself. I packed the fridge with a bunch of stuff I got from the garden but couldn't take to the market. Eat away. I'm going to go to sleep."

"It's almost dinnertime. Your body needs food to heal."

She reached her hand over to his arm.

"I'm good. Honestly, my stomach isn't the happiest right now. Not sure if it's the meds or just the accident, but I don't think I could keep anything down if I tried."

She watched a scowl shadow his face.

"You should have told Jake at the hospital. I'm sure there's some medicine that would help you not feel nauseous."

"No. I hate taking medicine as it is. I just need sleep."

By the time they made it back to her house, Daisy was ready to fall into her bed and not move for the next week.

"Let me show you where everything is."

"I can find my way around if you just want to head to your room."

"No, that's okay. Let me just give you a quick tour and then I'll turn in."

"Sure. Thanks."

Daisy led him from the living room into the kitchen.

"Please feel free to have whatever. Like I said before, there is a bunch of stuff in the fridge I had left over and it all needs to be eaten up. There's also a deep freezer full of meat out in the back sunroom."

"I'll be okay. Probably will just fix a sandwich or something and then crash, too."

"Okay, well, let me show you up to the room you can stay in."

"The couch is fine, Daisy."

"No way, Sheriff. I've got perfectly good guest rooms upstairs and that'll be easier for you than having to trek up and down the stairs when you have to come wake me up for Jake's scheduled check-ins."

"Okay."

Once upstairs, Daisy stopped outside the first door in the hallway.

"This one is my room. The next door is the bathroom you can use and you can pick which room you want to stay in out of the two that are at the end of the hall. The room on the left was mine growing up, so be warned, there are still boy band posters on the walls. Although, I'm not sure the other room, which was for my cousin, Grace, is any better," she laughed.

"It's all good. Thanks, Daisy. Do you need anything before you get some rest?"

"I'm all set."

"Alright, well, I hope you sleep well, and I'll see you in a few hours for a check-in."

"See you then, Hank."

———

Two in the morning. It was two in the damn morning and Daisy could not get back to sleep. Hank had last come in around midnight to wake her and check on her concussion symptoms, but she was fine aside from a small headache. It was his presence that had her all hot and bothered and wide awake.

That man had come into her room in nothing but his shorts and a fitted t-shirt and the shadows that graced his face made him look more handsome than normal, which she hadn't even known was possible. Maybe it was just her concussion playing games with her head and her heart. Whatever it was, she wasn't going to get back to sleep until her thirst was quenched. Settling for a glass of water, instead of the tall drink of water sleeping down the hall, Daisy picked up the empty cup on her nightstand and moaned at how sore and sluggish her body was.

Shuffling to the kitchen, a loud clap of thunder sounded directly over the house. She'd always loved stormy nights. The sound that the rain made on the fields outside her window had lulled her to some of the best sleep in her life growing up.

As the light over the sink turned on, she hissed at the pain that flitted through her head. She was clearly still sensitive to light. Just as she was turning the switch off, she caught the light spilling out into the yard behind the house. Daisy looked at the large tree where her swing still moved around in the wind. She remembered the day her grandpa had installed it, and how she played on it for hours, refusing to come in for dinner. Grandma Pat had to come out and pull her off when it was time for bed.

Had there honestly been a time when she thought about selling her home? It seemed like such a long time ago, even though a year hadn't even passed by. Her boss had called her in a panic after she'd sent in her resignation, but Daisy knew that there were eager new hires fresh out of college who would step into her position and blow it out of the water. She doubted anyone there even remembered her. After spending just a few weeks back in Bell Ridge, she knew it would be home forever. She would push aside the memories that haunted her and carry on the legacy her grandparents had started.

She felt the sip of cold water move down her throat and into her stomach. Yes, that was exactly what she needed to get her head and heart back under control.

Her eyes moved to the window overlooking her front

porch as she made her way back towards the stairs. She could have sworn a large creaking sound had just come from that direction. All the hairs stood up on the back of her neck and her breathing hitched for a moment. Had something just moved out there?

Taking a breath, trying to shake off whatever weird feeling had just come over her, Daisy pressed her body against the living room wall. Watching. Waiting for the wind to show her that all she'd seen was one of her hanging baskets moving; that the noise she'd heard wasn't from a footstep, but just the settling of old boards.

A streak of lightning cracked across the sky, and the farmhouse lit up. For a split second, everything froze in the light. Her eyes flew to the hulking shadow that remained in the window. A man was there, dressed in all black, looking in her front window. Daisy felt a scream bubble up from the depth of her soul as her glass tumbled to the floor and shattered.

Six

Hank was trying hard to fall asleep. He truly was, but Daisy kept flying into his mind. Thankfully, he'd been able to find her. He didn't even want to think about what could have happened if she'd been trapped in there and the gas leaking from the truck had ignited.

He definitely didn't want to think about how good it felt to hold her in his arms. He felt like a bastard. She needed help and all he could think about was how damn beautiful she was, and what it'd feel like to kiss her again, just like he did every other time he'd crossed paths with her. There had been something that night at the hospital, a spark he hadn't ever felt before with anyone else. Not even his ex, though he'd known for a long time now that they hadn't even really been in love. He was just going through the motions with her because he believed that was the right thing to do.

Anna was like a scorching summer day, burning anything that dared to move in the way of her path to happiness. Daisy was the spring sunshine that melted all the snow and encouraged the bluebonnets to come out of hibernation. Sure, there was some playful sass in her. But he always walked away from their interactions feeling like the sun had reached into his body and touched his heart.

And he was a bastard for thinking someone ten years younger than him would be interested. Even if she kissed him back that night. She was hurting, and emotionally compromised. Sighing, Hank ran his hand over his face. He was here to help her, not lust after her. He honestly needed to get a grip.

At the same time as he let out a groan, a flash of lightning lit up the sky outside his window. Not even a full second later, a scream ripped through the house and he was on his feet in an instant. It had come from downstairs, and his heart was in his stomach at the thought of something happening to Daisy.

As soon as he made it down the steps and into the living room, his alarm hit the roof. One look at Daisy, her pale face haunting the space, and he knew something was wrong. Gently touching her uninjured shoulder, he moved his hand down to grasp hers.

"What happened? Are you okay?" His feet were wet, and he realized he was standing in a mixture of shattered glass and water. He let his eyes run over her body, assessing for injuries. "Did the glass cut you?"

"There was someone on the porch," she whispered, never moving her eyes away from the window.

Hank turned.

"What do you mean? You saw someone out there?"

"Y-yes."

"Stay right here." He let go of her arm and started walking towards the front door.

"No!" He felt her body press close to his. "I'm scared."

Did she really want to be close to him to feel safe? That thought has his heart clenching. Grabbing her hand once more, Hank tucked Daisy behind his body as he opened the front door. A quick look around revealed nothing except a few tipped over planters, so he quickly shut and locked the door.

"Come on." The words came out a little gruffer than he meant for them to as he gently pulled her to the kitchen. They needed to check the back door. Someone could easily come through there if they were determined to get in.

Once satisfied that the house was secure, Hank turned on the floodlight for the backyard. He watched Daisy flinch and shut her eyes. Damn, he'd forgotten to warn her and that couldn't have felt good with her head.

Things were eerily calm, the only disturbance coming from the wind and rain. He scanned the fields until he registered Daisy's hand shaking in his.

"Hey, it's okay. Nobody's out there." He turned, studying the worried look on her face.

"I saw them, Hank. There was someone standing on my porch. They were tall, maybe just a few inches shorter than you, and had a hood up over their head."

"I believe you, Daisy. But no one is there now, and I don't expect they'd come back after hearing you scream like that. I'll stay up for a bit, though, and watch for them. You go back to bed."

"I need to clean up the broken glass." She grabbed a hand towel off the counter and walked back to the living room. Following close behind, Hank stopped her from getting down to pick up the pieces of glass.

"I've got it. You go on back up to bed."

"I think I need to sit up for a minute. All that adrenaline has my heart beating in my head."

His eyes flew to hers. How could he have forgotten about how all this would play out with her concussion? Of course she should sit down. Maybe he should even call Jake?

"God, Daisy, you should have said something before now." He grabbed her elbow and wrapped his other arm around her waist, helping her back to the sofa. "I'll go get you another glass of water. You tell me immediately if it gets any worse, understand?"

"Yes," she mumbled. He had expected a whole hell of a lot more fight than that, which may be why his own heart started pumping faster.

Quickly handing her a fresh glass with water, he tried not to hover, but as he picked up the shards of broken glass on the floor and cleaned the water up with the towel from the kitchen, he couldn't help but glance in her direction. Daisy was still pale and she was clearly deep in thought.

"How's your head?" he asked, studying her face for any signs of pain.

"It's getting better, thanks."

"Maybe I should call Jake?"

"I don't think we need to."

"But you had more pain, and he said if it got worse, you need to go back in."

"It's better now. It hasn't gotten worse and stayed that way. Honestly, Hank, I appreciate it, but I'm okay."

He'd send Jake a text just to ask. No need to worry her unnecessarily, but he wanted to be sure there wasn't anything more he needed to watch for.

"Alright. Well, do you feel like going back and laying down? It's pretty early to be starting the day, especially after getting a concussion. I'm thinking you need as much sleep as possible."

"I don't know that I can go back to sleep right now. I don't know if it's the adrenaline or just fear, but I don't feel like it's safe to close my eyes." She finally looked up at him. "What if they had gotten in here? What did they want? Would they have hurt me? Hurt you? There's nothing here that's valuable. Why were they looking in the window?"

Hank sighed, rubbing his hand across his chin and cheeks.

She needed rest, and he wanted to reassure her that nothing bad would happen as long as he was there.

"I'm not sure, Daisy, but we can answer all those questions later today or even tomorrow. Right now, you need rest. Move over a little." She moved slowly, tipping closer to the far end of the couch. Sitting down next to her, he wrapped his arm around her back. He felt her body melt from its rigid form as she leaned into him, her head plonking down heavily onto his chest.

"Is this okay? It's not hurting your shoulder, is it?"

"No, this is perfect. Thank you."

"Just try to get some rest. I'll be awake now. No one is going to hurt you."

He sat there, holding her, until her breaths evened out and lengthened. Hank tried not to focus on the feeling of her chest pressed into his side, or her warm hand laying on top of his stomach, but the pull he felt towards her was undeniable. What had he done by volunteering to stay here? To watch over her and make sure she was okay...it was too much.

Despite feeling the desperate need to gain some space and pulled at the same time to not be separated from Daisy by even an inch, he let his head win over his heart as he gently slid out from beneath her. Cold air swirled into the space where they had, just a mere second before, been touching.

The storm was gone, but the glow of the sun just below the horizon was still at least an hour or more away. Had the person come to harm Daisy? Could that person be involved in her accident? She had been adamant that her brakes were fine the last time she'd driven her truck, but they failed out of nowhere the day before.

Hank's gut instinct was telling him that the accident and the person on her porch were connected. But why? Nothing about the events from the last day added up in his mind. He knew one thing for sure, though. If Daisy was in danger, he'd do everything in his power to keep her safe.

SEVEN

Why was the light so bright when she still had her eyes closed? Slowly cracking them open, Daisy immediately wanted to force herself back to sleep. That accident had really taken it out of her. How was it possible she was feeling worse?

Forcing her eyes open, she recognized her bedroom, but had no recollection of walking back upstairs after the search to quench her thirst in the middle of the night ended with her cuddled next to Hank. She remembered so clearly falling asleep on him, his presence helping her relax. Had he carried her upstairs after? That thought, remembering the warmth that radiated off of him when he was near her, had her body sweating before she could remove the covers.

Expecting her head to pound as she set her feet on the floor, Daisy was pleasantly surprised that her body didn't protest. Her shoulder throbbed, and nearly every inch of her was sore, but the headache that had accompanied her home from the hospital was down to just a constant, yet dull, ache.

She couldn't help but smile as the smell of bacon tickled under her nose and caused her stomach to rumble. What time was it? She reached for her phone on her nightstand before realizing she hadn't plugged it in overnight, causing the battery to drain. Perfect. She'd just have to venture downstairs and see what Hank had been up to.

"Good morning, sunshine." He smiled as she walked into the kitchen and a flutter blossomed in her stomach. Whether that was from the sweet nickname he'd taken to calling her, his bright smile, or the delicious smell coming from whatever he was cooking, she couldn't tell.

"Sheriff." Her jaw was on the floor as she took in the scene before her. Hank was cooking in her kitchen. And not in a flimsy, incapable-but-trying way. This man knew his way around a stove.

"Like what you see?" He raised his eyebrow, clearly teasing her for staring.

"I just...I'm surprised, is all. Are you making omelets?"

"Yep. Hope that's okay. Your chickens are really mean, by the way. They almost pecked my hand off this morning when I went out to get the eggs."

Daisy laughed, before the memories of the day before filled her mind. She needed to find a time to tell Hank about someone killing her hens, but it could wait until after her rumbling stomach was filled.

"I wish I had been awake to see that. Did you give them anything to eat before you tried to collect the eggs?"

"No. Is that the secret?" His brows furrowed. "Makes total sense."

Hank cleared his throat. "How are you feeling this morning?"

"To be honest, I kind of feel like I got in a wreck yesterday." She smiled, but he just shook his head.

"How's your head?"

"It's the only thing that feels better this morning. I think you were right about the rest. Thanks for helping me go back to sleep after the whole creepy-person-on-my-porch situation."

Hank studied her for a minute before turning back to the stove. After placing the sizzling bacon onto a platter lined with a paper towel, he turned out an omelet and set both dishes down in front of her at the table.

"Do you need another pain pill for your shoulder?"

"No, it's sore, but I hate how they make me feel. I'll just take some Tylenol and call it a day."

"Daisy—"

"Hank, I promise, I'm okay. If it gets worse, I'll take some of the stronger stuff then."

"Fine," he said as he nodded toward the plate in front of her. "Eat up. You must be hungry after not eating yesterday."

"Thanks. I am. And this all looks amazing, but please don't think that you need to serve me. I can take over from here."

"Just eat, Daisy. I like to cook. It's no big deal."

She didn't even care that there was steam pouring off the eggs. Her stomach couldn't wait another second for a bite. It tasted just as amazing as it looked, and a small moan escaped before she could control herself.

Hank laughed.

"You approve?"

"It might be the most delicious thing I've eaten since getting back to Bell Ridge."

"Wow. That's a big compliment. I won't tell Emma you said that." He winked.

"Please don't. I'll never hear the end of that, and then you'll definitely have to take me back to the hospital for the headache I'll have."

Just a few minutes later, Daisy felt stuffed. As soon as she'd set her fork on her plate, Hank was up and sweeping it off to the sink.

"I'll get the dishes Hank, don't worry about it."

"I'm not worried about the dishes. It hasn't even been twenty-four hours since your accident. You should go back upstairs and rest."

"There are things I need to do around here."

"No, there's not. The only thing you need to do is tell me what needs to get done, and then go rest. Here, write a list of the chores for this morning and I'll start working on it after I do the dishes."

She sighed and picked up the pen, quickly jotting down the basic chores she worked to accomplish each day. As soon as she put the pen back down on the table, a pounding noise came from her front door, and she watched Hank stand. His eyes shifted from the front door back to her face.

"Were you expecting someone?"

"No."

"Stay right here. I'll go see who it is."

Why was her heart pounding in her chest? She still felt shaken from the accident and from the person who freaked her out at two in the morning, but she was almost one hundred percent certain someone who wanted to hurt her wouldn't knock before coming in.

"WHERE IS SHE?" Daisy heard the panic in her friend's voice before she saw her running through the house.

"Oh, my GOD! You bitch!" Emma's arms were around Daisy's chest in a warm embrace before she could even comprehend what she was talking about. She tried to hide the painful wince at being hugged so tightly. "Oh shit. Sorry. Probably shouldn't have mauled you like that. But how could you get in an accident, have to go to the hospital for treatment and NOT think to call me? Are you okay?"

That was why she adored Emma. So much fire, and so much love, packed into the body of this gorgeous woman. At first, Emma's friendship had been a surprise. Daisy was sure the woman, who looked like she should be in a magazine somewhere with her long, slender body and beautiful, sleek hair, would be totally insufferable. But Emma was kind and caring, and their friendship came easily.

"I'm sorry. I knew you were busy with the diner and I didn't want to be a burden."

"Daisy. There is so much wrong with that statement I don't even know where to begin. But let's skip that for now and say I'm very intrigued by who met me at the door. You replaced your best friend with the sexy sheriff? I guess I can't be too mad at that."

Someone cleared their voice from the doorway. Oh God, not just someone, but the sexy sheriff himself. Daisy might die of embarrassment.

"I'll just head out to start the chores, Daisy, unless you need help in here with anything before I go?"

"I'm good. Thank you. And really, you don't need to tackle everything without me. I can be out in just a few minutes."

"I've got it handled. The only thing you need to do is enjoy your visit with Emma and then go back to bed and rest. Make sure you tell her what you thought of breakfast this morning."

He winked before walking back towards the front door.

"Oh. My. Lord. Daisy!! I need to know EVERYTHING."

"Em. He's not here because he fell in love with me overnight and we've had a romantic tryst. I literally threw up on the poor man yesterday when he pulled me from my truck. I think that's the least romantic thing ever. He's just here because he feels sorry for me."

"Did you even see the way he looked at you just then? Like you were the most fragile piece of glass and it was his job to protect you? My panties almost melted off at the intensity."

"I'm sure Steve would love hearing that."

"I like Steve. I mean, hell, the man is living with me. But he doesn't look at me like that." Her eyes went wide and Daisy had to fight rolling her own into the back of her head.

"Em. He wasn't looking at me any certain way."

"You definitely have a concussion. How's your head feeling, by the way?"

"It's okay. On the mend."

"And your wing?" She gestured towards the sling.

"Sore. Definitely feels like my shoulder popped out of the socket and a very nice doctor had to shove it back in for me."

"Ouch."

"Yeah."

"Listen, babe. I'm trying to tell myself here I shouldn't be hurt that you didn't want to call me, but I'm struggling. You know I'd have been there in an instant."

"Exactly, Em. You would have had to close up the diner on the busiest day of the week. I know it's just been you working the front of house and Dave in the back cooking for a few months now. I couldn't ask you to lose out on your best day. Honestly, I wouldn't have called anyone. The only reason Hank volunteered was because he stayed to make sure I was okay at the hospital and Jake had to open his big mouth and insist someone be with me last night to make sure I was okay after the concussion."

"Oh, my god. Jake was your doctor? Damn, some people have all the luck. He's so freaking gorgeous too!"

"Emma!"

"What? I'm in a relationship, not dead."

"How did you even hear about the accident? I was going to text you this morning but left my phone off the charger last night and it died."

"Jackson and Caleb stopped in for breakfast this morning. They asked if I'd talked to you since *your accident* and I freaked out. Made them tell me what happened and took off like a bat outta Hell. Luckily, I told Dave to shut down the kitchen for a few hours and lock up until lunch so he wouldn't have to run the whole place by himself while I was gone. Although, it probably would have been hilarious to watch him try."

Dave Hines was fantastic in the kitchen, but had the inter-personal skills of a very sarcastic door knob. If she forced him to take orders, there would be customers who never returned.

"See! This is why I didn't tell you. You shouldn't have to shut down on the weekend for me. Honestly, I'm fine. I have half a mind to head outside and show Hank that I'm okay to take back over and tell him to leave."

"You really think you'd win that battle?"

"Well, he's leaving sometime today. Jake said I only needed someone around for a day to check on me and make sure my concussion symptoms didn't get worse. I'm fine, so I'm sure he's plotting his escape as we speak."

———

"Thank you for taking care of everything for me this morning. I really appreciate it." Daisy yawned as she sat on the couch curled up under a big blanket.

"You don't have to thank me."

"Yes, I do. It's your day off from work and you've spent it here taking care of me. I'd like to make you dinner before you head out, though. It's the least I can do."

His brows furrowed and his eyes tightened.

"What?" she asked.

"First, I'll make dinner." He paused, and she was sure he was waiting for her to argue. But she wanted to hear every-thing he had to say before chipping away at his defenses.

"And second?"

"Second, I'm staying the rest of the week." She knew her

face must have been giving away just how shocked she was because a smug smile spread across Hank's face.

"Jake said I only needed someone to look after me for the first night because of my concussion. There's really no reason for you to stay all week."

"I know you are hyper independent and don't want to lean on anyone because you can take care of yourself, but there is no way you're going to do those chores I took care of this morning with one mobile arm. I obviously won't stay if you are dead set against it, but I'd like to be out here to help. Jake said no farm chores for the week, and I'm inclined to say that you should follow his instructions unless you want your arm to take even longer to heal. I'll feel better going once your shoulder is good to go and you're not in the sling anymore. Besides..." Hank paused.

"Besides?"

He cleared his throat, running a hand over his jaw. "After what happened last night, I want to make sure no one comes back around. I'd like to think if they see my truck parked out front, they'll decide whatever they were up to isn't worth following through on. You should think about getting a security system installed while I'm here, too."

A shiver ran through her body. She'd tried all day to shove the fear she'd experienced the night before deep into the back of her mind.

"I'm going to go to my room for a bit. If you are sure that you want to stay, I'm okay with it. And I'll start looking into security systems tonight."

Daisy stood and walked towards the stairs. By the time she'd made it up to her room, her mind was racing with what she'd actually just agreed to. More Hank. More Hank, in her space, with his warmth, and his need to protect her, and his scruffy beard that made her wonder what it would feel like if he was to kiss the skin on her neck, her belly, her thighs. Oh lord, she needed to get a hold of herself. Or better yet, she needed him and his powerful muscles to get a hold of her.

She groaned, more from the idea of Hank being close enough to hold her than from the frustration that was overtaking her with struggling to get her shirt off for the bath she was planning on taking.

A sharp knock sounded on her bedroom door. She sighed and opened it, just to be met with the very sight she was trying to force out of her mind.

"Hey, is everything okay in here? I could hear you grumbling from down the hall."

"Yes." Daisy huffed, frustration brimming as she struggled to get her arm free.

Realizing she was struggling with her shirt, Hank chuckled.

"Here, let me help." He tugged the hem of the shirt down over her stomach, his fingers gently passing over her skin.

"I'm..uh...trying to take it off. I've been wearing the same clothes for over a day now and desperately need a bath. I fear Maisie might smell nicer than me at the moment."

"Oh. Well, I can still help." Hank stepped closer, reaching out once more to the hem of her shirt. "Here, I'll just lift it and you can slide your good arm out. Ready?"

This time, she felt the full warmth of his hands as he slid her shirt up and lifted it so that she could loop her arm through and take control of the garment herself. Daisy could feel the blush rise in her cheeks.

She was standing in front of Hank in just her bra. Lord, the heat of his gaze was so intense, she barely moved a muscle for fear she may burst into flames. His eyes were wide, scanning over the bruises that wrapped around her chest and torso. He lifted a trembling hand towards her skin, gently tracing over the marks with his rough, calloused fingers.

Daisy shivered at his touch, her skin dotted with bumps as electricity shot through her body.

"Daisy, these look terrible. Here, come sit down." A sigh escaped her lips as she realized he was touching her out of concern, and not desire.

"It's okay. Did you forget I was in an accident? Jake said there would be bruising."

"No, this looks awful, though. Are you sure we shouldn't be going back to the hospital? Maybe they missed something. Some of these are so purple they're almost black. What if there is internal bleeding? I should call Jake." He gently reached out towards the darkest bruise that angrily bloomed above her heart.

"I'm okay. It looks worse than it is, I promise."

When he didn't respond, she took his hand into her own and once again repeated, "I'm okay."

"Of course." He was back to being all business, dropping his hand back to his side. "Sit here. I'll get everything set for you in the bathroom."

"That's not necessary. I can run the water myself."

"Sit. I'm not asking."

She watched as Hank stomped into the bathroom, hovering over the tub for a moment before the sounds of flowing water met her ears. He stayed in there as the tub filled up, and after several long minutes, she heard the taps squeak into their shut position. Hank made his way back into her bedroom.

"Do, uh, do you need any more help?" He brushed her hair over her shoulder and she watched his eyes drop to her lips before settling back on her eyes.

Daisy couldn't help but smile at his clear shyness about the intimacy involved in helping her undress and drawing the bath. Perhaps the pink tint to his cheeks that normally wasn't there grew brighter as he thought about her laying in the warm water. Or maybe that was just what she was hoping he was thinking about.

"Ever the gentleman, Sheriff. Thank you for filling the tub for me, but I've got it from here."

"Of course. I'll just be getting dinner ready. Yell if you need anything." She had to stifle a laugh when he turned around and bumped into the armchair next to her dresser. Perhaps she wasn't the only one affected by their current arrangement.

EIGHT

“What do you think you're doing?” Hank's voice boomed through the kitchen the next morning.

Turning, Daisy's jaw nearly unhinged and fell to the floor. There he stood, feet away from her, glistening with sweat. His bare chest was heaving in and out as he wiped his face with a balled up piece of fabric. It must have been the shirt he was wearing on his run, and her mind wished he'd put it back on, even if her body wanted nothing more than to run her hands along the peaks and valleys of his exposed muscles.

“Daisy?”

“Oh, um...I thought you'd be hungry for breakfast when you got back from...” she waved her finger up and down at him, hoping he understood what she meant now that her brain was failing to produce the correct words for her mouth to say.

“You're not supposed to be doing anything strenuous. I would have come back and made breakfast for us.”

Daisy picked up an egg and attempted to crack it with one hand. Normally, she'd be able to handle it, but Hank's presence was an enormous distraction and she ended up with a shell in her batter.

"Oh, shit," she muttered.

"Here, let me."

Hank walked over and began scooping the bits of shell out of the bowl. Their hips were touching, heat radiating off his body in waves.

She needed to get herself together. He wasn't interested in her like that, and the last thing Daisy wanted was for Hank to think that she was some sex-crazed lunatic who was hopelessly pining after him.

"Honestly, it's nothing Hank. Just a batch of pancakes and breakfast sausages. I could whip this up in my sleep."

"And I can help." She felt his eyes on her. "How are you feeling this morning?"

"Sore. But on the mend. My head really is feeling so much."

"That's good." He looked into her eyes, and she knew he was reading her mind. "Don't even think that means I'm going to let you do farm chores today."

"Oh, let me, is it?"

"That's right. Seems I'm the only voice of reason in this house right now. Jake said no chores for the week. That's what you have me for."

"Hmmm. Well, I think I've got breakfast handled. You should go shower. No need to stink up our meal."

"I'll wait until everything is done cooking."

"Hank, I can handle pouring batter into a pan and flipping the pancake. It's all one handed operations, anyway. Besides..." she leaned in close to his chest and sniffed, feigning disgust. "You smell like sweat."

"Just because I smell like sweat doesn't mean I smell bad." He smiled, teasing her as one eyebrow raised in defiance on his forehead.

"That's true. You smell like sweat, but also like cedar and campfire. And a little like mint toothpaste, too." Her voice trailed off to a quiet whisper, pink heat rising in her cheeks.

Tipping her chin with his finger so her eyes met his, Hank stared into her eyes. The seconds that passed while she watched his eyes flicker to her lips and back up felt like hours of intense longing. Finally, he dropped his finger from her face and sighed.

"Off to shower, I go. At least now you don't have to worry about me using up all the warm water."

"So, how was your run?" Daisy asked as she forked another pancake onto her plate.

"It was good. I did about five miles, passed by Sam's place and said good morning to him."

"Oh, nice."

"Do you ever run that way?"

Daisy snorted and nearly choked on her mouthful of pancake.

"Oh, you're serious?" she asked when he just stared at her. "Uh, no. I'm not much of a runner. More of a yoga girl. You know, the kind where you just lay on the mat for half an hour in child's pose and contemplate life."

"So, napping."

A full laugh escaped as her face flushed.

"Yes, napping. I don't know if you've noticed or not, but I've got some extra weight and not a lot of extra time to dedicate to getting rid of it."

"I didn't mean anything by what I said."

"Mhmm."

"I mean it Daisy. I think you're perfect just how you are. I assumed you ran because of how toned your legs are."

The pancake on her fork froze in front of her open mouth.

"You look at my legs?"

"Only every chance I get."

Well, her appetite certainly increased with that revelation, only she wasn't hungry for breakfast anymore. No, something stirred within her belly, heating and churning her desire. As if he felt the electric charge he caused, Hank's smile fell and he cleared his throat.

"We need to talk about the accident."

Daisy cringed and sat back in her chair, dropping her fork onto the table.

"What more is there to talk about? I gave my statement to your deputies. I haven't remembered anything else."

"We won't have the full report for a few more days, but that doesn't mean we shouldn't be thinking about things. Especially if it comes back with conclusive evidence that someone tampered with your truck."

"I can't even think about that, Hank. What could I have possibly done to someone that they'd want to hurt me or worse, see me killed?" She reached out and pushed her plate away from where she was sitting.

"I'm sorry, Daisy. But this is important. Sam mentioned you've been having trouble with the truck over the past few weeks."

"Yeah, but like I said before, it was more like the battery was on its last leg. I had to jump it a few times to get it started for the market. Once it was running, though, I never had any problems."

She shuddered thinking back to just a few days before, on the morning of the accident. With everything that happened, she'd completely forgotten to mention the note she'd received to Hank. What if the person who was sending them had not only been bold enough to kill some of her hens, but they'd also tried to hurt her?

"You're thinking awfully hard over there," he said, looking at her with furrowed brows.

"I don't know if it's anything, but…" the taste of copper filled her mouth, and she winced, realizing just how hard she'd bitten down on her bottom lip.

"But what, Daisy?"

"Well, about six weeks after my grandparents died, I finally accepted that I'd be staying here and trying to make the farm life work. I woke up one morning and found an envelope stuck in my front door."

"Okay."

"There was a note inside that said I needed to leave. Like I said, I didn't think anything of it, other than it just being some prank someone was playing on me."

"Have you gotten more since then?"

Daisy looked at the hutch in the dining room that held all her grandmother's china. They never ate off of it, except for Christmas Day. Daisy would need to take it out more often. It deserved to be used and enjoyed. Her eyes drifted down to the drawer in the hutch, where the letters she'd received over the past year were tucked away.

"Daisy?"

"Yes. Several. Honestly, Hank, it seems like some kid is just trying to freak me out. But Saturday morning, there was a note. And then I found three of my chickens out by the coop. Someone had taken an ax to them."

"Jesus." Hank scrubbed his face with his hand and took a sip of his coffee. "Did you keep the notes?"

Getting up from her chair, Daisy walked to the corner of the room and opened the drawer. There, she pulled out eight envelopes and walked them over to Hank.

"Typed. Damn. I was hoping we could have done some type of handwriting analysis on it."

"It just doesn't make sense, Hank. I still think the accident was just that, an accident."

"And these letters? Your hens?"

"I just think someone is having a good laugh at my expense."

"Sunshine."

"Don't sunshine me, Sheriff."

"You are smarter than that, Daisy. These are creepy, and the fact that they haven't stopped is worrisome. You should have told me before now."

"Why would I have? Before the accident, you barely said two words at a time to me. I didn't want to bother you or anyone else with something that wasn't even an obvious threat."

"I'm sorry if I made you think you couldn't come to me with this."

Daisy just shrugged. Hank reached over, gently grasping her hand.

"No, Daisy. I really am sorry. If you felt unsafe, I would want you to tell either me or one of my deputies immediately. And that's true for anyone who lives in Clarence County. My actions, however unintended they may have been, made it less safe for you to live here, and I will do everything in my power to remedy that."

"I appreciate you saying that, but honestly, nothing ever made me feel unsafe until this past week. I wouldn't have brought it up to anyone, whether you were the sheriff or not."

"Then we need to talk about your internal risk assessment and situational awareness. Because these right here," he held up the envelopes before continuing. "These make the hair on the back of my neck stand up."

Nine

The most adorable surprise was waiting for Hank the next day as he took care of the morning chores while Daisy slept. Maisie's sweet calf had been born sometime overnight and as far as he could tell, everything with the newborn looked great. He was so excited to tell Daisy about it once he went inside.

Those last few days had been such a healing balm for his heart. He didn't want to admit how easy it was to spend less time at work than normal that week, because he knew he was going home to her. There was no longer an appeal to staying late and working overtime. In fact, he wished he had taken the whole damn week off. But that would have been a bad idea. If he was having a hard time restraining himself from telling her how he really felt just spending a few hours together in the morning and at night, he'd surely be incapable of staying quiet if they were together all day.

The previous night had been a perfect example. Daisy had bugged him for hours once he'd gotten home from work to let her make a batch of brownies, but he was still worried about her overdoing things. So, they compromised, and she sat in the kitchen, bossing him around with measurements and ingredient lists. He laughed so hard his sides hurt when she told him to turn around so she could add her secret ingredient in, but apparently she had been serious because the scowl on her face would have stopped any recipe thief in their tracks. Even though she hadn't been the one to stir up the batter, she still ended up covered in flour and cocoa powder. It had taken all of his strength not to pull her into his chest and let his fingers dust off her soft skin.

Hank returned to the house and made his way up the stairs to knock on her bedroom door. When that didn't get a response, he gently opened the door and walked in. She was snuggled under the covers like she was trying to hide from a snowstorm, and he chuckled as he felt the breeze coming in through the open window across the room.

"Daisy." Hank whispered her name, not wanting to startle her before the sun had even risen. Clearing his throat when she didn't stir, he called out to her again.

"Huh? Hank? What's going on?" Her voice was thick with sleep and confusion.

"I think I've found something you're going to want to see. Here, I grabbed your jacket. It's a little chilly out this morning."

Making their way down to the barn, Daisy's hand reached out and grasped his arm. He could see worry clouding her eyes.

"Hank, what is going on? Is everything okay with Maisie?"

"More than okay. Now just shush and enjoy this moment."

Swinging open the door into the barn, he watched Daisy walk to the cow's stall and freeze. There, laying in the hay, he knew she would see her sweet Maisie, newborn calf curled up next to her belly.

"Oh my goodness, Hank! She did it!" Tears spilled from

Daisy's eyes as she pulled him into a hug. It surprised him to feel tears pushing against the back of his own eyes.

"Congrats, Grandma. You've got a cute calf there."

Daisy's laugh filled the barn. "Wow, a grandmother at twenty-five. I never would have thought I could be so happy about that."

She stayed in his arms for a few minutes, the both of them just enjoying soaking in the beautiful moment.

———

"This barn needs to be cleaned up. My grandpa seemed to think this was a perfectly acceptable place to store a bunch of junk, but honestly, it's just getting in the way lately. I was in the middle of moving things around last week....but, well, you know." Daisy pushed an old wooden crate out of the corner with her foot. "Anyway, sorry if it's been a pain to get around out here."

"It hasn't bothered me at all. Why don't we tackle some of it before I head to work? Is there something you want to take care of while we're out here?"

Daisy thought for a moment. "Well, if you'd move those crates out, I'd have the space to move some things around in here to make it not so cramped."

"Sure thing. I'll put them just outside the door. Do not move anything on your own."

She smiled, holding up a hand in surrender. "Wouldn't dream of it."

A few minutes later, Daisy was sitting in the grass just outside the barn, looking through the crates. Hank walked out and crouched down next to her.

"Is this you?" he asked as he held up a weathered photograph.

"Oh my goodness, where did you find that?" Daisy gently plucked it from his fingers.

"It was just tucked in the wall there, behind some old rakes and shovels."

"Stay here on the porch, Daisy. Your dad and I need to talk to Grandma and Grandpa."

"But I want to come inside and play the piano."

"You can in a minute, sweetheart. Go see if you can find Banjo. That ol' hound is around here somewhere." Her grandma smiled down at her and then followed her parents into the house.

She ran down the old dirt path to the barn, right to the shade where she knew Banjo liked to hide. But the dog, who normally lapped up her love, wasn't there. Her little legs carried her up the hill, into her grandparent's backyard. She saw her favorite tree and the memory of her search for Banjo faded as the desire to climb overwhelmed her.

As soon as her hands touched the rough bark, her grip loosened, and she fell into the dirt below. She winced. Her hands would be scratched, and Mom wouldn't like that she'd gotten herself dirty. Standing up, she dusted off her pants. That's when she heard a car starting in the driveway.

Wondering where her grandparents were going when her mom and dad had just arrived for their visit, Daisy ran to the front porch. Only, it wasn't her grandparents leaving. Her mom and dad were driving down the road.

"Where are Mommy and Daddy going, Grandma?"

"Oh, sweetheart. You're going to be staying with Grandma and Grandpa for a while. Does that sound okay?" Her eyes were glistening with tears.

"Yes!" Daisy's voice squealed in a high pitch of enthusiasm. "But when will Mommy and Daddy be back?"

"How about we go inside and bake a pie? I think Grandpa

picked enough blackberries for one this morning. Come on, Daisy."

She cleared her throat. The memory sparked by the picture seared her heart with emotion.

"I think they took this the summer I came to live with Grandma Pat and Grandpa Joe. I was only six, maybe seven, here." Hank watched her eyes sparkle with tears.

"You were a cute kid."

"You think so? I look like I've been rolling in the mud here," She laughed as an ache settled in her chest. She had always been an energetic kid, never afraid to get dirty on the chance that she may be on the adventure of a lifetime. Maybe that energetic, adventurous streak was what her parents couldn't handle. "I think I look like my mom, definitely in the eyes and the smile."

"Why do you sound sad about that?"

"It's not so much sadness, as it is just an ache that comes up from time to time. It's really hard growing up without your parents. Especially when it's their choice to stay away."

"Have you ever looked for her? Or your dad?"

"No. And I don't think I ever would." Daisy sighed. "Grandma Pat became my mom and I have all the wonderful memories that I do because of her hard work. She didn't ask to take on a kindergartner when she was in her sixties, but she did it with a smile on her face and a homemade cookie in her hand. I miss her so much."

"Pat and Joe sure were something else. I still remember them dancing at every town block party. You could really see how much they loved each other."

"They sure did. They had that old time love, the kind you settle into only after growing together for a few decades. That's the kind of love so many people only ever dream of experiencing."

"It's hard to believe it's almost been a year since they passed."

Daisy nodded. "It still feels like yesterday I was in that fog of trying to figure everything out with their wishes and the farm." Daisy looked down at her hands. The anxiety of living up to all the hopes and dreams her grandparents had for the farm weighed heavy on her. Her voice was small, aching with emotion. "I hope I'm making them proud."

"Of course you are. You would have whether you stayed or went back to your old job. Your grandparents beamed any time they brought you up."

Her throat felt tight, and she tried to hide the tears that had flooded her eyes once again.

"Thank you for saying that." Her voice shook an embarrassing amount, and she cleared her throat trying to push down some of the raw emotion that overwhelmed her body. "I always worked so hard to be a good child, to be worthy of all they sacrificed. I hope it was worth it to them, to keep me when my parents just dumped me off like trash."

"Daisy..."

Her eyes remained trained on the hay scattered around the floor of the barn.

"Sorry. Didn't mean to trauma dump there."

Hank's hand gently found the underside of her chin and lifted her face towards his. She didn't want to look into his eyes. She wanted to resist the support she knew he was going to give her.

"That's not why I was saying your name."

She watched him study her, his eyes searching deep into her soul.

"You don't really believe that, do you?"

"That my parents saw me as trash? Something disposable to be left behind when I'd lost my appeal? Yes, Hank. I do. Why wouldn't I? The two people who were supposed to look after me, who were supposed to love me above everything else in this world, dropped me off to be a problem for someone else. What was so wrong with me that they could just say goodbye and not feel anything? I hate that I look like her, Hank. Because how am I ever going to be someone's mother one day when staring back at me in the mirror is the reminder of how much a mother can hurt her child?"

She couldn't sit there any longer and wallow in the hurt that threatened to pull her under for so many years. She set the photo into the trash pile she'd started and got up on her feet. Wiping her tears from her face, Daisy went back into the barn.

As she walked to check on Maisie, her foot caught on one of the uneven floorboards, and she let out a scream as her body careened into the wall.

Pain from her injured shoulder radiated through her body as sharp as a knife.

"Oh, god." Daisy forced out all the air in her lungs as nausea rolled violently in her stomach.

"What? What's wrong?" Hank ran into the barn, steadying Daisy with a hand on her waist.

"Ow. Oh, I think I'm going to be sick."

"Here. Sit down." He helped her towards a bench. "Head between your knees, and take some deep breaths."

Once she had the nausea under control, Daisy sat up slowly, grasping her injured arm by the elbow and whimpering slightly.

"I'm not usually this big of a baby about pain, but lord, I saw white and thought it might be my time a minute ago."

"You okay now?"

"I think I'll make it." She smiled weakly as he shook his head.

"We need to call Jake. How hard did you hit your shoulder? What the hell even happened?"

"I tripped on one of those uneven floorboards. Caught the

toe of my boot and I lost my balance. And as for calling Jake, absolutely not." He could glare at her all he wanted. She wasn't backing down. "It's just sore."

"I knew something like this was going to happen. I shouldn't have moved all the stuff around with you still out here. You should have gone back inside after you saw that calf." He raked his hand over his face. "Let's go back up to the house. Your time out here is over."

She wanted to argue with him. Honestly, it was her body, and yeah, that had hurt like hell, but it wasn't something she'd need to stay in bed all day to recover from. Knowing Hank, though, that was exactly what was about to come out of his mouth if she refused.

"Fine, but only because I need to go inside to call Sam. I have a million questions about Minnie and maybe he'll be able to come over and help calm my nerves now that she's here."

"Minnie?"

"The new calf. Her name is Minnie. Because she's a mini Maisie."

"Very fitting." He turned to walk towards the house, but Daisy grabbed his arm. When he turned to face her, his eyebrows met, questioning what she was about to say.

"Thank you so much for this, Hank. I'm glad I got to share meeting Minnie with you."

"Me too, Daisy. I'm glad I was here for this."

A half hour later, Daisy was on the phone with Sam leaning against the counter in her kitchen. Hank appeared in the doorway, freshly showered and dressed in his uniform.

"I'll be back by dinnertime. Don't overdo it," he whispered, as she waved to dismiss him.

"Yes, sir," she teased with a wink before returning to her call.

TEN

Hank had his work cut out for him. Between the kids they'd caught damaging some property in Bell Ridge the night before, their admission to being behind a slew of other crimes that were reported over the past few weeks, and everything set to come in on the investigation into Daisy's accident, he was scrambling to balance all the work on his plate.

"Hey, Hank?" Deputy Anderson stood in his doorway.

"Yeah, Mark. What do you need?"

"I have an update from Daisy's accident. They just sent over the final findings on her truck. Thought you'd want to see it first."

"Yep, I'll take it. Thanks."

"Do you want me to take over things with the Mitchell twins and their friend?"

"No, I can still handle that."

"You might want to reconsider when you see what that report says."

"Why?"

"I just think you'll be wanting to go out and let Daisy know what happened, is all."

Hank opened the folder and began reading the report. A pit of acid churned in his stomach.

"Okay, Mark. Take over the vandalism stuff."

"Sure thing."

Hank's head went into his hands as he continued to read over the details of Daisy's accident. Her statement washed over him, reliving the horrible feelings from finding her crashed off the road not even a week before.

The brake lines in her truck had been severed. The investigators concluded that the severing wasn't a result of age or wear. Someone had been trying to hurt Daisy...or worse. But it wasn't just that. The real reason Hank felt ill after reading the report was buried deeper in the paperwork. Further tampering was evident.

Daisy had sworn that the truck was speeding up erratically, which was initially why she noticed her brakes weren't functioning as expected. The accelerator linkage, which controls the engine's throttle and the vehicle's speed, had signs of recent alterations. Her truck really had been out of control, and there was nothing she could have done differently. Someone wanted to make sure she wouldn't survive that day.

Now, more than ever, Hank knew Daisy had seen the person responsible that night after her accident. They had come back to finish the job. Maybe his vehicle being there had deterred them? But what was keeping Daisy safe now that he was at work?

Grabbing his keys and phone from his desk, and scooping up the paperwork from Daisy's accident, Hank left his office.

Twenty minutes later, he pulled up next to Daisy's house, frustrated, thinking about everything the reports had revealed. Someone had deliberately made her truck unsafe to drive. And for the life of him, he couldn't figure out why. Daisy didn't seem to have an argument with anyone, ever. Well, aside from him.

The need to protect her overwhelmed him. Something, somewhere, had to be the key to unlocking why someone would want to hurt her.

As he walked to the porch, movement in the garden caught his eye. Turning, he immediately recognized the culprit. God, she was stubborn! As he scanned the surrounding area, his mouth flattened into an angry line and his jaw clenched. By the number of baskets that were filled with different harvests, she'd been out there nearly all day.

Slamming the truck door, he watched as Daisy's head whipped up from the patch of green beans she was tending to. Her sunhat caught and trapped the sunshine in it, making it look like a glowing halo was affixed to her head.

"Hey! How was your day?"

"What do you think you're doing?" He hadn't meant to sound so gruff, but his anger was boiling over.

"I'm working in the garden. Don't worry, I was careful."

"How long have you been out here, Daisy?" He scanned her arms, which were tinged with red, a clear indicator she'd been outside for more than a few minutes.

"Only a few hours."

"A few hours!"

"Calm down, Sheriff." She wiped her brow with her uninjured arm. "I needed to pull things for the market this weekend. You've done a great job looking after the garden, but I needed to harvest all this stuff before it got too ripe."

"Daisy, you needed to rest. Have you forgotten that five days ago you were in a car accident? Or that you almost passed out from the pain in your shoulder this morning after hitting it in the barn?"

"I'm not made of glass, Hank. I knew I could handle this. I promise, I didn't overdo it."

"Jake said no farm activities for a week."

"This hardly counts."

His legs propelled him forward. Gesturing angrily over the multiple baskets left in her wake.

"This is you, not overdoing things?"

She just stood there, smiling at him. No response, which he hoped was because she realized how in the wrong she'd been.

"Why didn't you call me? I would have come back early to do all this myself."

"You're already back a few hours before I was expecting you. But that's exactly why I didn't. You need to focus on your work, and I needed to get out into the fresh air and dig my hands into the dirt. Well, one hand at least."

Hank huffed. Turning from Daisy and the garden, he started walking away while pulling his phone from his pocket.

"Where are you going?" she called after him.

"I'm going to go call Jake. He's off today, so I'm going to see if he can't stop out here and shame some sense into you. I should have just done that this morning like I wanted to."

"I'm not some toddler that needs to be taught a lesson. You can't boss me around, Hank."

Turning back towards her, he took two steps in her direction. "Oh trust me, sunshine. I'm well aware of your womanly status." His eyes burned into her as they roamed over her body, and he delighted in the flush that rose on her already sun kissed cheeks. Even with the dirt smeared across her nose, she was adorable, which drove him crazy. "Though I do think there is a lesson or two I could teach you."

He turned and walked back towards the house in a huff. She could be so impossible. Fine, if she wanted to stay in the garden, she could. But he would do the work.

Lifting one of the rocking chairs off the porch, Hank carried it across the lawn and into the garden.

"I thought you'd gone inside." She had said it so quietly, and with her back turned to him, that he'd almost missed it.

"Look, you can stay out here as long as you want, but I'll be doing the work. Sit. You've already done too much for the day."

Touching her elbow, Hank led her to the chair.

"There's only a few things left to pick, and then I just need to move everything into the cold storage shed. You should go in. Honestly, Hank. I've got this. I'm not even feeling any pain."

Why was she so insistent on never letting him do anything for her?

"Sit. Down. I'm going to finish this up, and then I'll move all the baskets into cold storage for you. Like you said, it's not much, so you don't need to object to me doing it."

"Fine," she huffed as she sat down carelessly, bumping her immobilized arm on the chair. "Ow."

Hank lifted his eyes to meet hers. "You okay?"

"Yeah. Doesn't it figure I'd whack my arm the minute I stop doing work? Apparently I'm extra clumsy today."

"Mmm." Hank turned back to the garden.

"So, how was work?" she asked.

"It was work."

"Have you heard anything about my truck yet?"

He felt his muscles stiffen and his back became rigid. His heart lurched. On the drive out there, he planned on talking to her about the accident and what the investigation had officially concluded right away, but now he wanted to put it off for as long as possible. He'd been hoping to have more information before they talked about what the investigation had found. But maybe it was better this way? Maybe there was someone bothering Daisy that she hadn't told him about.

"Let's talk about it after dinner."

He studied her face and watched as her eyebrows knit

together, causing a crease between them that was pure concern.

"Get out of your head, Daisy. It'll all be okay."

"Okay, but why do we need to wait to talk about it?"

"Because I'm hungry and I can't think about anything other than your brownies."

He'd gotten a smile with that comment, and the line between her eyebrows went away. Mission accomplished.

"You should have told me before. I'll run up to the house and get you one."

"Sit. Down." His harsh tone stopped her just as she got to her feet. "I'll have one after dinner. If I start now, I may never stop."

"You know, Hank, you're an adult. If you wanted, you could just eat a whole pan of brownies for dinner. No one would need to know," she laughed.

"I take it you're an expert in this area?"

"Hey, I eat all my veggies, like a good girl, but yes. I've been known to eat dessert, and only dessert, from time to time."

His eyebrow lifted when she winked at him. God, this woman was infuriating and so damn adorable. What was he doing? Flirting back and leading her on. What an asshole thing to do. He was too old, too damaged for such a ray of sunshine.

"I'm afraid I'll have to start running ten miles on the weekends instead of five, and I'm too old for that."

Turning back to the bowl of blackberries, Hank lifted it and cleared his throat.

"This ought to be enough for the week, don't you think?"

"Yeah, that'll be good."

He walked to her chair, hunching over so their faces were mere inches away from each other. Lifting his finger, he dusted the dirt from her nose and traced the blush as it spread across her face.

"Good. You head up to the house and get cleaned up. I'll take care of all this and then come in and start dinner."

"Mhmm." Her eyes, bright and full of fire, didn't look away from his.

"And Daisy," he paused.

"Yes."

"Don't let me catch you doing this without my help again."

He watched the corners of her eyes squish in defiance at his demand. She didn't say anything after that. Instead, she placed her hand on his chest and pushed him away, standing and stomping off towards her house.

———

Daisy let her body sink into the hot water, and the ache that had been forming in her back over the last few hours relaxed almost immediately. She'd never admit that she'd overdone things out under the scorching sun for longer than she was originally anticipating.

The way Hank reacted to seeing her outside was both infuriating and so damn sweet. She could admit, even if only to herself, that she loved when he got mad at her for doing more than she should be doing.

This tension building between the two of them, however, was becoming unbearable. She was about to break. She needed relief, and there in the bath, she knew how to handle it.

Daisy settled down further into the bathtub, bubbles now tickling her neck and chin. Her hand slipped down her body and in between her legs. She needed this release. The energy between her and Hank felt as though they'd reached a boiling point, and she was sure she'd combust if she didn't. Her finger moved slowly back and forth across her clit. The feeling was almost too much for the throbbing sensitivity between her legs.

She imagined what it would feel like to have Hank touch her like that, a bolt of pleasure running through her veins. She could almost hear him whispering *sunshine* into her ear. Could almost feel his fiery touch rolling down her body as her back arched against the ceramic wall of the tub. Her lips ached for the intense kiss they'd shared almost a year ago, her mouth craving the taste of him. The roaring of her heartbeat grew louder in between her ears as her fingers moved more feverishly, building up the insatiable pressure within herself.

Daisy felt the familiar buzz starting in her core, burning lower as her fingers brought her closer to her release. She squeezed her eyes shut as she imagined Hank's head between her legs, his tongue working her body closer and closer to orgasm as her fingers ran through his hair, tugging at the root, encouraging him when he found the right combination of speed and pressure to make her melt. She could feel his hands on her breasts, teasing his rough fingers over the taut flesh of her nipples.

God, how she loved the moments where he was so protective of her, it felt like she belonged to him. Is that how he would make love to her? There was never a doubt in her mind that he would help her feel safe. And she'd seen the desire in his eyes. The thought of his eyes looking into hers as his tongue tasted her arousal, before he'd gently kiss her neck and then suck on her nipple, was powerful enough to tip her into full body tremors.

Hank!!

The warm water swirled around her body as she let herself fall over the edge. Her body tingled from her fingers all the way to her toes, and a soft smile spread across her face. Just imagining him touching her had been enough to set off fireworks through her entire body. She moaned with longing, imagining what it would be like if he were actually there.

The bathroom door burst open, causing Daisy to scream.

"Are you okay?!" Hank demanded. Daisy sank her shoulders under the water, strategically covering her body with the bubbles. She'd never been so thankful for her love of bubble baths before in her life.

"What are you doing? Why did you just burst in here?" She was almost certain her breathlessness and flushed face would give away exactly what she'd been doing.

"What do you mean? You screamed my name! I thought something was wrong." His eyes roamed over her face and she felt her cheeks darken with embarrassment. Had she really yelled out his name? Lord, how would she ever live that down?

"Uh, nope. I have no clue what you are talking about." Yep, she totally was going to gaslight him. There was no way she could live with the embarrassment otherwise. "I'm fine, though. Thanks for checking on me."

When he didn't move, except to furrow his brows further down his face, Daisy quickly added, "I'll be downstairs in just a few minutes. I'm really fine, I promise."

Hank apparently got the hint, because he turned, grumbling to himself something that was too quiet for Daisy to hear. As soon as the bathroom door clicked shut, Daisy silently screamed into the air as she submerged her whole body beneath the surface of the water.

ELEVEN

"Dinner looks delicious." Daisy's voice floated into the kitchen.

Hank turned from the counter, his uniform now replaced with a dark gray shirt and black running shorts.

"Wow." He looked Daisy over. Her beautiful blonde hair, freshly washed and still damp, laid over her bare shoulders. The sundress she wore hugged her chest and then flowed away from her hips. And to be honest, the sight of her made his mouth water more than anything he'd cooked that evening.

A bright flush made its way to Daisy's cheeks and she let out a small laugh.

"Wow yourself, Sheriff. Thanks for giving me time to get all the garden dirt off of me. What did you make?"

"It's a pasta salad recipe my mom used to make growing up. I've tweaked it a bit to fit in more of the extra vegetables you had from the garden this week."

"I can't wait to try it."

Hank scooped the salad into bowls and handed one to Daisy.

"Do you want to eat on the back patio?" she asked. "It's such a beautiful day. Seems like a waste to just sit inside."

"I like how you think. You take your bowl out and I'll meet you in a second after I grab us drinks."

Hank watched her walk out of the kitchen and grabbed two glasses from the cupboard by the sink. He took the lemonade he'd made a few minutes before out of the refrigerator and filled the glasses, walking to the door gingerly, trying his best not to spill.

"This is delicious, Hank. I'm sorry I couldn't wait to sneak a taste. And once I did, I couldn't stop." Daisy helped herself to another forkful.

"No need to wait on me. I'm glad you like it."

They ate in silence for a few minutes. Hank would do anything to prolong talking to Daisy about her truck and the danger that she could be in.

"So, I know your mom was an amazing cook, but I don't think I've ever heard you mention your dad. What does he do?" Her voice pulled him from his thoughts.

"He was a teacher. History." Hank struggled to swallow the food he'd just placed in his mouth, his throat growing sore with emotion just like it did any time he had to talk about his father.

"Was? Is he retired now?" she asked, and when he didn't respond right away, he saw recognition pass in her eyes.

"He died from a heart attack when I was twelve."

"I'm so sorry."

Looking at the fire pit in front of them, he suddenly felt the urge to build a fire.

"Do you want to have a fire tonight?" he asked, placing his fork down on the table before pointing to the pit.

"That sounds nice. I have some wood stacked over by the barn. I can come help you carry it."

A growl tore from his chest. Would she ever just sit and let him take care of her?

"Sit. I'll be right back with plenty."

Not that he just randomly wanted a fire. He needed to move away from the pain of talking about his dad. Even though it had been almost twenty-five years since he died, Hank still felt a sense of panic and indescribable pain when talking about him. Placing several large pieces of wood in his arms, the strain of his muscles helped ground him and pushed down the rawness he was feeling in his chest.

"That's why I run so much." He sat back in his chair, watching the flames dance in the fire pit. "I don't know if I'm genetically predisposed to something like that happening. He was forty-six when he died. That's only ten years away for me."

"Even if you are genetically predisposed to something, that doesn't mean it will happen."

"I know, but I can't imagine having a family, a wife and kids who I loved more than anything else in the entire world, and just dropping dead while walking to my car one day. Just laying there, in my driveway, until my son walks out for school and finds me there, face smashed in from the force of my fall onto the pavement."

"Hank." The sadness in her voice was almost too much for him to bear.

He cleared his throat. "Sorry. That was probably too much to share. But now you know why it's so much easier to talk about my mom."

The fire held his attention until he felt her hand on his arm. The heat from her touch was more scorching than the flames.

"Tell me more about him. Tell me about your favorite memory with him."

Daisy worked over the next ten minutes to pull Hank out of the sadness that had surrounded him when he first talked about his father. Before he knew it, they both were laughing with tears in their eyes after he shared a story about his father taking him fishing.

"And then, that damn fish pulled so hard, my rod flew out of my hands and plunked right into the lake. My dad didn't waste a single second. He picked me up by my shorts and threw me overboard to get it back."

"Did you?"

"Of course not! But I learned a valuable lesson about having a life vest on. Had I been wearing it, he wouldn't have even tried to throw me over because I wouldn't have been able to sink enough to get the rod."

"I wish I could have met him. He sounds like he was such a wonderful man."

"I wish you could have too, Daisy. He'd be so impressed with you keeping your family legacy alive through this farm. His love for history wasn't just about things that happened in the world. My dad lived for digging deeper into our family tree. One branch he'd verified all the way back to the thirteen hundreds."

"That's incredible."

"My mom still has all the books with his research on it. I'll have to dig back through them one of these days."

They fell into silence, both staring at the embers of the dying fire.

"Did your mom like her?"

"Who?"

"Your ex." Her voice was so small, despite the magnitude of the question she was asking.

Hank's mind froze. He'd rather shove a hot poker from the fire into his eye socket right now than talk about Anna.

"If you don't want to talk about her, I understand. I've just shared a lot of stuff with you over the past few days. I'm here if you need a neutral party to chat with."

"You're a neutral party when it comes to me?" He didn't really want her to answer that. He wanted to believe that the tension, the heat, the electricity between them was something she felt too. He wasn't neutral about her, not even close.

"No. Not neutral at all." That got his heart racing faster. "But I am curious about her, and what happened. I know you must have truly loved her for her to shatter your heart so completely.

"Anna didn't shatter my heart."

"Oh, really? That tough, grumpy exterior might fool people, but I've gotten a glimpse of your heart. There's no way another woman wouldn't have come along to claim you if you were putting yourself out there. But I know you haven't been in a relationship since her."

"Who told you that?"

He watched that familiar blush he loved bloom across her chest and rise all the way to her cheeks.

"A good detective never divulges their intel source, Sheriff. Shouldn't you know that?"

Her teasing eased the tension in his chest.

"Yeah, I guess I was heartbroken at first. I didn't understand how things fell apart so fast. But after the dust settled, I felt relieved."

"Why?"

"On paper, Anna and I were a good match. Ambitious, devoted to our families and their wishes. My mom adored her and made it very clear that she wanted me to marry her during every conversation we had. I didn't want to let her down. I guess I never wanted to admit that I was just going through the motions. Our relationship was nothing like the one my mom and dad had."

He watched her absorb his words and wondered what she was thinking about his confession.

"I also didn't want to let Anna down. She'd been with me

through the start of my career and I felt like she sacrificed a lot of the experiences of her early twenties for me. I felt obligated to propose to her. I felt obligated to marry her."

"But you loved her?"

"Yes." Hank blew out a long breath. "But after she left, I realized I wasn't in love with her. There were no butterflies when she walked into a room. When I'd had a long day at work, I didn't come home waiting for her smile to comfort me."

"That must have been really tough."

"I didn't know it was missing until she left and I thought back over why she did."

"Did she feel the same way? She was just going through the motions?"

"She didn't tell me. She just left. One day, I went to work, and when I came home, she was gone. Packed all of her stuff and moved out in one twelve-hour shift. I tried to reach out to her, to get some sort of closure, but her parents just told me she didn't want to see me again. Gave me back the ring I purchased for her and told me to take care of myself."

"Wow. It seems like she didn't actually love you at all."

Hank nodded. "So, when I say I understand what it's like to feel you aren't worth anything to someone who is supposed to love you above all else, I get it."

"I'm sorry that you do, Hank. You didn't deserve that." She stood and moved to the chair next to him. Pulling his hand into hers, they sat in silence as his fingers traced circles over her skin.

———

"So, is it time to tell me about my truck?" She knew Hank was stalling, which was probably the only reason he was so open about his dad and his ex.

"Daisy."

"I just need you to tell me. I've sat and worried about it for hours now since you came home. Please."

Hank sighed and squeezed her hand gently.

"The brake lines were severed."

Her eyes grew wide and looked back and forth between his as she tried to understand what that meant.

"Severed? As in, old and something on the truck rubbed against the lines until they failed?"

"No. Severed as in cut, on purpose. Someone was trying to make sure that you wouldn't be able to stop the truck the next time you drove it."

Daisy sat still, just blinking at Hank as the words he'd said sank in.

"But that wasn't all. Someone tampered with the accelerator linkage."

"I don't understand," she finally said. "What does that mean?"

"It means you were right about the truck speeding up erratically. Someone set it up so that you would speed out of control and not be able to stop because your brakes would fail."

The revelation hit her like a brick wall. She had to force herself to breathe. "I don't understand. Those are things that couldn't just be because of the age of the truck? I mean, my grandparents had it before I was even born."

"We had the best guys in the state looking at it, Daisy. I called in a favor to get it expedited, but I trust the results. This wasn't an age issue."

"Why? Why would someone want to do that to me?"

"I don't know right now, but we'll figure it out. Is there anyone you can think of who'd want to do this? Maybe an ex that you've had trouble with? Or someone who held a grudge against your family?"

She wasn't about to tell Hank that the last ex she had was in college, and she already lived through the repercussions of her actions following that break up.

"Hank, there isn't a single person I know today that I think would be capable of doing something like that."

"What if it isn't someone you know? But maybe someone your grandparents knew? Was there anything strange when you went to settle their estate after they passed?"

"There's honestly nothing. It was super straightforward. They left nearly everything to me. My cousin Grace was the only other person who was left anything."

"Could she be jealous of that fact?"

"No! Hank, honestly, Grace is the only family I have left. And she's in Miami, living her own life. I know she has nothing to do with this."

"Okay."

She was lost in her thoughts when Hank took a big breath and asked a question that made her stomach clench.

"What about your parents?"

"What about them?"

"Do you think they could have learned about your grandparents passing away and been mad there wasn't anything left to them?"

The thought hadn't even crossed her mind. If they were alive, would they have kept tabs on her? Did they still care about her enough to find out information about her life? Could the people who abandoned her really be back, trying to hurt her because she inherited something they felt they should have?

No. None of that made sense. She had been so sure for the last two decades that they left and never looked back. She didn't feel like anything had changed.

"They haven't been around in twenty years. I don't even know where they'd be or if they're even alive. If they are, and they'd been keeping tabs on me this entire time, I don't know how I would handle that."

"It's something worth looking into."

"No."

"Daisy, we need—"

"No, Hank. I'm serious."

"I wish I could say I don't need to look into them. You could have been killed in that accident, Daisy. I need to check every lead."

"I don't want to know what you find, Hank. If you have to look into them, fine. But I don't want to know."

"I can do that. I won't tell you anything I find out about them unless it is absolutely necessary for you to know for your safety. I need to know that I've done everything possible to keep you safe."

TWELVE

"Why are you making a mess in the kitchen this early?" Hank asked as he entered the kitchen, his packed bags in his hands.

"It is not a mess in here," she grumbled as she rolled her eyes. "Besides, a mess would be worth it. I wanted you to have fresh brownies to go home with today. Just as a little thank you for everything you've done over the last week to help me."

"I see you've already freed your arm from the sling. Are you sure that's okay to do? Don't you have a follow up appointment you should wait for?"

"I read the discharge instructions Jake sent home with me. It's perfectly fine for me to take it off now and see how I feel. So far, so good."

"Okay, you know your body and your limits better than I do."

"We could remedy that, Sheriff." Daisy couldn't even comprehend what had possessed her to say that so confidently. Maybe it was because she knew they were coming up hard against a deadline. He was leaving that morning. She would be back to a quiet house, a quiet farm, a quiet life. So yes, she knew just how important it was to find out if any of the deliciously torture-filled energy she'd felt pass between them was reciprocated. Daisy licked the spatula and winked, chocolate batter dripping down her chin.

He set his bags on the ground and closed the distance between them. Smiling down at her with a twinkle of mischief in his eye, he swiped the pad of his thumb across her chin, capturing the chocolate batter. Slowly, he lifted his thumb to his lips and licked his finger clean.

"Delicious, Daisy. Absolutely delicious."

She dipped the spatula into the batter again, this time holding it up to his lips. He licked at it, flames dancing in his eyes. Daisy smeared a little extra on his lips, and before his tongue could dart out to catch it, she stood on her tiptoes and kissed him.

His arm reached around her body, landing on the small of her back. His mouth quickly swallowed her gasp, opening to let her explore him. Chocolate and mint overwhelmed her senses, and she giggled as heat flushed from the top of her head all the way to her toes. That kiss was everything.

His arm was still firmly against her back when she placed her feet flat on the ground, tucking her face against his chest while she caught her breath. She couldn't look at him. Had he felt that heat, that connection, too? Because damn, that had been the hottest kiss of her entire life and she would likely burst into flames from the embarrassment if she looked into his eyes and saw anything other than desire there.

Almost as if he knew what she was thinking, Hank settled his finger under her chin and lifted her eyes to meet his. She searched for a moment, afraid to admit the passion she saw behind his blown out pupils.

Strong, rough hands were on her hips in an instant, lifting

her onto the counter. Her legs moved apart and her breath hitched with anticipation as he took a confident step between them. The throbbing in her core intensified as she raked her fingers over his chest, driving her wild with the need to explore every inch of his body. Hank's eyes held hers for another second, before he shook his head and took a step back. Tears pricked at the back of her eyes, but she wouldn't let him see her hurt over the loss of their connection.

"I should get my bags out to my truck. Then I'll load everything for the market."

"Okay. The brownies need to go in the oven, but they'll be done by the time I'm ready to leave." She kept her voice steady, despite her disappointment.

Hank planted a feather-light kiss on her cheek, right on top of the blush that she feared would be permanently seared onto her skin. Cool air swirled in front of her and, once he was out the front door, Daisy let the tears fall.

Hank had stayed to help her get the booth set up, meticulously lining up all the bins of goodies and arranging the jars of preserves and pickled veggies in groups. Maybe he didn't want to say goodbye as much as she didn't want to hear it.

She playfully bumped her hip into his and smiled. "Thank you for everything, Hank. I really appreciate all the help over the last week."

"It was nothing, sunshine. I'm just glad you're doing better and that I could help."

"Well, you're welcome back anytime. I hope you won't be a stranger."

"We've still got an active investigation open for your accident, so until we get that figured out, I couldn't be a stranger even if I wanted to."

"Oh."

"Not that I want to."

She desperately wanted to give in. To just lean closer to him and go for it. There had been that delicious flirtation in her kitchen, filled with the most erotically satisfying kiss of her life. But he didn't seem to understand just how much she wanted him. Would he hate for her to let him know here, out in the open, with so many people around and watching? She didn't think she could survive the week coming to a close knowing that they were just going to go back to the way things were before.

Their eyes locked, the warm breeze billowing down Main Street, almost willing them to close the mere inches separating their lips. She reached out and wrapped her arms around him. His whole body tensed, and she wondered for a second if she'd made a wrong move.

But then he melted into her, returning her embrace.

Pushing air into her lungs, she made the move. At first, her lips just dusted lightly across his. She felt the roughness of his stubble across her skin and the abrasive scraping did nothing to stop the familiar fire churning in her belly. In fact, the feeling made it burn brighter.

A whistle sounded out from Sam's booth and Daisy jumped back. While her friend was smiling, she felt the heat rising in her cheeks.

"I'm sorry, Hank."

His face returned to the stony, sharp look she had been so used to.

"I need to get going. Are you sure you won't need a ride back out to your house after the market?"

"I'll be fine with Sam."

"Alright." He turned and walked away.

"Goodbye, Sheriff." She could barely get her voice above a whisper, afraid her emotions would betray her, but she heard his reply filled with resolve and determination.

"Goodbye, sunshine."

THIRTEEN

The sounds of the county fair were loud and happy, and Daisy felt a familiar churning in her stomach as the most intense sense of nostalgia from the smell of fried dough and fresh popcorn hit her. She honestly didn't know why she was there. Would she rather be home, curled up in a ball, sulking about the fact that she'd finally gotten up the nerve to kiss Hank and he'd ghosted her? Yes, of course! She wanted to scream out in rage at him. It wouldn't be fair though, because he was actually still checking in, sending texts to make sure she remembered to lock her doors every day over the last week, but nothing more.

She felt like they had shared so much over the time he'd spent out at the farm, and there had been that insatiable push and pull that danced dangerously between friendship and flirtation. All the times he touched her, sparks coursed through her body. And she had been so certain he felt the same attraction. After all, why would he continue the physical contact if he was indifferent?

Her heart sank as she wondered if it was really all in her head. Maybe he just wanted friendship. The hot flush spreading across her chest wasn't just because of the warmer than expected temperatures outside, the realization she came to writing shame all over her face.

But that brownie batter covered kiss. It felt like her world shifted at that moment. It felt like being wrapped in so much warmth, so much safety, so much love. Like finally being home.

How could he just make her feel those things and then disappear into the shell she'd worked so hard to get inside of? He had been the one to insist he stay with her. She saw the desire in his eyes, felt the heat in his touch and the intensity in the air when they were close. Was he really just doing that out of some obligation as sheriff? She knew several women in the community who would toss themselves at his feet if that was the case.

Why had she thought there was something there between them? Clearly his ability to turn cold whenever she tried to get close was a defense mechanism, but the ice that had formed over his face when he pulled back from their kiss at the market, well, it had been cold enough to leave her feeling frost bitten. And the way he said goodbye, it felt like a forever sort of dismissal.

Smoothing her shirt and slinging her cross-body bag over her chest, Daisy's resolve to have fun with her friends strengthened. Walking through the food booths, she tried to distract herself from the humming pain in her shoulder. Her stomach was growling as the thought of blue cotton candy popped into her mind, so she stopped at the first booth she came to and handed over a few dollars for her favorite fair treat. Sticky hands were par for the course, but she should have had a better plan for what she would do once she'd consumed the entire bag to fill the void left by her pity party.

Glancing over at the main stage where her favorite local band, The Haberdashery, was playing, Daisy saw the sign for the restrooms. A few minutes later, her hands were relieved of their stickiness, plus she had a newfound appreciation for public venues that didn't solely rely on port-a-potties. Her body absentmindedly swayed to the music as she searched for her friends.

"Daisy!!!" She spun around to see Sam waving like a maniac at her.

"Hey! I was wondering where you were!" she said, raising her voice to be heard over the music.

"I'm so glad you came out! How's your arm feeling?"

"It's okay. Still pretty stiff, but I'm glad I don't have to keep it in the sling now."

"Is Hank still helping you out?"

That question earned Sam an icy glare.

"Whoa! Did something bad happen between you two?"

"You saw me kiss him at the market."

"Yeah, I know. I just, well, I mean..." he rubbed his hand on his neck, "there's always been that tension between you two. Anyone could see it from a mile away. I didn't want to ask when I brought you home, but are you guys now seeing each other?"

"It's a long story, Sam."

"Oh no," he groaned. "Am I going to have to kick the sheriff's ass? Because I'll do it, Daisy. You only need to say the word." She saw the mischievous glimmer in his eye and used her good arm to punch him in the chest.

"Don't you dare, Sam. I need you to come help me with moving the chicken run this week, and I can't have my strongest friend sitting in the slammer."

"I just want to make sure your honor is protected."

"You just let me worry about my honor." Her eyes rolled, and she reached for his arm. "Enough about me and my ill-chosen matters of the heart. Wanna split some greasy fair food?"

"I thought you'd never ask."

As the hours passed, Daisy's heart began feeling lighter than it had in days. She'd almost forgotten how funny Sam was. When they ran into the rest of their friends a few minutes after stuffing their faces full of fried dough, she didn't have enough room left in her stomach for the pit that had settled in over the last few days. They spent a little time listening to the local bands on the main stage before Aaron mentioned meeting up with a date and took off towards the games and carnival rides.

There was a shift in the wind and her skin pebbled as an unsettled feeling made its way back into her gut. Looking around as Sam and Emma sang along to the band on stage, Daisy couldn't help but take in the overwhelming feeling that she was being watched. She turned around to her chair and pretended to search her purse while occasionally looking up at her surroundings. Nothing. No one seemed to have eyes on her, but she still couldn't seem to shake the feeling.

"Everything okay?" Caleb asked loudly, trying to speak over the sounds of the band.

"Yeah, I think so. Just felt like someone was watching me. I don't know, I'm probably overreacting. I've had a strange couple of weeks."

"You want to get out of here?" Sam asked, worried lines forming near the corners of his eyes.

She realized exhaustion was setting in, and the sun hadn't even finished setting.

"Yeah, maybe it is time to head home. You should stay, though. I don't want you to have to leave just because I am."

"Nah, I've got an early start tomorrow, like always."

After saying goodbye to their friends, Sam and Daisy walked in silence until they were in front of the craft booths and realized they were parked in opposite directions.

"Thanks for the fun night, Sam."

"Of course. I'm glad you made it out. Call me tomorrow about moving the chicken run, okay? I'll figure out when I can swing by and help."

"You really are a lifesaver." She gave him a one arm hug and turned to walk back towards her car.

"Are you sure you don't want me to walk with you?" he called as she left.

"Nope! I'm all set!" Waving to him as she turned the corner, she smiled as she watched a little girl carrying a stuffed pony that was almost as large as she was.

What a lucky little girl. Her mom was laughing as she took the stuffed animal from her daughter's hands and the girl squealed in delight as her father swung her up onto his shoulders. They clearly had a wonderful relationship, and a familiar aching spread through Daisy's chest. Wasn't she just like that little girl when she was younger? Hadn't she been worthy of love like that from her own parents?

Lost in her own little world, she wasn't paying attention to her surroundings. A searing pain radiated through her shoulder as someone shoved into her.

"Sorry, I..." her voice trailed off as she took a step back from the person whose face, she realized, was hidden behind a black balaclava. Pushing down every nerve screaming at her to run, she tried to move away from the masked person. Their dark eyes stared into hers, and her stomach clenched.

Turning to find a different route, she tried to let out a scream when the person grabbed her arm and pulled her into their chest, but their hand quickly covered her mouth. They started moving towards the edge of the crowd. Dazed, she realized that no one around her was looking to step in to help. Self-preservation kicked in with a rush of adrenaline, and Daisy knew she needed to fight back if she wanted to make it back to her car and get out of there in one piece.

Twisting, she slammed her elbow up into the person's jaw,

connecting with an enormous crack. Whoever was holding her let go with a yelp, and she didn't stay still for another second. Daisy forced her feet to move towards her car.

Even with her heart beating out of her chest and the roar of blood in her ears at an all-time high, she was having a hard time coordinating her major muscle groups. Maybe Hank hadn't had such a bad idea with his daily runs. If she survived this, she'd start a running routine. Looking over her shoulder, an extra jolt of panic filled her bones as she watched the dark shadow follow her through the crowd. She willed her legs to move faster, but the shadow was still following her. Who the hell was this person? Why were they after her to begin with?

Oh shit. She'd gotten disoriented and was about to collide with the fair's perimeter gate. There would be nowhere to run after that.

Daisy forced her legs to slow, but they hadn't completely followed her instructions when she collided with a brick wall. Well, it felt like a wall, but it was warm and breathing, so most definitely not an actual brick wall. Strong hands grasped her arms as she let out a gasp.

"Daisy?" She winced and felt the arms release their grasp on her. "Sorry. Is your arm okay?"

"Oh thank god," she said, looking up into the brick wall's familiar melted chocolate eyes. All the anger she was feeling earlier towards him faded to the background once she realized she was near the one person who made her feel protected. "Hank! Yes, my arm is fine. Did you see anyone behind me?" She put her hands on her knees and took a few deep breaths to get her heart and lungs on the same page.

"I mean, I see a lot of people." He looked over her head, before crouching down on his haunches. "Why? What's wrong? Why were you running like that?"

"Someone was...someone was following me. I felt like someone had eyes on me, but I couldn't ever see where that feeling was coming from. I said goodnight to Sam and then, out of nowhere, someone in a hoodie and balaclava tried to grab me. I ran."

"You were here with Sam?" Was that really what he got out of what she just told him? Her head snapped up, and she stood tall, her breathing finally under control.

"That's besides the point."

"You were here with Sam and he just left you here on your own? He didn't walk you to your car? He didn't make sure you were home safe? That guy needs to be talked to about his date etiquette."

"We were NOT on a date. Sam is my friend."

"Please, Daisy, I've seen how he looks at you."

"Hank, even if we were on a date, why do you care?"

"Never mind. Let's go. I'll take you home." He held out his hand towards her, but she refused to take it.

"No, I-I'm good on my own. Thank you though. I'm sure you need to be getting back to whatever you were doing before I interrupted."

"Daisy, if you think for one minute I'm letting you walk back to your car alone after you just ran through here like your pants were set ablaze by the devil himself, you've got another thing coming."

"You have no right to be so pushy with me. What do you want, Hank? Do you want me? Because all you have to do is say yes. Say yes and I'm yours." She waited a heartbeat before continuing. "But if not, then you don't get to demand to watch over me. My protection is none of your business beyond what you would normally do as sheriff. So, unless you're going to arrest me, I suggest you let me go on my way."

She stood there staring at him, waiting for him to say something, anything. Her eyes grew wide as he slowly inched towards her until they were just a breath away from one another. He lowered his head towards hers, her eyes locked on his mouth. Was he about to kiss her? Had that speech actually worked?

Just before their lips touched, he moved his mouth to her ear and whispered, "I'd protect you with my dying breath if I had to, Daisy Hughes. Even if it wasn't my job. I'll do whatever it takes to keep you safe."

Fourteen

Hank had been so close to giving in. So close to telling her how she had completely bewitched his heart with just the memory of her lips on his. He wanted to sweep her up into his arms and give her an encore of the kiss they'd shared in her kitchen. It had physically hurt him to stay away from her since they said goodbye at the farmer's market. He'd run more miles and taken more ice cold showers in the last few days than ever before in his life. What he wouldn't give to just fix his messed up heart so that he could be the man she wanted him to be.

Instead, he was now driving behind her, away from the fair and towards her house. She was stubborn beyond anything he'd ever seen before, but hell, it was so damn attractive it almost aggravated him. Hank had never seen someone turn from pure fear to full spitfire in such a short expanse of time. It would have made him laugh if he wasn't so on edge from seeing her run like someone was about to attack her.

Initially intending to slow down as he drove to the edge of her driveway, Hank slammed on his brakes. Daisy's car was just sitting there, right in the middle of her driveway, brake lights lit. Why wasn't she parking off to the side like she normally would?

Hank pulled in behind her, parked, and immediately got out of his vehicle, flashlight in hand. It was nearly nine, and the sky was now dark, a thick cover of clouds hiding the starry night. The ground crunched beneath his feet and the hairs stood up on the back of his neck. Something was off, but a quick sweep of the area revealed nothing strange or unexpected.

Hank knocked on Daisy's window, and she screamed. His heart jumped a mile.

"Hey! It's just me. What's going on?"

She cracked her car door like she wanted to get out, but left the vehicle running, and her seat belt engaged.

"S-someone was walking around the back of the house when I pulled in."

Yup, that was enough for Hank to pull his weapon.

"Come with me." When she didn't move from her car, he repeated himself. "Come with me, Daisy. Let's go."

Once out of her car, he marched Daisy back to his vehicle, opening the passenger door and ushering her inside.

"Lock the doors and stay right here. I'll go check around back."

"Okay." She grabbed his arm before he could step away. "Hank, it looked like a woman. I can't be sure, but the build wasn't the same as the person I saw on the porch after my accident."

"I'll check it out. If anything happens, you lay on the horn and I'll come right back. Lock the doors now, Daisy."

He heard the click of the locks and nodded at her before turning towards the front porch. With his flashlight on, his heart galloped at the sight of fresh footprints leading around the house. Someone had definitely been there. Hank rounded the corner and swore as he saw the kitchen door swinging wide open in the breeze. He listened to the sounds outside while he scanned the fields behind Daisy's house. When he didn't hear any telltale signs that the person Daisy saw stayed around, he made his way into her house.

———

Maybe it was all in her head? Had she really even seen someone walking around the house? She was tired, after all, and maybe that was finally wearing her down. No, she had seen someone skittering around the corner when she pulled into the driveway. The person was dressed in the same dark clothes as the man she'd seen on the porch a few days before, and, come to think of it, the guy with the balaclava on that evening at the fair. Who was this person? What did they want?

She exhaled all the air she hadn't realized she was holding in when she saw Hank come out the front door of her house. How had he gotten inside? He walked to her side and she opened the door.

"Hey, so, there are definitely footprints outside your house. They lead all the way to the backyard, and then I lose them in the grass."

"God, why would someone be creeping around my house at night like that? What do they want?"

"I'm not sure." He was deep in thought and she didn't want to interrupt, but tired didn't even begin to explain how she felt. The adrenaline coursing through her veins was waning, and with it, her ability to stay awake.

"I should probably go inside. Thanks for looking everything over for me."

"Don't move." He shut the door with her still sitting inside his vehicle. She watched him walk around the truck and get in on the driver's side, placing the key into the ignition before clicking his seat belt into place.

"What are you doing?"

"Look, are you comfortable staying out here tonight? Your kitchen door was open, but it doesn't look like that lock was broken. I swept through the house. No one is in there."

Daisy bit her lip, rolling the flesh between her teeth. No, she really wasn't keen on staying there after she'd seen that person lurking, and knowing they were probably in her house at some point that evening made her skin crawl. Add that to the constant feeling she had all night of being watched, and her danger meter was going off the chart.

"I-I'll be okay." She tried to sound tough, but knew her shaking voice betrayed her.

"No. You're coming home with me."

"Hank, no. I don't think that's necessary."

"Daisy, you're exhausted. I'm exhausted. I think you coming to stay at my place makes the most sense seeing as how I have a security system already installed and we can both sleep better knowing that if someone tries to get to you, we'll have an alarm that goes off to warn us."

"But the farm..."

"I'll drop you off early in the morning. Maisie and Minnie won't even know you've been gone. It'll give me a chance to get some alarms for your doors and windows, too. I know we talked about it before, but I should have just done that from the start. I'm sorry I haven't."

"Don't apologize. It's my responsibility, not yours." Her shoulders fell, and a sigh left her lips. "Are you sure you're comfortable with me staying at your place?"

"I just want to make sure you're okay. I can also stay out here if that would make you more comfortable. But either way, I don't really want to leave you on your own."

"Maybe it's just a neighbor who needed something?"

"And what about the person who watched you at the fair? The person you were running from tonight? I just don't think we should take that risk."

"Okay, you're right. What is going on, Hank?"

"I'm not sure, but I intend to find out. Let's get going."

———

Daisy sucked in a sharp breath in awe of the house they were parking in front of.

"This is your home?" The modern architecture of the building was a beautiful contrast to the land the house sat on.

"Yep. Were you expecting something else?"

"Something completely different, actually. Are you a fan of the modern look?"

"I like it. It was more Anna's style. I like old farmhouses." Her heart skipped when his mouth turned up into a small half smile. "Come on, let's go in."

The house was just as stunning on the inside. Classic masculine touches were all over the space, with leather furniture in the living room and dark accents in the kitchen. She took a breath in and immediately recognized his scent. It was all over the place, this cedar and smokey campfire musk that enveloped her whenever he was near. It was beyond intoxicating, and now she couldn't escape it. No woman should be held responsible for the things she says or does in the presence of such a dangerously delicious scent.

"This space is amazing." Daisy couldn't get over how beautiful the kitchen was. She could whip up an enjoyable meal or two in there, no doubt. Heck, maybe that kitchen was to thank for all of Hank's amazing cooking skills.

"I'm glad you like it." He was clearly proud of the space, as he should be. It was beautiful.

"You mentioned Anna like modern homes. Was this yours together?"

There was a slight change in his features when she brought up his ex. Almost undetectable. But she'd spent so much time with him recently that she noticed it. Immediately, she regretted asking the question.

"Yes." He cleared his throat as he grabbed two glasses down from the cabinet next to the sink. "Only for a few weeks. She left just as I was gutting the place." She took the freshly filled glass from his hand, jumping at the heat that shot through her when his fingers gently brushed against hers. It was so interesting how quick her body responded to him.

"You didn't buy the house like this?"

"No, it was a mess when I first got it. Good bones, but it needed a lot of work. I'd always wanted to try my hand at flipping a house. I guess I didn't calculate how long it would take, or how I'd end up loving the space."

"Hmm."

Daisy laughed at the face he made in response to her.

"What's so interesting?" He placed his glass of water down on the counter and stepped closer, the air between them heating as his eyes bored into hers.

"You protect and serve our community for a living, you can cook and clean, and you know how to build entire houses. How are you still single?" Her question was serious. There wasn't one hit of joking or teasing in there. And that's because the more she learned about Hank, the more he let her in, the more she knew she was falling for him.

Shivers ran down Daisy's arms as he placed the pad of his thumb on her cheek and gently swiped across it.

"Maybe I was just waiting for the right woman."

"I hope she finds you soon."

"Maybe she already has."

They stayed like that, eyes connected, his hand pouring heat into her body for several more heartbeats. Finally, his eyes fell and Daisy felt him pull away. She wanted to scream, to pull him back to her. Instead, all she did was sigh breathlessly.

"Do you want to see the place I love most in this entire house?"

"It's not this kitchen? I could stand here in awe of this room for the next ten years."

Hank laughed.

"No, it's not the kitchen, although that is a close second. Come on." He reached out and took her hand in his, leading her down to the end of a hallway. "This is the attached garage."

"Are you one of those fancy car collectors who never actually take their cars out for a drive? Is that why you need three bays, but don't park inside?"

"No," he laughed again.

The smell of fresh cut lumber and sawdust hit her before her eyes could even focus on the space.

"A wood shop?"

"Yep. I really fell in love with renovating this house, and once that was done, I didn't want to give up on woodworking. Now, I mostly just tinker with tables or porch swings. I've even made a couple of signs. I don't know if you noticed at last week's market, but the diner has a new sign."

"You made that? I talked Emma's ear off for a good five minutes and she never mentioned it."

"Probably because you were mad at me then."

"Mmm, I still might be mad at you."

"I deserve it."

His smile faded until she wrapped her fingers through his and squeezed.

"Can you tell me what all these tools do?"

Thirty minutes later, Daisy had become very well versed in

the differences between a circular saw and a table saw, how to use a router, and just how important a good jointer could be. Would she ever need this knowledge? Probably not. But seeing Hank light up talking to her about it almost washed away all the anger she was grappling with.

Her traitorous body couldn't hold in a yawn any longer. It had been a long day, and her adrenaline from earlier was gone, her body finally crashing from its absence.

"Ready for bed?"

Bed, yes. Ready to say goodnight to Hank? No.

"I could listen to you talk about this stuff for hours, but I think my body is about to crash."

"I'll show you my room."

"Your room?" Perhaps all hope was not lost.

"I use my guest room as an in-home office. I'll change the sheets on my bed and you can sleep in there tonight. I'll take the couch."

Daisy tried to hide the disappointment from showing all over her face.

"You'll do no such thing. I'm intruding on your space. I'll take the couch."

He stared at her for a moment, a slight scowl forming on his lips.

"Sunshine, do you really think I'm going to have you sleep on the couch? Besides it being the most ungentlemanly thing I can think of, the living room is very exposed. I don't want anyone looking in the windows and seeing you there. I'll be close to the door so I can protect you if someone tries to come in."

Lord, those were definitely not the words she needed to hear right now. She'd almost forgotten the reason she was here. It had almost been enough to just flirt with Hank, to pretend like someone wasn't trying to scare her, or maybe even worse, hurt her.

Hank took her hand.

"Sorry, Daisy. I didn't mean to upset you."

"You didn't. I'd just forgotten for a moment what I was doing here." She took a deep breath and smiled. "Let's go see this bedroom."

FIFTEEN

Daisy helped Hank switch out the sheets on his bed with a few more jokes about how masculine his place was, but he could tell that she was worried. Her smile didn't reach her eyes like it normally did, and she kept moving her gaze to the windows. There was also this little crease in between her eyes that kept watch over her face, and all he wanted to do was erase it with sweet kisses. Why did he have to remind her of the danger that seemed to surround her now? He should have just mentioned wanting to be a gentleman and left it at that.

They'd been having such a nice time. His brain had to ruin it. If he'd listened to his heart, and the aching in his pants, he'd be doing unspeakable things to her in his bed right now. He wanted her so damn bad, and as things stood, all he'd have to show for it was the permanent imprint his zipper was leaving on his flesh any time she was around. It was torture to spend the week at her house, listening to the way her breath left her chest in the most adorable sigh when she was mad at him for trying to take over something she'd felt perfectly capable of handling. Each time she opened up to him, it was like the barriers to his own heart cracked and crumbled just a little more, and now there was a longing begging to be set free.

Had he ever felt such intense chemistry with someone before? Even when he'd been sure of his decision to marry Anna, there had always been this lingering feeling of things being just good enough. Never extraordinary. Never mind blowing. Never like all the air was leaving the room and the fire they were creating with their attraction would sustain them for the rest of their lives.

No, with Anna it had been about practicality. She was career driven, just like he was. She complimented his ambitions, and he complimented hers. He couldn't even remember a time when he'd thought about sparks existing between them. Just a regular comfort of familiarity. Of knowing his mom liked her and that her parents liked him. Of knowing they could make it work if they never disturbed the status quo.

But then Anna left. Without talking to him. Without seeing if he was willing to change things, to see if there could be an explosion of passion. At first, it had nearly killed him. He was worried that something had happened to her, and everyone in her world stopped him from finding out where she had run off to. She didn't want to speak to him, so aside from the letter she left behind just stating that things were over, he had no way of getting more answers.

This home, in the beginning, was where he saw his future children living. Having breakfast all around the island in the kitchen, family game nights in the living room. But as the years passed, no woman ever lived up to the dream. He couldn't see kids growing up there anymore. But he'd seen them playing on the tire swing in Daisy's yard. He'd thought about a little blonde-haired girl, with Daisy's piercing blue eyes, running through the sunflower fields chasing after a little boy with his dark features. The dream of what this house would hold was too precious to him to dirty with one-night stands or women who were just passing through his life. But now that Daisy was there, and he'd heard her laughter bounce off the walls, he'd smelled her delicately floral scent fill the rooms as they walked through, he didn't want to think about letting her go.

When she'd gone on and on earlier about his kitchen, he'd wanted nothing more than to lay her on the counter, and show her how perfect a space it was for activities more satiating than cooking. He would have given anything to have feasted on her body, to have shown her his tongue had skills beyond being able to taste the correct seasoning for an omelet.

The flirtation was fun, and he loved how it felt to watch a blush paint across Daisy's face, knowing his words, or his actions, had caused her body to respond like that. But there was also a point where the tension was painful. And that evening had been one of those times.

It was his fault, his hangups that he couldn't get over. Jake had been so willing to point that out to him. He needed to be thinking about her objectively, to figure out who was behind the sabotage of her truck, and who was now stalking her. But all he could think about was her beautiful, pale curves and what it would feel like to run his hands over them. Each time he'd held her in his arms before, it'd been through the lens of tragedy or fear. He wanted her to fall into his arms with pure and fiery passion.

Instead, they'd finished changing the sheets and had drifted out to the living room, where she was sitting on the opposite end of the couch from him, watching some nature documentary. Apparently, she'd gotten a second wind after nearly collapsing with exhaustion in the garage.

Now, she was there, an arm's length away, wringing her hands together. The worry was rolling off of her in waves.

"Everything okay?"

"Oh, sorry. I think I'm ready to go to bed." He watched

her stand and stretch, a small amount of smooth skin on her stomach peeking out from under her shirt. He wondered how her body would respond if he were to touch her there with his fingers. Or better yet, if he was to taste that creamy skin with his tongue.

"Of course." He expected her to leave, but she lingered. "What's wrong?"

"Uh, it's just that I have nothing to sleep in. I should have gone into the house and gotten some things, but I wasn't thinking. Maybe I could lock the door so you don't come in and see me sleeping in my...not in my clothes, but that just doesn't feel safe. I mean, what if something happens and someone's in the room with me and you can't get in to help because I've locked the door?" He watched her cheeks turn a bright shade of red. It was utterly adorable.

"I have a shirt you can wear. You'll drown in it, but it should do the job." What job was that? Because the thought of her wearing his shirt, her skin being touched by something his own skin had touched, was doing unseemly things to his heart.

"Are you sure? I'm already taking your bed."

"Daisy, believe me when I say I'm pretty sure knowing you are in my t-shirt, in my bed, is going to be more of a treat for me than it is a favor for you." More heat flushed her cheeks.

"Okay then," she smiled. "That would be perfect. Thank you."

They walked back to the room together, and Hank searched his drawer for his relaxed, oversized shirts the sheriff's department sold each year for community outreach fundraising. Pulling the first one he found from the drawer, he handed it to Daisy. Their hands skimmed past each other and there was that familiar pull on his heart.

"I, um, I'll just change in the bathroom. Thank you again, Hank."

"Sweet dreams, sunshine." He loved how he could make the flush of her cheeks show up whenever he wanted.

"Sweet dreams, Sheriff."

———

Feet were pounding on the pavement. She could hear the slapping of them as she ran across the road. Sharp pain tore through her skin as pebbles and debris sliced into her flesh. Where were her shoes? And why did her legs refuse to move faster? Her lungs were burning with the desire to pull in extra oxygen, but she couldn't get her body to cooperate with any of the demands she was making. She needed to get away, away from the shadow. Scared and desperate, she felt her heart pounding out of her chest and her lungs burning for air. But what was she running from? The shadow that just wouldn't let her go.

Why did he want her? She was already broken, already damaged. Hands reached out to grab her.

No! Get away! She tried to scream, but nothing came out. The hands continued to grab, faceless shadows pulling at her. She kicked fiercely, thrashing as she tumbled to the ground.

Only it wasn't the ground she landed on. It was a bed. It was hard, and the room was dark. Her mind felt like it was swimming until recognition hit like a lightning bolt. A dorm room. She was drenched in sweat, losing the ability to focus on the man in front of her. She could hear his zipper lowering, nausea swelling in the pit of her stomach.

NO!

Trying to move her arms and legs was no use. She knew this. She'd lived this moment a thousand times over the past six years. But that didn't mean she wanted to stay in this nightmare. The shadow grew bigger. She felt it press into her, and with every ounce of strength she possessed, she willed herself to wake up.

Daisy's eyes flew open and her chest heaved air in and out

of her lungs. She was soaked from the sweat she'd worked up trying to fight her way through her dreams. Looking out the window, darkness still surrounded the house. She pulled her knees into her chest and willed her adrenaline to wane.

It was lost on her just how long she sat there, watching the branches on the trees outside Hank's house sway with each tendril of wind that floated by, but suddenly, she knew she couldn't watch for one minute more.

The door from the bedroom let out a loud groan as she slowly opened it. In the dark hallway, Daisy took a moment to listen for any sign that Hank was awake. It had been a long day for them both, so she doubted he would be. She'd just get a drink from the kitchen, and then head back to bed. Even if she didn't sleep the rest of that night, she might get a nap in after morning chores once she was back out at her farm.

Turning on the faucet, she ran the glass she had used earlier under the stream of water. As the glass touched lips and cool water ran down her throat, she felt a hand rest gently on her back and choked. Sputtering, trying to clear the water from her lungs, she turned to face the person.

"Sorry," Hank said, his eyes fixed on her.

"You scared the crap out of me!" Her throat burned from the coughing.

"Is everything okay?" His eyes darted out the window they were standing next to, then returned to her face.

"Besides you giving me a heart attack?"

"Yes. Besides that."

"I couldn't get back to sleep after a...a dream...woke me up."

"Want to talk about it?"

"Actually," she bit her bottom lip and watched as his eyes traveled down to take in the sight. *Just ask.* That's all she needed to do. To be brave and ask for what she needed. "I was hoping you'd come back to bed with me. Just to sleep. I don't feel safe being in there all alone." And the dreams would hopefully not return if her brain knew she was in someone's arms.

"Daisy." Hank growled her name, low and filled with emotion.

She placed her hand on his chest and looked back up into his eyes.

"Just sleep, Hank. Just lay in bed and sleep."

"I don't know if I'm capable of that."

"I trust you. I need you. I need you to help me feel safe."

She could see how that affected him. Her words went into his mind, and they touched his heart. But the tortured look didn't leave his face.

"Let's go." He took her hand and led her back to his bed.

"Do you have a side you always sleep on?" She asked, hoping he would not want to sleep on the side she'd thrashed into a rumpled mess with her nightmare.

"I'll take the side closest to the door."

"A protector through and through." As they climbed under the covers, Hank laid down and held his arm out. She slipped into bed and curled up with her head on his chest. "Thank you, Hank."

"Of course, sunshine. Sweet dreams."

Within a few minutes, Daisy's world faded away, this time into blissful rest.

Sixteen

Daisy was wrapped in warmth when suddenly, the stone wall she'd been laying on moved. Shifted. And all the heat that was gloriously radiating off of it was pulled from her. Opening her eyes, she realized Hank had gotten up from the bed.

"Hank?" Her voice was groggy, coated in sleep.

"Sorry, Daisy. It's almost time for me to get you back out to your house."

"Oh. Right."

She sat up, swinging her legs over the side of the bed and wiggled her toes. Stepping down onto the floor, she gathered up her clothes from beside the bed where she'd set them the previous night and then gave her body a good, tall stretch. She felt Hank's shirt skim over her thighs, aware he was watching her from the doorway of his bathroom.

"I'm going to shower and then I'll make breakfast. You can hop in the shower after, if you want."

"Perfect. Thank you."

He smiled as he turned, and Daisy made her way into the kitchen.

Once she'd grabbed a couple of eggs from the fridge and some bread off the counter, Daisy started making breakfast before Hank could insist on doing it himself. She had already imposed, and now it was her turn to do something nice. She'd successfully gotten two eggs cracked into the warmed skillet when Hank's alarm system suddenly chirped out a warning sound. Someone had unlocked and opened the front door.

Daisy waited, frozen in place by the stove. He hadn't mentioned someone else having a key to his place, or to expect anyone in the morning. Was someone breaking in? She needed to turn around and see who had walked in the door, but her body just wouldn't move.

"Hank! You better get your butt out here and give me a hug. I brought you donuts. And I know you're not at work yet, because your truck is still outside!" A lovely, light voice flitted through the house.

In an instant, Daisy wished it had been an intruder. Not a woman Hank obviously cared enough about to give a key to his home. She needed to get out, and get out fast.

"Oh, hi there. I'm so sorry. I didn't know Hank had someone over."

"Hi," Daisy choked out. The woman standing in front of her was gorgeous. Dark brown hair flowed over her shoulders, she had striking chestnut colored eyes and her thin frame was on full display in her Lycra workout clothes. Of course, she was probably a runner. Maybe that's how Hank met her.

"Are you okay?" The mystery woman asked. "I hate to say it, but you look a little pale."

"I'm fine. I-I was just going."

"With eggs on the stove and Hank nowhere to be found?"

"He's in the shower. I'll just plate these up and be on my way."

"Wait, please don't leave on my account. I usually call my brother before I come over, but I didn't want him deflecting this morning, so I just barged in. He's never had anyone here before, so I didn't even think. You don't need to run away on my account."

Holy shit. How did she not know Hank had a sister? Daisy's mind ran through all the conversations they'd had, and not once did she remember him talking about a sister.

"Your brother?"

"Yup. Mr. Tall, Dark, and Humorless looks just like our father. I got all of our mother's brains, class, and powerful perfection. I'm five years younger, but you'd think it was fifty, with how grouchy he is and how exuberantly youthful I am." Hank's sister laughed at her own snark and smiled at Daisy. As soon as she did, Daisy saw the resemblance. They had the same smile, complete with matching left-side dimples.

"Oh no. You didn't think I was someone he was sleeping with, did you? Ew, I really need to wash my brain out now. I'm Kara, by the way."

"It's nice to meet you, Kara. I'm Daisy."

She watched as Kara's eyes went wide.

"You're Daisy? As in *the* Daisy? And you spent the night here?"

"Um, I'm not really sure what you meant by '*the* Daisy', but yes, that is my name. And I stayed the night...but just because someone was creeping around my house and it didn't feel safe to stay there. Is that okay?"

"Oh my goodness, that's more than okay! Oh, I'm so happy for Hank! He's told me so much about you and I just can't believe it. Can I give you a hug?"

"Oh, um, sure."

Kara moved so quickly. If Daisy hadn't known it was coming, she would have easily barreled her over. There was something so sweet about the gesture, Daisy just melted into the embrace. Tears stung at the back of her eyes, and she fought to swallow the lump forming in her throat. This was a member of Hank's family, and she'd been immediately welcomed in.

After squeezing her tightly, Kara stepped back.

"So wait. What did you mean by someone creeping outside your house?"

"It's a long story. Can I ask why you're so excited to see me here?"

"Hmm. We'll need to circle back to your safety here in a second. I own a self defense company in Lark Lake and I'm going to punch my brother for not connecting us before this chance meeting. As for your question, let's just say, I've been praying for Hank to get his shit together and tell you how he's felt about you for almost a year now. He calls me and I can barely get a word in about my life. He's always wanting to talk about you!"

Shock registered in her brain, and she was certain that it was clear on her face as well. "Never in a million years would I have thought that was what you would say. Before my accident a few weeks ago, Hank had barely said more than two words at a time to me."

"Oh, honey. He's been telling me about you since last year. He was beside himself when you got in your accident, and then he brought you here when you felt unsafe. Hank wants to protect you. He's a goner, for sure."

Daisy's heart clenched in her chest and she tried to laugh lightheartedly, turning back to the pan of sputtering eggs on the stove in case it wasn't convincing. Just as she placed the last one on a plate, she heard Hank's bedroom door open and his heavy footsteps filled the hallway.

"Kara," he said, eyes wide and voice tight. "What are you doing here?"

Kara sighed, before pulling her brother into a hug.

"I brought you breakfast and wanted to chat without worrying that you were going to make up an excuse not to be home when I stopped by. Sorry, I didn't know you had a sleep-over guest."

She turned to Daisy and raised her eyebrows a few times, all the while a huge smile sat on her face. Daisy laughed, loving the surprised look that danced across Hank's dark features.

"I see you've met my sister. She's a menace, but I love her."

"Yes. She was just going to tell me about the self defense business she owns in Lark Lake."

"Yeah, you big jerk." Kara interjected, and as promised, she promptly punched him in the arm. "How could you not tell me that Daisy's been feeling unsafe at home? You know I could set her up with some kick-ass tools to help protect herself."

"I know you won't believe it, but one of my first calls today was going to be to you for that exact thing."

Kara rolled her eyes, and Daisy laughed again. Her breath hitched when Hank walked towards her and placed his hand on the small of her back.

"You didn't have to make breakfast. I told you I'd come out and whip something up after I showered."

"It was no big deal. I'm happy to not be a total mooch. I'll just head in to shower and you can catch up with your sister."

"I left a set of towels on the counter in there. Sorry, there's no girly smelling soap."

"I don't mind having to smell like you."

Daisy turned to walk away, but Hank's arm stayed in place and directed her into his chest. Looking up at him, the air between them stilled, and she watched his eyes run through a thousand different emotions before he stepped back, giving her space to walk away.

"Well, that was...interesting." Kara said, clearing her throat.

"I'll be out in a few minutes, and I hope you'll still be here when I'm done, Kara. I want to hear all the stories about

Hank as a kid. I just picture this grumpy, giant four-year-old and it's too cute. I have to know if I'm right."

"I'll be here, for sure. If nothing more than to get to see Hank's face turn red when I tell you about the time he got all dressed up for my tea party themed birthday."

"My shower is about to be lightening fast," Daisy laughed as she walked from the room.

———

"So." Kara turned to her brother. "She slept over."

"Keep those wide eyes of yours tucked in your head. Nothing happened."

"From the way you put your hand on the small of her back and pulled her into your chest just a minute ago, I would venture to say a whole hell of a lot happened between you two."

"Kara, leave it."

"What are you going to do? Arrest me for being happy for you? This is so wonderful, Hank. Are you totally freaking out?"

"I'm not freaked out about anything, because nothing is happening."

"No, wait one second. You spent an entire week with her after her accident, and now she's scared and trusts you to help her and spends the night at your house for her safety. Something is going on between you two. Would you let Mrs. Wilkinson's daughter Joy stay here if she was feeling scared?"

"Joy has a big family who can provide her with protection."

"So this is just about Daisy not having family?"

"Kara..."

"Exactly big bro. You're in so deep and I know you. You're

trying to convince yourself that what you're feeling goes against what she deserves."

"You sound like Jake."

"There's a reason I've always had a little thing for him," she smiled mischievously.

"I'd kill him, Kara. In an instant. He may be my best friend, but I'd happily plan his memorial if he ever touched you."

"Yeah, yeah, killer. Calm down. He's not actually my type. You know I have a thing for military bad boys."

"Did you just come here to press all my buttons first thing in the morning? 'Cause I've kind of been having a shit week, and I'd like to head into work in not the worst mood possible."

"How can you even be feeling anything other than completely elated after the scene I just witnessed?"

"Because you're ruining it with your third degree inquisition into my feelings."

"That's what little sisters are for! I wouldn't be doing my familial duty if I didn't."

"Consider your duty done. Now, what did you want to talk about before you barged in here on my peaceful morning?"

"I actually need your help."

SEVENTEEN

"Hey girl!" Emma's bright smile greeted Daisy as she sat down at the diner's counter. When Daisy returned to the kitchen after her shower, Hank had a scowl of concern that didn't budge from his face the rest of the morning. She wasn't sure what Kara and Hank had discussed while she was out of the room, but it had left them both shaken.

Since then, Hank resumed his habit of checking in only about safety, making sure she was home at night, that she had locked her doors, and that she had alarmed the security system he had made sure was installed. Nothing more. No stolen kisses in her kitchen. No snuggle sessions at night to help her sleep. He was even back to one-word answers with her.

"Hey, Ems."

Emma's eyes fixed on Daisy. "Uh oh, what's wrong?"

"Nothing a good cup of coffee won't fix."

"You want something extra strong?"

"Actually, yes. Please."

"You got it. But then you're going to spill."

There were only a handful of customers in the diner, so it

didn't surprise her when Emma brought out two coffees and plopped down onto the stool next to her.

"Extra strong, and extra big. Just how we like our coffee, and our men," Emma winked. "Now spill while I wait for Mrs. Mulcahey to flag me down for a slice of pie."

"Ugh. I just don't understand what's wrong with me. I feel like I'm going insane. Am I that bad at reading signals? Is it all in my imagination?"

"Shall I assume this is about a certain hunky sheriff?"

Daisy sighed. "Who else would it be about? I'm being desperate, hoping that he feels something for me when he's just constantly flipping between hot and cold."

"Oh honey, anyone who pays attention knows Hank's been pining after you since you came back to Bell Ridge. He's just got a lot of his own junk that he went through with his ex. I'm sure that's playing a big part in his whole hot then cold routine."

"Maybe." Daisy took a sip from her coffee. "God, this is just what I needed. So delicious."

"Thanks, gorgeous."

"How are the renovations lining up?"

Emma sighed, worried lines forming across her forehead. She'd been talking about shifting the diner to a bakery for a while. Daisy suspected the sign which changed the name from the Main Street Diner to Emma's was just one of the first steps in that transition.

"Don't think that change of subject is going to get you out of talking about him." She raised a knowing eyebrow and groaned. "I think I'm going to have to push them out a bit. Business is good, but not that good. The estimates are astronomical, and I wish I could do some of the work myself, but I'm much better at decorating cakes and baking cookies than I am at laying flooring."

"If you ever wanted to give doing-it-yourself a go, I'd

totally be down for helping," Daisy smiled. "Just remember, we'd have to go slow because of this bum arm of mine."

"A bum arm and payment in coffee and cookies is better than a twenty thousand dollar estimate for demolition." Yikes, Emma was right about the costs being high. "How is your arm feeling, by the way?"

"Great. Two or three more weeks and I should be good as new. Hank was so damn attentive after my accident. He barely let me use my legs to walk around, and he definitely didn't let me use my arm for anything other than sling duty."

Daisy groaned, anger warming her chest. "I just don't understand him. I felt like we had this amazing week together, although he was totally overprotective and ridiculous at times. But it was nice to have someone care so much about me. And then he just left. My sling came off, and it was like his ticket to freedom away from me. But it didn't feel like he wanted to escape when we were kissing."

Emma coughed as she set her coffee cup down on the counter. "I remember you saying how fiery that market kiss was."

Daisy nodded while opening her eyes wide. "Ems, it wasn't just at the market. Earlier that morning, we shared the most amazing, erotic, demanding, sexually arousing kiss of my entire life. Not that there is much to compare it to, but I literally thought I was going to come undone just from the touch of his lips. And I haven't even told you about spending the night at his house. In his bed. In his arms."

"WHAT!"

"Yeah." She shook her head, tracing her lips with her fingertip. "That night we all met up at the fair? Well, after we'd said goodnight, a guy started following me. He grabbed me and I made a run for it."

"Holy shit, Daisy! That was on Monday! Three whole days ago! Why is this the first I'm hearing of this?"

"I didn't want to tell you in a text, and we've both been busy. Anyway, I got turned around trying to get to my car and ended up running into Hank. Literally. I thought I hit a brick wall." She let her mind wander to the feeling of her body pressed against his, warmth spreading between the two of them.

Emma snapped her fingers in front of Daisy's face.

"Yeah, okay daydreamer. Back to the story at hand for a minute."

"Sorry. When I explained to Hank what happened, he insisted on driving back to my house with me to make sure I was safe."

Daisy sighed, breathy and dreamily as she thought about how frequently Hank was stepping up as her protector over the past few weeks.

"Oh girl. You've got it bad for him."

"Of course I do. It's because of all those damn romance books I read. Classic fall for the protector plot line. But he just forced his way into my heart and then left. And where does that leave me? Am I even allowed to feel brokenhearted?"

"You feel however you need to, but don't wallow, babe. You're gorgeous and smart, the whole freaking package. You're killing me here, though. Spill the beans about how you ended up at his house!"

"When we got back to the farmhouse, someone in a mask was walking around outside. Hank pulled me from my car into his and then went searching for them. The back door was open, and it looked like maybe they had been in the house. I couldn't stand the thought of staying, so he offered to let me stay at his place until he had the chance to install a new security system at mine."

"Daisy! What the hell is going on? First your accident, and now someone tried to grab you at the fair and skulked around your house?"

"I wish I knew. You know, the weirdest part is, I don't think it's just one person. It was definitely a man who tried to grab me at the fair, but I would swear on my life it was a woman walking around my house."

"I don't care who it was, Daisy. I just want you to come stay with me. I have a guest room in my apartment upstairs. With Steve being there, it'll be tight, but I want to know you're safe! You shouldn't be alone while all this is happening." Tears filled her friend's eyes.

"I didn't mean to scare you. It's probably just tied to the trouble other farmers in the area have run into. Sam mentioned some stuff happening at his ranch and he ran off a couple of kids from his pastures last week. I know Aaron and the Lawtons have been having issues, too."

"I don't know, Daisy. What does Hank say about it all?"

"He installed a security system at my house. Texts me to make sure I'm inside and all locked in at night. It's sweet and so infuriating all at the same time."

"Well, I'm glad he's keeping his eye on the situation. But I'd still feel better if you were in town and not all alone out there."

"I have to be out at the farm. I can't lose the small income I make from the market each week. It's literally all I have keeping me afloat at the moment."

"At least tell me you have Hank on speed dial in case anything happens? That way he can get to you and help."

"If you mean 9-1-1, then yes, I have his number memorized."

"Hilarious, but that's not what I meant."

Daisy shrugged her shoulders.

"I obviously have his number. He gets an alert if there is a problem with the alarm system, along with the security company who notifies the sheriff's department for me. So it's up to him if he shows up. I wouldn't be surprised if he found a reason to avoid seeing me, even in that situation.

Emma cleared her voice, looking out the windows at the front of the shop.

"I have a feeling our very handsome sheriff will make an appearance back in your life before you know it."

"I don't think so, Ems."

The bell over the diner's door jingled, alerting the women to a new customer's arrival. Daisy swung her body towards the door to offer whoever it was a warm smile, but her heart stopped when she saw the six foot three familiar frame step into the shop.

"Emma."

"Hank. What can I get for you?"

"A cup of coffee and a slice of key lime pie to go, please."

"Sure thing, Sheriff." Emma shuffled away, giving a wink to Daisy.

"Daisy." His voice was gruff and strained as he sat on the stool next to hers.

"Hank."

"How are you?"

"You don't have to ask. You can just get your coffee and pie and leave."

"Daisy..." his voice strained.

"What do you want from me, Hank?" she whispered, dropping her voice. "You take care of me so gently, you protect me, and you want to be the first person I call when I'm scared or in danger. You kiss me like I've never been kissed before in my entire life. And just when I think we've turned the corner, you run. I don't want to be on this ride anymore."

"It's complicated, Daisy. I-I'm...there's just. Fuck. I don't want to get into it here. Can I stop out at the farm later?" He stepped closer to her, leaning in to place his hand on her arm.

"No. I don't think that's a good idea. I need some space

from you and your intoxicating scent. It makes me feel safe, and I don't think that's what you can actually give me. You're not safe for my heart."

Tears slid into her eyes as she turned and hopped off the stool. Her shoulders were shaking by the time she walked into the bakery's kitchen. It only took one look in her tear-filled eyes for Emma to stomp out to the counter. Daisy overheard every biting word her friend said to Hank.

"You need to do better. It's not just enough to show up when she's scared or hurt. What do you want? Because from what I've seen, you want her, Hank. If that's the case, you need to show her it's an all the time sort of feeling."

"Thanks, Emma," was all he'd said in return. Daisy heard the bell ring once more when Hank left, her heart shattering as the door closed.

Daisy slid to the floor and wrapped her arms around her legs as she cried. She felt her friend slide up next to her, but Emma just let Daisy release all her pent up emotion. When the tears finally ran out, and her breath shuddered in a final expulsion of emotion, Emma stood and held a hand out for Daisy to grab.

"Come on babe, up you go. He'll come around."

"He wanted to talk, but I told him no."

"Good. Make him earn it. If he doesn't step up and work it out, then he isn't worth your time or your tears."

"I love you, Ems."

"I love you too, Daisy."

"Now, enough of this sadness stuff. I know just what you need to shake it off."

"You do?"

A sparkle of mischief twinkled in Emma's eye.

"Girls' night! How does tomorrow sound?"

"I don't know Ems. I don't feel like getting into trouble."

"Who says we're going to get into trouble? Besides, it

won't be a real girls' night. I already know Steve will want to tag along to make sure we're safe."

"Well, how can I turn down being a third wheel?"

Emma rolled her eyes.

"Excuse me, but Steve is the third wheel, and he is well aware of that status already."

Daisy laughed. She liked Emma's boyfriend, although she wasn't sure he was the perfect fit for her friend. Whatever they had going on was sweet, and if Emma was happy for the time being, so was Daisy.

"Alright, well, as long as he understands that."

"Hooray! I think this is the best idea I've had in a while!"

Eighteen

This was a bad idea. Daisy didn't enjoy hanging out at bars, and certainly not at the Broken Spoke, which was a favorite spot for anyone local. Sure, it was the only place within fifty miles that had a decent sized dance floor and a DJ who actually played music that the patrons liked, but things also got rowdy and out of hand the later you stayed.

Parking on the edge of the lot, Daisy stepped out of her car. She checked her reflection in her car's window, regretting the ripped jean shorts and white t-shirt she'd paired with her favorite cowboy boots. Sure, it was a good look, but she felt like it showed off her curves in all the wrong ways. Maybe she'd be able to get away with just sitting in a booth for the next hour or two before heading back to the farm.

A whistle pierced the low hum of music coming from the bar. Daisy looked around and laughed when she saw Emma's goofy smile lighting up her face.

"Damn girl!! You look amazing!"

"I feel like I should go home and change. Or just stay there and go to bed." She hugged Emma, then turned to Emma's boyfriend, Steve, and smiled.

"Thanks for letting me crash girls' night." He looked happy to be there, if not a bit apprehensive about being in the middle of their shenanigans.

"Anytime! Honestly, it'll be nice to have someone rein in Emma and all her crazy ideas."

"Excuse you. My ideas are wonderful. And the first idea I have is to get you all liquored up and out on the dance floor now that you are off your pain meds and out of your sling!"

"Emma, just one drink, okay? I have the market in the morning and I don't want to be hung over hanging out with all my berries."

They made their way into the bar, which was already packed with locals enjoying the dance floor and loud music.

"Girl, you kill me! You are twenty-five, gorgeous and single. You need to be putting yourself out there so that you can find a husband who can tend your vegetable garden and your lady garden, too." Emma looped her arm through Daisy's and led her over to the bar. After ordering drinks, they walked to the booth Steve was able to grab in their absence.

"Emma! Sheesh! I'm fine. It's okay, I'm not really interested in all that right now. I need to get the farm set up and finally operating as a successful business, then I'll worry about finding someone."

"Well, I, for one, think it would be nice for you to have someone who could help you out. I don't like everything that's been going on, and I worry about you being all alone and something happening. You know, the offer to stay with me still stands."

"I'm perfectly fine. I've got that security system now. So what's going to happen? A sunflower falls over on me?"

The two women laughed, and Daisy took a sip of her drink.

"I'm sure you're right. I'm just a worrier, and I want to see you happy! Plus, Steve and I want someone to go on double dates with!"

"Jeepers! My drink is strong tonight. I'm going to have a migraine tomorrow. I can already tell." Daisy coughed from the burn of the alcohol as she took another long pull on the straw.

"Oh, don't be such a Debby Downer! Maybe you'll be too hung-over to even notice."

"That sounds even worse. Plus, I'm only having one drink."

"You are no fun!"

"And sometimes you are too much fun!" Daisy replied.

———

Hank parked his truck in the packed lot and buried his hands into his pockets as he walked into The Broken Spoke and cringed. This definitely wasn't his scene anymore. Scanning the crowd, he locked on to Daisy almost instantly.

He hadn't been expecting to see her, but there she was on the edge of the dance floor, smiling and laughing with Emma. God, she looked beautiful. Her curves were on display, and it took all the strength he had not to stomp over and claim every inch of her in front of the entire crowd.

Hank tried to do the right thing. He tried to escape her orbit, and yet here the universe was, pushing her right in front of him. Wasn't it enough that he'd forced himself to turn cold around her? That the only contact he would allow himself to have with her was a quick text at the end of the day to make sure she was safe?

Damn, her legs looked amazing in her little cutoff shorts, swaying to the music filling the bar. He needed a cold beer, and some time spent thinking about something other than the magnetic pull she had on him. Shoving his hands into his pockets, Hank walked to the bar and sat on a stool, waiting for the bartender to come take his order.

The next time he looked for her, she was sitting next to Dale Giunetti. The slimy bastard had his arm around her, pulling her into his chest. What the actual fuck? She couldn't really be interested in that low life, could she? The idea of him putting his hands on Daisy instantly soured the alcohol in Hank's stomach.

He deserved the ache he felt spreading through his heart. After all, she'd shown time and time again that she was interested in him, and all he'd done was give her hope and then run away when the fear of his feelings overwhelmed him. There was too much of a connection, too much of a spark with Daisy, and if he was being honest with himself, it was scary to feel things he'd worked so hard to build a wall against.

Deciding to keep his butt planted on the seat at the bar, Hank ordered another beer and sat back, trying to look anywhere other than in her direction. It was no use. His curiosity made sure Daisy was still in his line of sight.

Hank watched Dale pull Daisy into his chest, but she pushed him away, moving closer to the wall in the booth she was sitting in. The hair stood up on the back of his neck and a burning need to protect her surged through his veins. The muscles in his jaw ached from how hard he was grinding his molars together. She looked uncomfortable, and it'd be a cold day in Hell when he didn't step in to protect her.

He watched Daisy as she checked out of the conversation happening around her, taking out her phone and looking down at the screen. Hank felt his phone buzz and his jaw dropped when he saw a new message come in from her.

How was work today?

She was texting him while she was on a date? Damn, why

did that make his heart pound in his chest? Had she not seen him come in? Or was this a game she was playing?

It was fine. Came out for a beer by myself afterwards. I'd ask how your day was, but I don't want to take your attention away from your date.

He sent the message and couldn't help but watch Daisy to see her reaction. When her screen lit up, so did her face. Then she read the message. He watched her eyes jump from her screen to the people surrounding her. Her eyes roamed until, finally, they met his. He gave her a nod and then turned away.

After downing the last mouthful of his beer, Hank watched Dale turn his attention back to her, pulling her close to his body once more, ignoring her protests to be left alone. Hank was up on his feet walking towards their booth in an instant, but when Daisy's eyes met his with a fierce fire burning in them, he kept walking towards the restroom. He looked Dale in the eyes as he went by. A few minutes later, as he walked out and back towards the bar, his heart sank.

"Okay, Dale, let her out now. It's not funny anymore." Emma was nearly shouting, her boyfriend looking like a fish out of water, trying to decide if the situation was worth getting into a fight for or not. Hank wouldn't let him make that decision. He'd handle the situation himself.

"Let me out of this booth right now, Dale." Daisy was standing on the bench seat trying to climb over him as Dale held on to her body.

"You're not going anywhere, you little tease, unless it's right onto my lap." Dale's response was enough to make Hank's blood boil with rage.

"What's going on here?" His heart was beating out of his

chest as he watched Dale let Daisy go, her face turning bright red as she looked away.

"Nothing is going on here, Sheriff. Daisy and I were just having a drink together. Isn't that right Daisy?" He didn't wait for a response before continuing, "You look like you're dressed awfully casual for acting in such a demanding manner." Dale put his finger through a belt loop on Daisy's jean shorts and tugged her towards him.

"I'm not on official business right now, Dale. I came in for a drink. But I can clearly see that Daisy is uncomfortable with how you are acting and just thought I'd come make sure everything was okay."

"She's fine, ain't you, sweetheart? You like Dale being so close, don't you?"

"No, I don't. I've asked you nicely three times to leave me alone, but you don't seem to know how to take no for an answer. I don't appreciate you kissing me without my permission, and I'd like to leave now." Daisy removed his hand from her body, but as she attempted to step over him, Dale grabbed her wrist.

"You don't just walk away from me, you stuck-up bitch."

Hank watched Daisy swat away Dale's hand as it moved further up her thigh. When he latched on to her bottom, Daisy let out a shriek and Hank watched Emma's boyfriend leap over the table to try to physically separate them.

"Wrong answer." Hank burst in between them and yanked Dale's hand away from Daisy. "Did you really think manhandling a woman in front of the Sheriff was a smart move?"

"Oh, come on. You know, she's just a prude and a tease. It ain't fair, her always turning her nose up at everyone when she's no better than the rest of us. Her own parents didn't even want to stick around and keep her."

Hank heard Daisy gasp and pain ricocheted through his

body when he registered what Dale had just said. That pain was quickly replaced with anger.

"He kissed you without your permission?" Hank asked Daisy.

"Yes," she answered with her eyes trained to her shoes.

"Do you want to press charges?" Hank held on to Dale as he struggled to free himself from Hank's grasp.

Looking up at Hank, Daisy quickly responded.

"I, uh, no. I don't think that's necessary. He's just had too much to drink." Hank watched as she placed her arms together across her body and moved her gaze towards her friends.

"Daisy is doing you a big favor here, Dale. So listen. I'm going to give you one chance to apologize and walk out of here for the night. If you say another word besides 'I'm sorry' and 'goodnight', I will make the decision to arrest you for harassment and assault." Hank's anger was boiling over, but he tried to rein it in, knowing how many eyes in the bar had been watching him, including Daisy's. When Dale protested, he simply replied, "Don't test me."

Defeated, Dale turned to Daisy and said, "I'm sorry."

"Now, walk out of this bar, Dale, and go home."

"Sure thing, Sheriff." Dale walked out with his tail between his legs, but Hank didn't care. Serves him right for thinking he could treat a woman like that.

Turning towards Daisy, who was in the middle of collecting her jacket and purse, he asked, "Are you okay?"

But he never expected for there to be a fire in her eyes when she looked back at him.

"Yes. I'm perfectly fine. I didn't need you to step in there and threaten him. I can take care of myself."

"I know you can, sunshine."

He glanced at Emma, who herself looked to be on the verge of tears.

"I'm so sorry, Daisy. I shouldn't have pushed so hard for you to let him join us. I d-didn't know he'd act like that."

"It's not your fault. I could have said no, too. I just wanted to forget for one night."

"Forget what?" Hank asked. She paused, her eyes lingering on Emma's face before moving to his.

"You."

There was a moment where all the air left his lungs and he feared he'd never pull in a full breath again.

Emma's words pulled him back. "Do you want Steve and I to walk you to your car?"

"No, Em, I'm really fine. You guys enjoy the rest of your night and I'll see you at the market tomorrow."

"I don't think we're going to stay, so we can walk out with you. It's no problem."

"No. Please stay and have some time together. I'm fine, and I have to get home, anyway. I'll text you later."

"Okay, if you're sure?"

"I'm sure." Daisy blurted out her goodbyes as she rushed past Hank towards the doors.

"Well, Hank? Are you going to go after her?" Emma asked.

With the way she had just ran without looking at him, no, he didn't think she wanted to see him again. And he couldn't blame her. She might be mad, but she should know there would never be a time when he wouldn't intervene to keep her safe.

"No. She made it pretty clear she's mad at me. I think I'll cut my losses while I can and just let her cool off."

Hank marched back to the bar. Instead of ordering another beer, he waited a few minutes and then closed out his tab. Why had she gotten so upset with him for protecting her? Of course, she could handle things on her own, but she shouldn't have to. He wanted to protect her.

With his head wrapped up in thoughts as he walked back to his truck, he almost missed the sound of muffled cries coming from the alleyway beside the bar. Almost.

Turning to look at where the sound came from, his heart jumped into his throat when he saw two shadows struggling.

"Come on, you prude bitch. Give me what I want. I'll make it fast, but I can't promise it'll be painless."

"I SAID NO!" Hank was running at the sound of Daisy's frantic protests.

"Hey! What's going on over here?" his voice boomed. Dale's pants were undone, slung low on his hips, and his hand was wrapped around his exposed self. Daisy's shirt was torn and Dale had his hand around her breasts, fondling them.

Hank saw red. His head exploded with rage and his hands clenched into fists as he readied to end Dale's pathetic life.

"AHHHHHHH!" Dale let out a scream. Daisy must have bitten the hand that was frantically trying to cover her mouth. Hank moved towards them, watching in horror as Dale hit Daisy in the face. He ran full speed into Dale, tackling him to the ground in a heap.

Daisy stood still, one hand holding her shirt, the other covering the spot where Dale had hit her. Her chest rose and fell frantically and he could tell she was caught between adrenaline fueling her desire to run and fear freezing her to the spot where she stood.

Dale needed to be dealt with, then he could comfort her. Fighting every instinct in his body that was telling him to go to her, he turned and knelt on Dale's back. Spreading his legs and arms out, Hank moved down Dale's body, searching for weapons. He found a switchblade in Dale's shoe and zip ties in his back pocket.

"What were you planning on doing to her, you piece of shit?"

"Nothing she doesn't deserve."

Hank pulled one of the zip ties out and bound Dale's hands behind his back. He did the same to his feet.

"Don't fight me Dale. I gave you a chance to go home, and you lurked out here in the alley and assaulted Daisy. Wrong choice."

"She asked for it. She was begging me for another chance after you interrupted. I didn't do nothing she didn't ask for. Nothing she wouldn't be crying out for if she wasn't such a stuck-up bitch."

"Stop. Talking." Hank growled into his ear. He wanted to rip this man into tiny pieces for touching Daisy.

"She's going to get what's coming to her though. You just wait and see."

"What did you just say?" The words seethed from Hank's mouth. "Did you just threaten her?"

"It's not a threat. It's a promise. I'm not the only one she's pissed off. I'm not the only one who wants what's rightfully theirs."

"Nothing of Daisy's is rightfully yours. She doesn't owe you a smile, a pleasant word, and she especially doesn't owe you any part of her body." Grabbing Dale's shirt, Hank shoved him against the alley wall. "Who else poses a threat to Daisy?"

"How about you let me go? We forget about this, and I'll give you a name."

"Not a snowflake's chance in Hell."

"Well, then, I guess you'll just have to wait it out and see. Too bad it's not going to end well for your girlfriend."

Hank felt the veins in his neck bulge. His muscles were burning with the desire to pummel this pathetic excuse of a man into the ground. Instead, he shoved him down to the ground against the brick building.

"I suggest you sit there and shut your mouth, Dale. Right. Now."

Hank looked over his shoulder. Daisy stood there, holding

her left arm, silent tears once again falling down her face. They were shining in the moonlight, and the sight of her there, once again injured, pulled the truth from within Hank's armored heart. He didn't just want to protect Daisy because she was part of his responsibility as sheriff. Daisy was his to protect.

When he was finally satisfied that the scumbag wouldn't be going anywhere, he left him in the dirt, moving quickly to Daisy's side.

She was pale. Too pale. Her body was shaking, tears falling down her face and dotting her shirt. Hank called out her name, but she didn't respond.

"Daisy. Listen to me. You're safe now. I'm so sorry, sunshine. I really am. But you're safe."

He watched her blink, the fog in her gaze slowly clearing up as she came back from whatever she had been lost to.

"Hank?"

Before he could respond, she crashed into his chest, his arms wrapping around her in an instant.

"What happened?" His chest rumbled with rage. "Daisy, look at me..." he lifted her chin with his finger and swept her hair from her face. "What happened?"

"He...he...Hank..."

"Shh. You're okay, now."

Fishing through his pocket, he pulled out his cell phone and called in to dispatch. Luckily, deputies were on patrol just a few blocks down from the bar and arrived quickly to help.

"We'll take him in for you, Hank, unless you want to see to this yourself?"

"Nah, I trust you Wilkins. I need to make sure Daisy gets checked over, anyway." He patted the young deputy on the shoulder and watched as the cruiser took Dale away.

Walking calmly over to Daisy, Hank stopped short of pulling her into his arms. He'd struggled to maintain his composure as she walked the deputy through what happened for the official report. Now that she was done with that, he needed to get her to the hospital.

"Tomorrow, I want you to come in and we'll work on a restraining order for you against Dale. He won't be able to get within a mile of you when I'm done with him."

"I appreciate that, Hank, but I don't think it's necessary. He's just drunk. Let him sleep it off and then let him be on his way."

"No, sunshine, I can't do that. He assaulted you. Who knows what would have happened if I hadn't been walking out to my truck when I was."

"It doesn't matter. Can I go home now?" She bit her bottom lip and looked up into his eyes. "I'd really like to go."

"You need to be seen by a doctor."

"No, Hank. I'm okay. I just want to go home." The tears in her voice were enough to rip his heart into tiny pieces. He saw how desperate she was to leave, to be somewhere she felt safe. Although, did she even have that anymore with everything going on?

When he snapped out of his thoughts, he realized she was almost to her car.

"Hey, Daisy, wait a second!"

Fumbling with her keys, her shaking hands betrayed her and dropped them outside her door.

"Here, let me." Hank reached her car and quickly scooped the keys up. "Are you okay?" he asked as he tried to hand the keys back to her, but she remained still, her back towards him. "Daisy?" Hank gently rested his hand on the back of her arm and walked around to face her.

He watched as tears poured from her eyes down to the pavement in silent rivers. She crouched down to the ground and brought her hands up to cover her face. It wasn't easy, or painless, for him to do, but Hank followed, crouching down as low as he could go to give her support, despite the pain crying out from his knee.

"Aw hell, Daisy. Don't cry."

"S-sorry. I should be able to keep it t-together."

"No, sunshine. You don't have to keep it together around me. That's not what I meant when I told you not to cry. It's that I want to fix it all for you. But I don't know how to do that without beating the hell out of Dale. And trust me, as much as I would love to, it's not the best idea."

"That wouldn't fix anything."

Hank stood, extending his hand out to Daisy. As she found her footing, she shuddered through the last of her tears.

"No? He violated your personal space. I mean, when I came outside and heard you scream, fuck, I wanted to throttle him into next week..." his calloused hand moved to the back of his neck and he attempted to wring out all the tension in his muscles, "but that wouldn't be too proper of me as the sheriff."

"No, I suppose not. I can't even think about him touching me like he did, or kissing me." She shuddered, wincing and cradling her left arm.

"Is your arm bothering you?"

"It's just my shoulder. I must have aggravated it when I tried to push him off of me. Hank, his words just keep ringing in my ears. I never realized—"

"Nothing he said matters."

"That's not true, Hank. He said exactly what I've always been afraid of, but just blindly shoved it down. I don't know why I didn't realize everyone thought those things about me."

"I refuse to believe that you think anything that comes out of that asshole's mouth even closely resembles the truth."

"Tell me you don't see me that way." She paused. "Because you can't. You see the same thing everyone else does. That I'm worth abandoning."

Hank pushed back a strand of hair that had fallen into her face.

"Nothing could be farther from the truth."

"Why? My parents did it. The people who are supposed to love me the most in my whole life just left me on my grandparent's porch. I'm not worth anything to anyone. I'm just someone that gets used until the next best thing comes along." She sniffled, running her fingers under her nose and across her cheeks to sweep away the tears.

"Daisy." He lifted her face towards his, waiting to continue until her eyes met his. "Please believe me when I say that nothing could be farther from the truth. Your parents were the ones who left, not because of you, but because of their own issues. You were not to blame."

"It's no big deal." She moved his hand away from her face and he cleared his throat, pulling himself out of the intimate moment and back into a distanced stance. "I didn't mean to get all weepy." Daisy continued. "Thank you for everything, Hank. I'm just going to head home now."

Watching her hands shake as she tried to put the key into the door lock, Hank took her hands into his own and said, "I think we need to get that shoulder looked at before you head anywhere. And we need to get a doctor's report for what happened with Dale. Come on, I'll give you a ride to the hospital."

"No, that's not necessary."

"Daisy, forget the stuff from tonight. If you really don't want to see a doctor for that, I can't make you. But you remember what Jake said about your shoulder, right? You injure it again before it's fully healed and it could cause permanent damage. You need to be seen."

"I'll go get it checked in the morning, Hank. I'm tired and I just want to go home."

"Fine. But if you're going home without seeing if it's re-injured, I'm staying with you until you get it checked."

"What? No, you don't need to do that."

"Yes, I do Daisy. This was my fault, and I need to make sure you're okay."

He watched the wheels turning in her head. He had meant what he said. She was hurt because of him. There was no way he would let her try to suffer through it without him there to help.

"Alright," she sighed and relief flooded his chest. "Let's go."

Nineteen

"Hank is going to wear a hole in the floor with the way he's pacing outside this room. Are you sure you wouldn't like some company?" Jake was busy typing away on a small computer when he asked.

"I don't even know why he's here. I mean, I know he's here because he felt some need to drive me here and make sure my shoulder was okay, but why? I'm nothing to him."

"I think we both know that's not true." Jake moved closer to Daisy, and she raised her eyes to meet his.

"What do you mean?"

"We'll circle back to that in a minute. But why don't you go over with me how this happened? Hank mentioned being at the Broken Spoke, but didn't give any other details."

"Oh, um, there was just a guy who wouldn't take no for an answer. Hank intervened, and made him leave, but I guess he stuck around outside because when I was walking to my car, he grabbed me." Her voice stuck in her throat and her gaze lingered on the floor. Surely she didn't have to go further than that. She didn't know if she'd be able to keep it together if she did.

"That's all that happened, the guy grabbed you?"

"Jake."

"Daisy, I just want to understand. If there was more, if he hurt you more, I want to help you." He gently touched her arms and looked over the bruises that were already forming.

"H-he tried to, I mean, he was trying t-to do more. B-but he didn't have time to." Tears dotted her lash line and then they flowed freely, completely disregarding how hard she was working to keep it all together.

"That must have been really scary. I'm so sorry that happened."

"I don't even know why I'm crying. Nothing happened. Hank was walking by and stepped in. I'm fine."

"Daisy, you were physically assaulted tonight. You've been working to recover from the accident and then to have this happen. Of course you're going to be emotional." She quickly accepted the tissue he was handing to her. "Do you have someone you can talk to about this?"

"Not really, but it's okay. I'm okay."

"I know you are incredibly strong, but when things like this happen, it's not only the physical things you have to get over. There's a psychological component, too. I just want to make sure you are taking care of that part of yourself, too."

"It's not my first time dealing with something like this." She watched the concern on Jake's face turn to shock and then understanding.

"I didn't see anything in your medical history."

"I didn't report it."

"Have you told Hank?"

She was sure her face betrayed her own shock now.

"I've never told anyone."

"Daisy, I think it would be good for you to let him in. He cares about you. He will want to help you through this."

"As much as a sheriff cares about anyone who lives in the area he serves."

"No, you're wrong. If you don't want to talk to him, I can get you some resources, names of therapists or support groups that can help." She just shook her head slowly.

In the years since it happened, Daisy had pushed through. She was okay. She would be okay. She didn't need to burden anyone else with it.

"Listen, that guy out there is my best friend. And he would absolutely kill me if he knew I was saying this right now, but I don't care. I can't keep watching you two dance around each other, never landing on the same page. He has never talked about another woman since his ex left. Not a single one. Now, in the past few weeks, you are all he talks about. Wanting to check in on you, wanting to see you at the market, wanting to go spend time with you and your cows. Do you not know how wild that is for me to witness? You have to know he's not just doing that as a sheriff looking after someone who lives under his protection. The guy is nuts about you."

"I-I, no. I didn't know. I thought, well, every time I've started something," she felt her face flush with embarrassment, "he's never really reciprocated. Or if he did, he pulled away immediately after. How am I supposed to take that, other than that he regretted what happened?"

"Daisy, that is a man conflicted about his feelings and not wanting to hurt you. Is it right? Hell no. I keep trying to tell him that, but we both know he's as stubborn as they come. Talk to him."

There was that undeniable electricity between them. What if she was letting her own insecurities run wild through her mind, and not focusing on what everyone around her was saying? Could Hank really be struggling with whether he was good enough for her? She had waited for Hank to make some sort of move since the first time they met. Hasn't she made it perfectly clear she was attracted to him, that she'd wanted him, right from that very first kiss?

Jake stood up, waiting for Daisy to reply.

"Okay, you can tell him he can come in."

"Perfect. Now, about that shoulder. I'm going to tell you something you don't want to hear, and I'm sorry about that. You need to let it rest for at least another week. It's not to where I'm going to say it needs to be immobilized like before. However, you've got some inflammation setting in and I'm sure that's only going to increase over the next twenty-four hours. I'll send you home with some anti-inflammatory medication and I want you to rest that arm. I know we had the whole 'busy with farm work' talk last time, but let's try to work within the same restrictions as before as much as you can, okay?"

"I'll manage."

"I can talk to Hank if you want? Maybe he can swing some time to help you out."

"No, that's okay. I'll let him know what's going on and figure it out myself."

"Sure. I'll be back in a few minutes with your discharge papers."

"Thanks, Jake."

He squeezed her hand and gave her a smile before stepping out into the hallway.

Daisy's stomach was in knots. She didn't want to tell Hank her darkest secret. She didn't want to relive the details of that day in college when her life changed. Where she went from trusting men to never feeling truly safe around them. The day she realized she was nothing more than a person who could be so easily used and discarded. Always a burden. Those that should have loved her seemed to be the ones to leave her at her most vulnerable. Here she was, needing help again, and she'd rather be cold and in the ground before having to rely on someone else for help.

———

Hank paced the hallway in front of Daisy's room so furiously he thought they might need to replace the flooring from excessive wear. He was mad. Mad that she didn't want him to be in there with her. Jake wouldn't tell him anything about her shoulder and he knew she had sustained other injuries. There was a mark on her cheek from where Dale had hit her, and angry looking bruises on her arms and wrists from where he had tried to restrain her.

The smell of antiseptic and chemical cleaners filled the hallway. He'd never been a fan of the hospital, and it pained him even more that his most recent trips here had been to make sure Daisy was okay.

His blood boiled thinking about another man touching her. And she hadn't even wanted that touch. No one deserved to be violated like that. No, Dale's touch had been rough and scary, and it had broken his heart to hear her trying to scream for help. The terror in her eyes had made him want to beat that asshole to a pulp. To forget he'd ever been a member of law enforcement. To do unspeakable things to protect her.

"Hank?" Jake placed a gentle arm on his shoulder as he closed the door behind him.

"Is she okay?"

"She will be."

"I don't like that she keeps ending up here. What am I missing?"

"I think you're missing the part where she wants you to tell her how you feel about her."

"Hell, Jake, that's not what I mean. I'm not...I'm not what

she needs. I have to protect her, and I need to figure out who is behind everything that's happened to her."

"You don't think it's the guy who attacked her tonight?"

"He's a scumbag, but he doesn't strike me as someone smart enough to coordinate tampering with her truck, although he could be the person who's been outside her house on multiple occasions. He also made a comment about him not being the only one who wanted to take something from Daisy."

"So, he's impulsive. So impulsive that he tried to rape her while you were there in the bar. But he's not a mastermind."

Hank wanted to vomit.

"I can't believe I didn't walk out right after she'd left. I didn't make sure she was safe."

"Listen, she doesn't think she's yours to protect. She thinks you would be this torn up about any other citizen here in Clarence County. But she's wrong. I know it, and you know it. She deserves to know how you feel about her."

"Jake..."

"She's not Anna, Hank. We both know that. She's worth putting your heart out there again for."

"You're right. She is." He scrubbed his hand across his face. "I need to tell her. But no matter what, there's no way I'm letting her out of my sight now. I should have told her after the accident. I should have been there to protect her."

"Okay, enough beating yourself up about it. You did what you thought was best. It wasn't." Hank glared at Jake, who smiled as both his hands shot up in the air like he was innocent. "But listen, you figured out you were wrong and now you can fix it. So go, fix it. I'll take a few extra minutes gathering her discharge paperwork."

Hank looked down at his feet, and then at the door to her hospital room.

"Just go in there and talk to her." Jake slapped a rough hand on Hank's shoulder and smiled.

Hank watched Jake walk down the hallway to the nurses' station and wondered when his friend had become so wise. He'd been burned by a woman too, and made his fair share of mistakes, but Jake had never lost his hope for love like Hank had. There was something there with Daisy, though, that brought hope to life again in his heart. Every time he looked at her, when they touched, when they kissed. It's always been electric. And it hadn't faded one bit since the first time he'd held her. Yep, he was in deep for Daisy. And now he needed to do everything in his power to convince her of that.

Gulping down a big breath, Hank knocked gently on the door. He didn't hear a reply, so he softly opened the door, giving her plenty of time to protest.

"Hey, sunshine. Jake said it was finally okay for me to come in. You okay?"

He watched her eyes lift to meet his, and it felt like someone had punched him in the gut. Her face was filled with a black and blue mark from where Dale had hit her, and as he scanned her body, he saw horrible bruises showing their anger on her arms. Dale had held her, forcing her to stay in place, and now she would have to look at those marks and relive those moments. Hank wanted nothing more than to scoop her up and hold her until they disappeared. Until they figured out who was behind everything that had been happening lately, and even beyond that.

He studied her face. She was grimacing now, trying to move her left arm. Her right hand held onto it like she was afraid her left arm was about to fly away from her body.

"I'm okay." Hmmm, not a totally truthful assessment there, but he'd let it slide for now. He'd already made up his mind.

"Well, that's good. Did Jake say anything about your shoulder?"

"He'll be back in a minute to discharge me. It looks fine."

"Is it hurting? You're holding it awfully tight there." He nodded towards her arm and tried to give her a reassuring smile. "Want to try again and tell me how it actually is?"

"It really is fine. I just...I have to rest for the next week. Jake said there's inflammation in it."

"Okay." He truly believed she would ask him to stay out at the farm again. When she opened her mouth, his heart fell.

"Before you can even say it, I just want you to know that I'm okay being by myself. It was nice having you around to help last time, but you don't need to rearrange everything again to help me out."

She didn't want his help. So much for Jake being an expert in these things.

"Okay." He wasn't about to get into a fight with her. She looked exhausted and stressed, two things that weren't great for recovering from trauma. And that's what tonight had been for her. Traumatic.

"Looks like you're thinking awfully hard there, sunshine. Want to share?" She looked so conflicted by his response, or lack thereof, that the question slipped out before he'd really even thought about why he was asking it.

"No."

Just then, Jake walked back in, complete with release paperwork.

"Okay. So like I said before, no using that left arm for a week. If the pain gets worse, just come back and see me, and we'll re-evaluate from there."

"Thanks, Jake."

"Sure thing." Jake turned to Hank with a smile on his face. "I assume you'll be staying with her to help again, Hank?"

His eyes turned towards Daisy, whose mouth had opened, shocked at Jake's question and devilish smile.

"Oh, no—" she started to speak, but Hank stopped her mid sentence when he scooped her right hand up into his, lacing his fingers through hers.

"Yep. I'll be there."

He smiled down at Daisy, who was busy looking up at him with a puzzled look on her face.

"Hank? I just told you, you don't have to."

"I know, sunshine. And now I'm telling you I'm going to. What do you say? Can I take you home now?"

TWENTY

All the way to the farmhouse, Daisy was quiet. Hank listened to the sound of tires on asphalt, his blinker turning on and off, hitting the dirt of Daisy's driveway. God, he just wanted to know what she was thinking. Was she still grappling with what Dale had said to her? His heart was in a million pieces, knowing she thought no one cared about her. That she was someone worth abandoning. That was the farthest thing from the truth and tonight he would tell her just how much she meant to him.

Pulling up next to the front porch, Hank parked. They sat there, waiting for something to break the silence. Finally, he decided he would.

"I'm so sorry he put his hands on you again. He should have never had the chance. I failed to protect you."

"I'm not yours to worry about, Hank. I was the one who left by myself. I was the one who turned him down, taunting him. This is on me."

"Don't. Don't you dare take any of the blame and put it on yourself."

"But it was, Hank." He watched her closely, and felt a

crushing pain in his chest when she whispered, "Just like before."

Just like before? Had Dale attacked her another time? How would he have not known about this?

"Daisy, what do you mean it's like before?"

"I, what? I didn't say that." Her eyes were glazed and he could see the pain in them.

"You did. You said it was your fault, just like before. Has Dale hurt you before?"

"No."

Thank god. He was already having a hard enough time not going to beat the life out of Dale for what he'd done to Daisy. There would be no stopping him if Dale had touched her in the past, too. But if it wasn't Dale, that meant...Fuck. There was that sharp pain in his chest, once again squeezing the air from his lungs.

"So, it wasn't Dale, but someone hurt you before? In the same way?"

"Hank."

"I'm just trying to understand. I just want to make sure you're okay."

"I'm fine. You've made sure I got home safe. It's late and I'm tired and I just want to go to sleep."

Hank walked around his truck and helped Daisy down before heading up to the front door.

"Here, let me have your keys." He took them from her hand and opened the door. Stepping inside, he punched in the code for her security system. He'd expected to feel her walking in with him, but she wasn't there. Turning, he saw the tears in her eyes as she pressed herself against the door.

"Daisy?"

"C-can you turn on the lights? It's too dark."

"Of course. Come in and let's get the door locked so I can

rearm your system. I'll go turn on all the lights for you once you're inside."

She let out a sigh and Hank worked as quickly as he could, illuminating the path up to her room.

"Are you...I mean, will you stay here tonight?"

"I'm not going anywhere, sunshine."

"Thank you." The relief in her eyes punched him in the gut.

Hank cleared his throat and ran his hand across his chin.

"Do you want anything to eat? I could make something quick?"

"No, I'm good. You can make whatever for yourself, though. The fridge has all the stuff I wasn't planning on taking to the market tomorrow. I think I'll just take a quick shower. I need to wash away the feeling of him touching me."

His muscles instantly tensed.

"I'm so sorry, Daisy."

"Hank, please. Stop apologizing. You're the reason he only touched me, and wasn't able to go further. You protected me tonight. I'm thankful you were there."

He gently took her hand and squeezed reassuringly. Her skin was cold, and he felt the trembling she was trying to conceal.

"If you need anything, just call out to me, okay? I'll just be down the hall."

"Okay."

———

Daisy walked to her room and gently closed the door. Once in the bathroom, she turned the shower on as hot as it would go, and under the scalding stream of water, she scrubbed her skin until it was numb.

The hot water helped her aching muscles relax, but what she hadn't counted on was how that relief from the pain would open the floodgates for her emotions. Her breath hitched as she tried to stop the sobs from breaking free, but it was a futile attempt. Her body folded in half, tears flowing as she braced against the wall of the shower. She lowered herself down until she was seated, with her arms wrapped around her knees.

She hated feeling like this. So desperately inadequate. Not being strong enough to protect herself before, she'd sworn that would never happen again. And yet here she was, fighting to control the rage and devastating sadness that she'd been too weak to protect herself again. There had been no one to help her last time. But this time, she'd had Hank. Once again, jumping in to save her.

He was her fierce protector. There was no denying that. He'd chosen to stay with her like it was just the obvious choice that he would. Daisy knew he wanted to make sure she was okay and felt safe, and damn it, the only reason she did was because he was there. She wanted to tell him what had happened all those years ago. She finally needed to ask someone to help her with the weight of carrying her pain.

Pulling herself up and out of the shower, she reached back in to shut off the water. The sound of herself breathing in the now quiet bathroom had her instantly thinking about Dale's hot breath searing into the side of her face as he pressed his body against hers. Forcing herself to not fall apart again, she toweled off and dressed in an old T-shirt and shorts, her wet hair flying up into a messy ponytail. The pulling sensation in her shoulder made her wince while her mind wandered back to the alley. There was too much pent up nervous energy in her body, begging to be released before she went to find Hank. The stress and adrenaline from the night was clearly wreaking havoc on her body. Maybe she would just slip down to the kitchen for a glass of water.

Her feet froze in place when she saw him sitting at her dining room table, head lowered into his hands. The floorboard beneath her foot let out a squeak, and Hank's head bolted upright at the sound.

"Sorry, I didn't mean to make you jump. Just wanted to get some water before bed."

"It's fine. I had to take a call from work, and didn't want to disturb you by talking if you were trying to sleep."

Her eyes flicked towards her front window, and the fear of everything that had been happening washed over her. Nausea rolled in her stomach and tears stung in her eyes. Her hands pulled at the hem of her shirt, rolling the fabric between her finger and her thumb. Hadn't she cried enough? Why was the sight of this amazing, caring man sitting there looking so defeated, causing a whole new round of emotions to flood her system? She needed to stop the tears, stop the fear, and just be strong for once in her life.

"Would it be okay for me to give you a hug?" he asked.

More than anything, she just wanted to be held by him. Had he known? Could he sense her desperation?

"Yes. I-I'd like that Hank."

The moment she accepted, he closed the distance between them, gently wrapping his arms around her body. Her new resolve shattered, and she fell apart all over again.

Daisy melted into Hank's touch. It was kind and filled with warmth. His arms weren't taking from her body, they were giving her safety. Tears spilled from her eyes and soaked the shirt she was now clinging on to.

Suddenly, Daisy's world was tipping. She didn't pay attention to the movement, though. She wrapped her arms around Hank's neck, pressing her face farther into his chest.

"Just breathe, Daisy. You're safe. You're going to be okay." Hank's voice soothed her heart, over and over, with the same three sentences, as her hand grasped tighter to his shirt.

The next time she opened her eyes, Hank was setting her back on her feet in her bedroom. Her body chilled as he moved away from her. Rolling down the edge of the comforter on her bed, he held his hand out and helped her into bed.

She didn't want him to go, unsure if she'd be able to sleep without him near. The tears were still there, and she desperately needed him to stay.

"Please," she whispered as he stood next to the bed, watching her. "Please stay."

He didn't respond. Instead, he walked around to the far side of the bed. Daisy didn't move, but she felt the bed dip and then Hank's warm body was there next to hers. His arms engulfed her in strength and he pulled her into his chest. That's when she finally turned to face him, snuggling her head under his chin.

"Sleep, Daisy. I'm right here. I'll keep you safe." A soft kiss landed in her hair and before she knew it, sleep came.

———

"You're going to regret that jungle juice in the morning!" Jasmine, the larger-than-life redhead who she'd met at freshman orientation and become instant friends with, yelled over the booming music of the frat house. Daisy didn't care. She just wanted to forget about the fight she'd had with Grady.

"He's a piece of shit, Daisy. But you don't need to get shit-faced to prove anything to him."

"I'm not drinking for him. I'm drinking for me. I don't want to feel anything other than peaceful numbness, and this is going a long way to help with that!" Daisy sat on the couch, acutely aware that it was wet and sticky. She didn't want to think about why.

"What did you even see in that jerk, anyway?"

"My future."

"Oh, Daisy."

"Whatever Jazz. I don't want to talk about him anymore unless it's talking about what an insecure prick he is. I can't believe he thought I was cheating with my lab partner. Just because we were studying more than usual. What was so hard to understand about me being absolutely terrible at chemistry?"

"Well, I mean, Luca is ridiculously gorgeous. But that doesn't mean anything happened between you two!"

"Exactly."

"Are you going to be okay if I mingle a little? I think I saw Bodhi head into the kitchen. I'd like to flirt with him before we head out."

Daisy laughed. Jasmine was the biggest flirt she'd ever met, and all the guys knew it, including Bodhi, who she'd sparked an interest in a few weeks before.

"Don't stay here on my account. Tell him I said hi...and good luck!" She winked at her friend, who scoffed, and bounced down the hallway towards her latest conquest.

Another sip from her party cup, another moment the pain edged further and further away.

"This seat taken?"

She heard the voice, but couldn't make out his features. Maybe she did need to slow down. Being a lightweight, she didn't always stick to pacing herself appropriately.

"No, please, sit. It's all yours." Her voice was distant now, almost as if she wasn't fully in her body.

"I don't think we've met before." She heard the voice say.

"No. I don't think so either. Are you a student here?"

"Nope, I'm visiting my friend. He's in this frat. I'll be heading home tomorrow."

"Oh, well, it was nice of you to come and visit your friend."

"Yeah, I had to once he told me the prettiest girls he's ever seen came to these frat parties. And now I know he wasn't full of shit."

"How do you know that?"

"Well, because I saw you."

If she could control her eyes right now, she'd definitely be rolling them into the back of her head at such a cheesy line. But they seemed to have a mind of their own, not focusing on anything in the room, no matter how hard she tried to get them to.

"That's very sweet, but I'm seeing someone."

"Not according to that conversation you were just having with your friend." Why couldn't she make out what this guy looked like? Her head swam and her arms and legs felt heavy. Nausea rolled through her stomach as her eyelids grew heavy.

"Once your friend came up to me to get a drink, I knew I had to come over and say hi. Why don't you come upstairs with me?"

"Oh, no...I d-don't think..." What was wrong with her? Sweat formed on her brow. Maybe she really had indulged in too much alcohol.

"I'm not f-feeling very well. Excuse m-me." But as Daisy tried to make her way past the strange, amorphous man on the sofa, she fell, landing directly on his lap.

"Oh sweetheart, if you wanted some of that, you only had to ask. Let's go." In the next moment, Daisy was floating through the air. She watched as the stairs slowly moved by, and before she could blink, she was being placed down on a bed.

"I-I'm okay. I need to...find...my friend." Why was it so hard to talk? She'd never had this reaction to alcohol before. "Jasmine? Help me, please," she whispered.

The man pulled down her skirt. She wanted to fight, to kick her legs, to scream out telling him no, but the darkness was closing in. The last thing she could make out was the sound of his fly unzipping. His warm breath lingered on her skin, and then there was darkness.

Twenty-One

She'd fallen asleep in his arms, trusting him to keep her safe. And if that didn't just tear him apart. He'd failed her, and still, there she was, clinging to him like he was her lifeline.

Her breathing evened out over a few minutes after the tears stopped falling, but Hank continued to hold her. An hour passed, maybe even two, before he slipped out from her bed and headed to the room that he'd stayed in so many nights over the past month.

He was nearly asleep when he heard her cries fill the house. Should he go to her? Would she want him to comfort him, or would she realize he was responsible for her pain?

When the cries didn't calm, Hank slipped his pants back on over his boxers and quietly moved down the hall and into her room.

"Daisy. Sunshine. You're having a bad dream. It's time to wake up." He gently placed his hand on the side of her face, watching her eyes flutter open as he swept her sweat soaked hair off of her forehead. She searched around in the dark, finally landing on Hank's face.

Raising her hand to cover his, her breath sawed in and out of her chest.

"Hank?"

"You were having a nightmare."

"Oh, I'm sorry."

"You don't have to apologize."

She cleared her throat.

"I do when I clearly woke you up." He watched her close her eyes tightly and ever so slightly shake her head, as if she was trying to shake away the last lingering moments of tormented sleep. "It was just a bad dream. You can go."

Like hell. The very last thing he wanted in the entire world was to walk out of this room and leave her alone.

"Want to talk about it?"

He watched her pull inwards, covering more of her body with her comforter.

"I-It's just a nightmare. I've had it before. It's been a long time since it happened, but I think tonight, with Dale," he watched her swallow, "I think it just brought it back up."

"What was the dream about, Daisy?"

She tried to pull her body up to a sitting position, but he heard her swear under her breath, pain flaring in her eyes.

"Here, let me help." Placing his hands on her waist, he lifted her up a little and gave her time to get her legs situated before setting her gently back onto the bed.

"I was a sophomore in college. One night, my friend Jasmine and I went to a frat party. It wasn't unusual for us to be at one or two a week, but I was particularly upset at this one and had a lot to drink. Mistake number one."

Hank felt his pulse tick up. He didn't enjoy hearing her blame herself for any part of what he feared this story was going to contain. Acid churned in his stomach as he encouraged her to continue.

"Why were you upset?"

"My boyfriend at the time thought I was cheating on him with my chemistry lab partner. We'd been spending a lot of time studying, but that was because I was about to fail, and he was the smartest guy in the class. The argument had been bad, and we broke up. I couldn't stand the idea of a jealous, controlling man trying to restrict who I could and couldn't see."

"Smart girl." Hank smiled, hoping she would truly see how proud of her he was.

"My friend Jasmine warned me to slow down on the drinking, but I didn't listen. She went off to flirt with her new boy of the week and that's when things get fuzzy."

"What do you mean by fuzzy?"

"My vision was literally that, fuzzy. I couldn't make out faces. My arms and legs were like lead weights. I was dizzy and felt nauseous. I told the guy sitting next to me on the couch and he carried me upstairs. He looked like he was going to help, but..." her voice trailed off and Hank watched her eyes move to the window.

"Daisy, what happened then?"

"I remember...I just remember him taking off my skirt. Everything was getting really blurry by then. I had almost blacked out when I heard him undoing his pants. I tried to tell him no. I tried to call for my friend."

"I'm so sorry, sunshine." Hank wiped away the tear that had fallen onto her cheek.

"The worst part was the next day, I woke up outside the frat house. I don't even know how I got there. But waking up out there, I felt like I was nothing more than trash that needed to be taken out."

"Please tell me you filed a report. That the school threw the asshole out. That he's in jail now." Hank's rage was burning in his veins.

"I was underage, Hank. I shouldn't have been drinking,

and I was afraid of getting in trouble and losing my scholarships. The thought of my grandparents finding out and being disappointed in me was too painful. Besides, he didn't go to my school. That was one blaring detail seared into my memory. He specifically mentioned he was just visiting a friend at the frat house. And I never filed a report because I didn't know what really happened. I mean, physically I could tell, but I was so ashamed that I had let my guard down, that I'd had too much to drink. It was my fault it happened, just like tonight."

"Daisy. That night was not your fault, and neither was tonight. Where was your friend? She should have been looking out for you. But she thought flirting with some guy was more important than that? No. And the man that violated you should be rotting in prison."

Her lower lip trembled, and Hank wanted nothing more than to capture it with his mouth. Instead, he traced the rough pad of his thumb over it for a moment, before training his eyes back on hers.

"I wish I had known you back then. I would have done everything to protect you from that asshole."

"I know you would have. Just like you're always protecting me now."

Out of nowhere, her arms wrapped around his waist. Daisy burrowed her head into his chest and he felt her tense body slowly relax. God, the feeling of being a safe place for her, of being someone she felt she could count on, was enough to send his soul flying into the clouds. Her shoulders shook and dampness tickled his bare chest.

"Everything will be okay, sunshine. I will not let anything bad happen to you ever again."

He wasn't sure if she understood the depth of what he'd just admitted, but he'd never said truer words. The thought of ever walking away from her again made him instantly nauseous.

"I hadn't ever been with anyone before. It was the first time anyone ever..." She said the words so quietly they almost didn't reach his ears. Almost. But when they did, her confession shattered him in a whole different way.

"That's not what it should be like, ever. I'm so sorry, sunshine. You deserve to be loved so completely that it feels good. So deeply good. Softly, warmly, with care. That's what you deserve."

Her hand moved, and he felt the light pressure of her finger trace the veins on his arm, setting his skin on fire.

"You know, I hadn't kissed anyone in years, since that night. I was so terrified to trust that there were good men in the world. But then I kissed you the night we met and there was something. This spark. This electricity that I couldn't explain. It restarted my heart, my desires, my needs. I waited, wondering what was so wrong with me that you never came back. And then, all the moments we've shared lately, you've just gone so cold afterwards. It has to be me. I'm not enough."

Hank scrubbed his hand across his face. He felt like such an asshole. And he deserved to.

"Nothing about you is wrong, Daisy. I've been thinking of you every day since you went flying past my radar gun. I didn't want to take advantage of your grief, or the loss that you had suffered. It feels like something inside me is broken. When my relationship with Anna failed, it changed me. I was afraid of showing you that. I was afraid that maybe I wasn't worthy of someone loving me. I'd convinced myself that something was wrong with me, because how could she just leave without trying to work things out? It would be too much for my heart to take if my brokenness hurt you."

She moved back from him, and he felt his heart cracking.

He'd put it all out there, and he had been right. He didn't deserve her. He wasn't enough.

"Hank, you are not broken. You are the most amazing, thoughtful man I know. And I know you could never hurt me by just being who you are." Her eyes lit up, but her voice hushed to a whisper. "Will you kiss me now?"

"Daisy, I don't know if that's smart. After everything tonight...I—" He growled, his body already burning for her touch.

"Please, Hank. I want to wash off the nightmare of tonight. I want to replace it with a beautiful memory instead."

"And kissing me will be a beautiful memory?"

"The most beautiful." Her bright blue eyes twinkled at him, and that was all it took to break down the last wall in place over his heart.

Placing his hand under her chin, Hank tilted her lips towards his. He pressed gently into them at first, trying to be restrained and gentle. But when the taste of her, that enchanting mix of honey and violets that had haunted his thoughts since their first kiss, hit his mouth, his desire exploded. He pressed his tongue into her mouth as soon as she opened it with a sigh, exploring, claiming every surface as his. A groan escaped from her and it nearly undid him.

She is mine. Mine. I'll never walk away from her again.

———

Oh shit! Was this really happening? Fireworks shot off in Daisy's mind as Hank pressed a kiss deep into her lips. Her core melted into delicious lava, a moan of desire escaping as she opened her mouth to his. She leaned in for more and he delivered, exploring her mouth with his tongue. Daisy's whole body shivered as she thought about where that moment was heading. She wanted all of him, and she didn't want to wait.

Her right hand lifted from her lap, gently exploring Hank's muscular arm. With their lips still pressing together feverishly, she let her fingertips glide across his chest. His heart was beating fast, kicking up a notch as she lowered her hand down to his stomach, down to his hips. She needed to be closer to him. She needed to be bold. Slowly, she pulled away.

Hank's eyes were glassy, his pupils wide with desire. Gathering up all her courage, she moved her legs across his lap and sat, leaning in for another kiss.

She heard his breath hitch as she traced her hips in a circle over him. His hands grasped her waist and her skin pebbled beneath his firm grip.

"Daisy..." he growled.

"Please, Hank. I want more. I want all of you." His eyes roamed over her. She was sure he was looking for any sign of hesitation or regret, but Daisy knew he would see nothing but confidence and the wild flames of her attraction. Slowly, he shook his head.

"No, sunshine. Not tonight."

The rejection stung her as if she'd fallen into a wasp's nest.

"You don't want me?"

"Of course I do. You're so fucking gorgeous. I want you more than my very next breath. But what you've been through, what you've shared with me about your past, I don't...I don't want to hurt you."

"Hank." Her hands swept lightly over his chest, dancing across his collarbone, tracing rivers down his shoulders and onto his arms.

"I want this. I need it. I need you." Her mouth moved close to his ear, a breathy whisper leaving her lips. "I need you to show me that someone could love me the way you said I deserve to be loved." She moved her hands to the hem of her shirt and lifted it over her head.

Hank turned, his eyes gliding down her body. She felt

herself shrink back under his gaze, remembering all the ways her body curved and swelled.

"You are so beautiful, Daisy. Don't hide your body from me. It's perfect. You are perfect." She flushed, and he captured her mouth. "You are in control here." Another deep kiss. "You tell me to stop, I stop. Understand?"

"Yes. I want you, Hank. All of you." Shudders coursed through her body as his kisses peppered her neck. "I want to give you all of me."

"Not yet." Slowly, he tugged the shorts she'd been wearing down from her hips and off her legs. That was it. The last barrier she had. Now she was fully on display for him. The lust filled look in Hank's eyes crushed any lingering thoughts of her imperfect body. She melted into the bed and laid herself before him.

Her body was already on fire, yearning for his touch. Waiting, anticipating what would happen next. It was delicious torture.

Hank moved his body between her legs. She let out a gasp as his hand found its way to her chest. Gently, he leaned over and kissed her lips, gently massaging her breast at the same time. He dusted his fingers over her nipple, sending waves of bliss through her as it hardened beneath the rough pad of his thumb. Daisy arched her back, pressing herself harder into his hand while heat flooded her core. Hot, wet desire pooled between her legs.

"So damn perfect, sunshine."

She giggled, loving the praise he lavished on her. At that moment, she felt like the most beautiful woman in the world.

Hank's lips pressed down her neck, over her collarbone, all the way to the breast he had been tenderly working with his hand. He switched sides, lapping her now free nipple up into his mouth. Swirling, licking, sucking, it tickled her somewhere deep that she'd never felt before.

A moan escaped from her lips and she felt her face flush, a tinge of embarrassment washing over her as she heard the notes of desperation in the noise she'd just made.

"Hank..." The longing in her breathy voice had him tracing his name across her chest with kisses.

"Yes, sunshine. God, I love the way my name sounds on your lips."

"Oh, Hank...I need more. I need..." she gasped as his kisses went down her belly, down her hips, down to the source of her throbbing need.

Her back arched as his tongue found its way to her clit. Repeatedly he tickled her nerves with lick after generous lick, circling with his tongue, edging her to the brink of an orgasm. As the fire became white hot within her core, his mouth met hers once more. His thumb took over, gently stroking her while she felt his finger wait at her entrance. He paused for a moment, bringing his eyes to hers.

"Hank...please." She was so close, so very close to falling over the edge. He made her feel safe, he made her feel treasured, and lord, he made her feel like all of her muscles and bones were about to melt away into a puddle. She wanted it. She wanted him.

"Fuck, sunshine. You're killing me."

He slipped his finger into her core and she gasped, bucking her hips forward, encouraging his movements deeper. When Hank added a second finger, she felt her muscles tighten around him as fireworks danced behind her eyelids.

A grin settled across her face as she floated back to reality. Her hands guided Hank's mouth back to hers, slipping them across his broad shoulders and raking her nails down his back. This was it. She was going to be brave. She was going to have courage and push for what she so desperately wanted.

Her hand found him...rock hard.

"Sunshine." He growled. "We don't have to do this."

"I meant what I said, Hank. I want all of you."

A pained expression washed across his face as she continued to palm him. "You tell me the minute it's too much. Okay, Daisy?"

"Yes." The desperation to quench the throbbing that had returned the instant she touched him grew exponentially as she waited for him to make his move.

"Say the words." His eyes held hers, so much desire staring back at her it took her breath away.

"I-I'll tell you if it's too much. I'll tell you to stop if I need you to."

"And you trust that I'll listen."

"I trust you to keep me safe."

"Fuck. That means everything to me, sunshine. Everything." he sat back, his brows pinching together in thought. "I don't have a condom."

"I'm on birth control. For my cycle." She nibbled on his earlobe. "We're covered."

"Are you sure?" He held her face in his hands and locked eyes with her.

"Hank. I've never been more sure of anything in my entire life."

He kissed her again, laying her back down on the bed before leaving a trail of kisses along her neck and collarbone, while grinding his hips against hers. She could feel the effects of their actions pushing against her, and groaned when Hank sat up, stopping the sweet pressure she'd been using to try and find relief.

His hands moved to the waistband of his pants, and Daisy's hands moved to stop him.

"Are you okay?" he asked, worry etched in his gaze.

"Yes. But...I-I want to do this part." She pulled her bottom lip in between her teeth and smiled shyly. His hands dropped away instantly, and she took over freeing him from his clothing.

Her hand dipped into his underwear, wrapping him in a firm hold. She giggled as he went completely still at her touch. There wasn't even the slight rise and fall of breathing across his muscular chest. She freed him, eyes hooded with lust as she continued to rub her hand around his thickness. "That feels amazing, sunshine. But it's time to make you feel amazing, too."

Hank nipped at her earlobe, causing her to gasp. Before the sound could escape her lips, his mouth was crashing onto hers, capturing the noise.

A throaty groan escaped as she felt him position himself between her thighs. He moved painstakingly slow. She had been right. He was so attentive to her needs. She felt him restraining himself to make sure it wasn't too much for her. The muscles in his jaw flexed, and she knew it must be torture for him to move with so much restraint. He was keeping her safe, making sure he didn't hurt her. It only fueled her desire, the ache inside her growing unbearable.

"More, Hank," she encouraged.

"Daisy..."

"More, God, please Hank. I want all of you." Her nails raked down his back, scratching his skin as he filled her with his full length. She feverishly thrust her hips in rhythm with his movements, the friction only adding to the intense heat building once again in her core. "I will not break. Don't treat me like I'm made of glass, Hank. I'm strong."

"You're perfect." His mouth grabbed hers, teeth gently nipping her bottom lip.

Hank increased his pace, and Daisy met him thrust for thrust. The agony of the building tension seared her body. Just as she thought she couldn't possibly take the pressure anymore, his thumb found her clit again, and the pleasure made her see stars. She shattered so completely, shouting out as Hank continued to pump into her, stretching her orgasm out until darkness crept into the corners of her vision. Her eyes clamped shut as she felt him stiffen and shudder through his own release.

"God, Daisy. That was—" His eyes filled with lust as he looked down at her.

"Perfect. Hank. It was perfect."

Hank was careful to keep his weight off of Daisy as they both came down from their ecstasy. Heavy breathing and racing heartbeats filled the air, until Hank slid out of her, rolling to her side. Daisy cuddled into his chest, happiness washing over her. In the warmth of her arms, she felt herself drifting back to sleep.

"Goodnight, Sheriff," she mumbled as her eyelids closed.

"Goodnight, sunshine." He kissed her temple and pulled her closer.

Her heart already knew what her brain was just figuring out. She was in love with this man.

Twenty-Two

"Daisy, is everything okay?" Mrs. Callum had walked across the small street to her booth.

"Hi, Mrs. Callum. Yes, everything's fine."

"But your arm is back in the sling. I thought you were cleared to have it taken off from the accident."

"I just had a minor incident yesterday and now I'm dealing with a bit of inflammation. It was sore, so I wore the sling today. I'm really fine."

"Where's that handsome sheriff of ours? Is he still helping you out at that farm?"

"No, he isn't."

Please let her have the awareness not to pry.

"Well, that's his loss." She smiled at Daisy. "Chin up, dear, and if you need any help this morning, you just holler over to me and I'll be more than happy to come over."

"Thank you, Mrs. Callum."

When she woke earlier that morning, Daisy searched for the warmth of Hank's powerful arms wrapped around her. Instead, she was met with a swirl of cold air and emptiness. He wasn't there. He wasn't in the bathroom or the kitchen making breakfast. He wasn't out tending to the chickens. She checked the alarm system. It was still armed. There was no sign of him anywhere.

After a good cry, Daisy got dressed and headed out to the market far earlier than she normally would. It figures the only time she could manage to be early for setting up would be when she was running from a broken heart.

Daisy turned back to her car, which was stuffed to the windows. She needed to find out when they would return her truck to her, since it wasn't sustainable to pack everything into such a tiny vehicle.

Although her display was looking as lackluster as she felt, Daisy had a gut feeling that the news of her eventful week had made its way through town. So many people stopped at her booth that they sold her out of produce in the first hour of the market. That had never happened before, but she was grateful for the opportunity to pack up and head home early.

She hadn't seen Hank yet, and she wanted to keep it that way. Unlike the last few months, where all she could think about was running into him, this time, she was praying he wouldn't show up.

Tears choked her. He'd done exactly what she'd told him she was terrified of. He'd given her hope, and the best orgasm of her life, and then he'd just left.

"Hey, gorgeous!" Emma's voice filtered over the crowd as she stepped into the booth. "Wow! Are you out of everything already? That's amazing!"

"Please tell me that the coffee in your hand is for me."

"Of course it is. You know I wouldn't show up empty-handed, especially when I was expecting you to have the most gorgeous blackberries that I was hoping to take off your hands. Please tell me you held some back for me."

"For my best friend? Of course I did." Walking to the back

seat of her car, Daisy removed the flat pack of blackberries and brought them to Emma.

"You're the best, gorgeous."

Daisy smiled and turned from her friend.

"Hey, is everything okay? You never messaged me back last night. And why is your arm back in the sling?"

Daisy sighed.

"Dale attacked me after I left the bar."

"WHAT?" Emma's eyes grew wide.

"Shhh!" Daisy said, mortified as faces passing by turned to gawk at Emma's outburst.

"What exactly do you mean, he attacked you?"

"When I left the bar, he was waiting for me in the alleyway. He grabbed me and I ended up hurting my shoulder, trying to get away."

"Oh shit, Daisy, I'm so sorry. Steve and I should have walked out with you. I'll never forgive myself."

"I didn't want anyone to walk out with me, Em. This isn't on you. Besides, Hank was there."

"He was? He told me he wasn't going after you."

"Yeah, well, he came around the corner just as Dale was pants-down stroking himself, getting ready to..." Tears stung her eyes.

"No." Emma was pale, tears cascading over her own lash line now. She immediately pulled Daisy into an embrace. "That asshole. I'll kill him. No, better yet, I'll have Steve kill him. No one will suspect a nerd like Steve to do something like that."

Daisy released an emotionless laugh. "Hank arrested him. There's no need for anyone to do anything crazy. I'm fine. I'll be fine."

Even with tears stinging her eyes, she refused to let them fall. No, she'd cried enough over the last twenty-four hours to last her a good long while.

"I am so sorry. How are you even here right now? Shouldn't you be sleeping in, then eating your weight in chocolate and ice cream and bacon? You deserve all your favorite things after what you've been through lately."

"No. I just needed to do something normal. Life has been so weird these past few weeks. I still can't shake the feeling that someone is watching me, and then all these really horrible things keep happening. I don't know, Emma, I just needed the normalcy of the market today."

"Where's Hank? Why isn't he here making sure you're okay?"

"Why would he be? I'm not his responsibility." Her voice shook, and she turned her face away before the onslaught of emotions was seen by potential customers.

"Did he say anything to you after what happened with Dale?"

"He took me to the hospital for my shoulder. Then drove me home and spent the night. In my bed."

"In your bed?" Emma's eyes were wide. "Did you guys..."

Daisy nodded. "It was amazing, Em. Like the most intense connection I've ever experienced as a human. And when I woke up this morning, he was gone."

"No."

"Yes. No note. Not even a text. Obviously, what we shared was a pity situation. I poured my heart out to him. I shared something I'd never shared with another person before, and he made me feel so safe, and cherished, and worth something."

"And then he just left."

She nodded. "And then he just left."

"Maybe something came up with work. I don't want to make up excuses for him because leaving without talking to you is inexcusable, but I also know you might be heading towards a self-fulfilling prophecy."

"What the hell is that supposed to mean? I've given him chance after chance to—"

"Daisy." The voice growled from behind her and she turned slowly to see Hank standing in front of her booth.

"Uh, I'll just leave you two to it..." Emma walked towards Sam's booth and didn't even try to hide her gaze locked on Daisy's face.

"What are you doing here?" Hank asked, now standing mere inches away from her. Her heart pounded in her ears. He looked angry, as if she was the one in the wrong. Hell, no. He wasn't about to turn this on her.

"I'm selling my stuff at the market, like I do every Saturday morning. What does it matter to you?" Her voice was low, barely above a whisper, but tinged with the bite of heartache.

"Maybe because when I got back to the farm this morning, you were just gone, and I nearly lost my mind trying to get to you to make sure you were okay!"

He breathed in, something shifting in his face from anger to worry as he reached out and tucked a piece of hair that had fallen loose from her headband behind her ear.

Daisy sighed, pushing her hand into his chest. She needed to force some room between them, to let the air between them cool. Hank didn't budge at first, then took one small step back.

"I wasn't the person who was supposed to keep someone safe by staying with them. You just weren't there this morning. Of all mornings to just disappear, Hank. What I shared with you last night, what we did together...and then you're just gone when I wake up. I feel like my chest is about to crack."

"Daisy. I tried to wake you up, but you were out cold and I wanted you to rest after everything that happened. I got called in for work. I didn't want to, but I had to go."

"You should have told me."

"I see that now. I'm so sorry. Truly."

She finally peeled her gaze off of the road. His deep chocolate eyes were staring back at her, filled with worry and regret. She could see it. She could feel it coming off of him in waves. Her heart was ready to leap into his arms and tell him to take her home so they could repeat exactly what they'd done the night before. But there was a new wall in her mind that had welded into place.

"I didn't think I'd be gone that long. There was an authorization problem I needed to take care of and once that was done, I was going to surprise you with some of those raspberry cream donuts from Champ's that I always see you eating here. You know, the ones he only makes on Saturday morning for the market? I didn't think you'd be here today, but still wanted you to have them."

Daisy just stared at him as he continued. "I thought I could make it back before you even woke up, and I'm so sorry that I didn't. But I sent you a text as soon as I got held up. And about fifty more after that. You never responded."

"I turned my phone off."

"Why?"

She knew it had been reckless to turn it off. What if something else happened out at the farm before she left, or on her way to the market? She wouldn't have been able to call for help. Maybe she had wanted to be unreachable, not to punish him, but for her to feel justified in her anger towards the whole situation. If he could explain things, maybe she wouldn't be strong enough to sit in her pain and allow herself to feel the disappointment.

"I didn't want you to convince me that my anger was unjustified."

"I wouldn't do that. I see how it all looks now, and I am so sorry for that. I never intended to just disappear." He looked at the empty table in her booth. "It looks like you're already done here. Can I please take you home?"

"No." The quiver in her voice brought tears stinging back into her eyes.

"Daisy."

"Hank, I'm serious. I understand now what happened, and I'm not saying I don't forgive you or that I don't want to put it behind us, but I can't even explain what it was like to put my trust in you, and to open up about something I've never shared with another soul...and then to have you just leave."

Hank put his hand to her face, sweeping away the tear that finally freed itself from her eye.

"I'm sorry, sunshine. I never meant to hurt you like that. I understand, though. I have to work tonight, but I'll be around if you need me. Make sure you lock up and set the alarm when you get home."

"I will."

He leaned in and placed a gentle kiss on her cheek. As Daisy watched Hank walk away, she felt arms wrap around her gently.

"Oh, babe." Emma had returned, and in her arms, Daisy fell apart.

"How much did you hear?"

"Enough to know that he's an idiot, but that he made an honest mistake."

"I know. And I want to say it's all okay. To tell him to come back to the farm and stay with me, but I can't. What's wrong with me?"

"There's nothing wrong with you. When you've been burned, sometimes the spot still hurts even though the scar is healed over and it's been ages since it happened. It can ache like the burn is fresh. Your parents left you when you were vulnerable. Hank's now done the same."

"It's not the same. Hank isn't required to stay. It's not his responsibility to."

"It might not be the same, but maybe it hurts even worse because of that."

"What do you mean?"

"Let's take out the fact that we now know he left because of work and then did something sweet for you, with every intention of coming back. Let's just go back to the start of this feeling. Maybe it's because he isn't required to stay that it hurts so badly to think he left. Because you finally had someone who'd chosen you. He'd shown time and time again that he wanted to protect you, and last night he showed how much he wanted to cherish you, to treat you well. Then he just left."

"It's my biggest fear, come true."

"Exactly, babe."

Daisy sighed, shrugging her shoulders as Emma continued. "But he didn't really leave."

"No, I guess he didn't."

"So, can you be pissed at him for not thinking to tell you where he was going?"

"Yes."

"And can you also see that maybe you were letting some of your own insecurities fuel your response?"

"Yes."

"Good. Are you going to go after him now?"

Her eyes filled with more tears, but her shoulders stiffened with resolve.

"No."

"Daisy. Why not?"

"I just need some time."

Emma sighed. "Fair enough, but he's good for you, babe. Just like you're good for him. The both of you have this spark that flares in your eyes when you are with each other. For him, it's like you're the most beautiful thing he's ever seen. Try not to stay mad at him for too long."

TWENTY-THREE

There wasn't anything in that damn file he hadn't already read fifty times over, but it didn't matter. Hank sat back at his desk, a loud sigh penetrating the air. His frustrations at not having any idea who was targeting Daisy or what they were trying to achieve were eating away at him. There had to be something that he was missing.

Most shifts as sheriff were quiet, and he was thankful for living in a town where most crime was petty and the daunting paperwork was often the scariest part of his day. The shift he was working had been no different. But just this once, Hank thought it might be nice to have something to take his mind off of Daisy and the relationship he feared he messed up before it had even officially begun.

Daisy had been right. Of course, he didn't mean to hurt her, but he had. And now, Hank had no idea how to make it better. This was why he never should have offered to help her after her accident. He was no good at this stuff.

Hank jumped when an alarm rang out from his cell phone. Apparently, the night was about to get more interesting. A warning for flash flooding and torrential downpours had been issued for Clarence County. The short notice meant people would travel to get home and out of the storm, and some of those folks would inevitably get stranded and need help.

He took a minute to send off a text to Daisy, reminding her to stay safe and make sure the house was locked up for the night. He thought it might be an easy olive branch after what happened that morning. The message was marked read, and he held his breath as three little dots appeared on the screen.

Everything is okay here. Be careful with the storm coming in.

He couldn't help but smile.

I will. Sweet dreams, sunshine.

Stay safe, Sheriff.

He could fix things. They would figure out whoever was behind the threats to Daisy. Things were going to be okay.

———

Things were not going to be okay. The storm cell moved through Clarence County with efficient destruction. Multiple emergency calls came into the station for a pileup on the highway between Bell Ridge and Rogersville, casualties reported.

The truck handled the wet roads well enough, but there was thick debris on some of the back roads, and Hank had to stop multiple times to clear it away before he reached the on-ramp to the highway. Thankfully, he hadn't come across anyone else in need of help before he arrived on the scene.

Stepping out of the truck, his heart sank. There had to be at least fifteen vehicles in various states of destruction. Some crumpled from bumper to bumper, others with sides smashed in. Aside from some standing water issues, the fire and ambulance teams could do their jobs without having to fight the elements.

Hank directed his deputies to coordinate a shutdown for that section of highway, making it easier for the multiple ambulances and rescue personnel to access the scene. When a frantic shout came from a few yards away, Hank recognized the voice and ran to see if he could help.

"Caleb? I didn't think your crew was on tonight. What do you need?"

"Yeah, Jackson and I heard the calls go out and showed up to help. Listen, help me pull away this front windshield. We've got a family trapped in here, minimal injuries but scared kids. I'd like to get them out quickly and away from here."

"I can definitely help with that. Just tell me what to do and I'll do it."

"Great. I'll need to climb on the hood and slide into that space between the cars. Once I'm over there, we'll work on getting the windshield off so we can help the family out through that opening."

They immediately jumped into action. Hank and Caleb worked to get the glass cleared away, laying down blankets on the dash and across the broken glass so that the occupants of the car wouldn't get cut as they extracted them.

Once the parents were out, Caleb crawled into the vehicle to access the children in the back. From what Hank could see, there was a young girl, who was maybe five or six years old, and a little boy who was maybe two. Although he didn't know this family, he felt overwhelmed with gratitude that they had not been injured.

Caleb handed the little boy to Hank, who promptly handed him over to his grateful father.

"You can head over to that ambulance and get everyone checked out." Hank pointed to the row of ambulances.

The family walked away as Hank held out a hand to help Caleb down from the vehicle.

"That's the best outcome you can hope for when something like this happens. A whole family just walks away without major injury."

"Yeah. It really is. It was nice of you and Jacks—"

A flash of bright light illuminated his field of vision and Hank felt his body moving, flying to the wet ground as the sound of crunching metal filled the air. His head slammed onto the pavement, the sensation of fire dancing down his face as his skin scraped along the road.

For some people, he was sure the saying about life flashing in front of your eyes was true. But for Hank, he didn't see the life he'd lived. No. In the split second between Caleb pushing him, and the moment his body landed on the pavement, Hank saw the life he was meant to have.

A vision of Daisy filled his mind. She was there, standing on the front porch of her farmhouse, chasing after a little girl with blonde curls. She stopped, her hands resting on her belly, which was beautifully round with another baby. As she lifted her face, she met his eyes and the overwhelming feeling of love slammed into him as she gave him the most beautiful smile he'd ever seen. A blink passed, and he was next to her, their lips pressed together. When Hank's body came to rest on the pavement, he could still feel the heat from the kiss on his lips.

Breath after breath, Hank tried to make sense of the things he'd just seen. He watched deputies and firefighters running towards where he'd just been standing, not able to shake the vision of Daisy. His brain finally registered what had happened.

A paramedic he didn't recognize crouched down next to him. He desperately wanted to check on Caleb, but when he tried to stand, powerful arms kept him in place. "Let me look you over, Sheriff. Make sure everything is okay."

"Did you see the firefighter who pushed me out of the way? Is he okay?" Hank asked.

"I don't know. But there are lots of people coming to help whoever was caught up in that, so let's just focus on making sure you're okay. That's a pretty nasty abrasion you've got on your face, and I'll need to check for a concussion."

"I'm fine."

It took thirty minutes, which was twenty-nine minutes longer than Hank wanted to give the paramedic, but they had finally completed their thorough assessment and aside from a bit of soreness from crashing to the ground so unexpectedly, and the throbbing in his face from the abrasion, he was okay.

As soon as he stepped away from the ambulance, a pit formed in his stomach. The scene was too quiet. It was eerie to see people standing still and to have no noise, not even the chatter of a radio cutting through his thoughts.

Standing with a group of firefighters, Hank recognized Jackson.

"Hey man. Where's Caleb? I want to thank him for pushing me out of the way. I don't think I would have walked away from that if he hadn't."

As soon as Jackson turned to face him, Hank realized his friend had tears in his eyes.

"What's going on? You okay?"

Jackson shook his head, and that dread-filled pit in Hank's stomach churned acid into his throat.

"Caleb was caught between the car you guys removed that family from and the truck that lost control across the median. He—" his voice caught in his throat, causing a lump of emotion to grow in Hank's. "He's gone."

"Fuck." Hank's voice shook as tears stung his eyes. He took a breath in and placed his hand on Jackson's shoulder. "I'm so sorry."

They stood there for a moment, Hank supporting Jackson as the emotion of losing his best friend overtook him.

"He wouldn't have changed things, you know? He pushed you out of the way of that truck, and I know he would do it again, knowing the outcome would be the same." Jackson finally spoke, wiping his eyes.

"I didn't even see it coming. I wish I had. I wish I had been able to get us both out of the path."

"I have to be there when his parents get to the hospital."

"Do you need a ride? I can take you, or one of the deputies can."

Jackson shook his head. "Captain Ellersman is heading that way now and I need to get the rest of my crew there too, but I need to wait here until..." his voice caught.

"I understand. You want to ride in with him."

Nodding, Hank squeezed the hand on Jackson's shoulder one more time and watched him walk back towards his crew. God, the guilt he felt was overwhelming. It felt like it might swallow him whole. He had a job to do here, though, and he was no good to anyone if he couldn't shove down his own emotions and focus.

There would be time to mourn Caleb. There would be time to figure out how to honor his sacrifice. There would be time to process the thoughts bouncing around in his head about his unworthiness of such an amazing, selfless act.

Locking his emotions into the darkest corner of his mind, Hank worked with the rest of the emergency workers until the early hours of the morning. When it was evident that things were winding down on the scene, he left one of his deputies in charge and made his way to the hospital.

———

"Mr. and Mrs. Davis?" He approached the couple, who were sitting in the waiting room with Jackson at their side. Caleb's mom had one hand tightly on her husband's leg, the other hand gently held in Jackson's. One nod from Jackson and Hank knew he had already shared the news with them.

"I'm Hank Porter, the Sheriff of Clarence County. I wanted to personally share my condolences on the loss of your son. Caleb was an outstanding member of our community, and more personally, someone I considered a friend." When Mrs. Davis let out a sob, Hank crouched down and placed his hand on her arm. "Your son saved my life tonight. He pushed me out of the way when I didn't see the truck coming. His actions were heroic in every sense of the word, and I'll spend every day of my life honoring the sacrifice he made for me tonight."

"Thank you, Sheriff." Mr. Davis said, extending his hand out. Hank quickly stood, shaking his hand.

"If there is anything that you need, please let me know."

"My son. I need my son." The statement was barely above a whisper, but the soft lamentation shattered Hank so completely.

He didn't know what to say. Afraid any words he could offer would only make their pain worse, he silently gave a nod to both Mr. Davis and Jackson before walking out of the hospital. After several long minutes of just sitting in his truck, he began driving out of town. He wasn't heading to the station or his house. No, there was only one place he wanted to be just then, and only one person he wanted to be with.

Hank walked slowly up to the front porch. He wasn't even sure she'd be willing to see him, but he had to try.

The floorboard groaned and strained as he approached the door. He gave two gentle knocks and walked back to the steps, sighing deeply and wringing the back of his neck with his hand before sitting down. Hank removed his hat and set it down next to him while he waited to see if Daisy would answer the door.

Twenty-Four

The sound of tires crunching on gravel and brakes groaning right outside her window brought Daisy out of her dreams. Her body shot straight up in bed, adrenaline coursing through her as she picked up her phone. Who would come out to the house at four in the morning?

She slipped her flannel robe over the running shorts and cotton t-shirt she'd been sleeping in. Pulling her long blonde hair out from under the collar of the robe, she captured it all into a low bun, slid on her slippers and headed to the window. Daisy could clearly make out the vehicle and she held her breath as she decided what to do next.

Hank slowly got out, the tension in his back and shoulders immediately visible. As he disappeared beneath the roofline, she held her breath, waiting to hear a knock at the door. Why was he hesitating? The waiting had her anxiety skyrocketing. When he did finally knock, Daisy moved as quickly as she could to get downstairs and out the door.

Lights flooded the porch, and her heart pounded in her chest as Hank moved to wipe away a tear on his cheek. He kept his back to her.

Sitting down on the steps, she remained silent. Whatever this was, whatever had happened, she wanted to give him the space to choose her for support. Breathing in the cool night air, she turned her face to take in his.

The shadow from the light by the front door stressed the stubble on his chin and cheeks. Dirt dusted his forehead and nose. He turned his face fully to meet her eyes, and she couldn't stop the gasp that escaped.

"You're hurt." She gently touched the area around the scratches. It was clear that he was searching for the words to explain why he'd come there in the middle of the night, but failed to find them.

Instead, he took her hand in his, and they sat in silence. Her thumb strummed back and forth over the veins in his hand as she waited.

"Hank? What's going on?" Daisy finally asked, breaking the silence as she placed her hand on his arm.

He didn't answer, and her heart dropped. Whatever he was going through, whatever had happened during his shift, must have been bad. An ache spread throughout her chest.

"Hey, what's going on?" she asked again as she put her arm through his and laid her head on his shoulder. "Talk to me. Whatever it is, we can get through it."

Hank cleared his throat and finally spoke. "There was a bad pileup between Bell Ridge and Rogersville." Tears strained in his voice, ripped raw with emotion.

"Oh lord," she whispered. "Were there casualties?"

Hank wiped the tears from his eyes and let out a jagged breath. "Yes. Two people were killed in the initial accident."

Daisy's heart was sinking as she felt heat build in her throat.

"That's terrible. Did you know them?"

"No. They weren't from here."

Something wasn't adding up. Her stomach rolled, worry

and unease bubbling up into the back of her throat. Hank would have seen accidents like this before, and although never easy, she was sure something more had to have happened for him to be struggling like he was.

"Why does it have you so shaken, then?"

"I'm not upset about that, Daisy. It is upsetting, it's just, I see that stuff more often than I'd like. I'm hardened to it."

"It makes sense that you would have learned how to process those scenes, Hank. But you said the initial accident. Did something else happen?"

"Yes."

There it was. That nagging feeling in her stomach churned once more.

"You don't have to tell me about it if you don't want to. If it's too much, we can just sit here."

"I don't know why I came here, Daisy."

"It doesn't matter why you did. I'm just happy you're here. We can just sit like this for as long as you need. And when we're done sitting here, you're going to let me take a better look at those scratches on your face. You don't need to tell me how you got them, but you are going to let me make sure they are clean and not causing you pain."

She looped her arm through his. Resting her head on his shoulder, she rubbed circles into his arm as they breathed together. Was this shock? Maybe she needed to be getting him something to eat, or drink, but she couldn't imagine leaving him to sit on the porch by himself while she ran to her kitchen.

After several long minutes, Daisy felt Hank's body stiffen beneath her touch. He cleared his throat and looked into her eyes.

"Caleb and I were helping a family with two little kids get out of their car. The sides were pinned between other vehicles, so we had to take out the windshield."

"Were they injured?"

"No. Caleb wanted to get them out and away from the crash, but they were all fine." He swallowed roughly. "I didn't even see it happening, Daisy. I should have been paying attention."

"What happened?"

"When I arrived on the scene, I had my deputies stop and reroute traffic on our side of the highway. I never even thought about vehicles heading in the opposite direction." His head fell into his hands as he continued. "A truck lost control. They crossed the grass median and—"

"Hank! That's why your face is all scratched up? Were you hurt? Did anyone check you over? Do you need to go to the hospital?" She could hear how poorly she was hiding her instant hysteria, even over the blood whooshing in her ears, but his injury had been caused by something far worse than she had even been imagining.

"No. Caleb must have seen the truck heading for us. He pushed me out of the way at the last minute."

Her heart squeezed. Caleb was there, and he'd made sure Hank was safe. There would never be enough words to describe how thankful she was for her sweet friend, but the next time she saw him, she'd be giving him the biggest hug she could.

"I'll need to bake him a few hundred batches of brownies to tell him how thankful I am that he protected you."

"Daisy." The pain in his voice was back.

"What?"

"He didn't make it."

She searched his eyes for clarity, but all she was met with was regret and heartache.

"What do you mean, he didn't make it? He pushed you out of the way, but that truck injured him? Is he at the hospital now?"

"The truck pinned him against the car we had been working on. His injuries...he didn't make it. The driver of that truck killed him."

"Caleb died?" The words tumbled from her mouth as nothing more than a whispered plea for misunderstanding.

She felt stunned, frozen in place as a deafening silence built in the space where she expected to hear him say she had heard wrong. When that correction never came, she cried. The ground spun and, if she hadn't already been sitting down, Daisy knew she would have fallen. Her heart shattered for the sweet friend she would never get to speak to again. For his parents, who lost their only child. For the community, who lost an outstanding neighbor and servant. For Hank, who clearly was feeling the weight of surviving when Caleb didn't.

"I should have had better situational awareness. I should have pushed him out of the way. It was supposed to be me, Daisy."

Her stomach clenched, instant nausea swarming her senses.

"No, Hank. God. None of this is your fault. And it certainly shouldn't have been you. I can't even think about that. I can never repay what Caleb did by pushing you out of the way, but it's easily the best gift I've ever been given so far in life. If you had died tonight, if it had been someone else here pulling into my driveway tonight to tell me it was you, I would have died right here, too. I hate that he's gone. But I know he wouldn't want you to feel that way, and I certainly never want you to say that it should have been you instead. That probably makes me so selfish, but I can't help it, Hank. I need you here with me."

She hoped her words were sinking in. Her anger from the day before felt like such a waste. At that moment, the same thought kept bouncing around her mind. She had wasted almost a whole day staying away from him, allowing her anger to control her happiness. Never again. That's what Caleb's gift to her would always be.

When Daisy pictured all the people connected to Caleb, Jackson immediately came to mind.

"Was Jackson there?"

Hank nodded.

"That's his best friend. I can't imagine." Daisy gasped as she thought of Caleb's parents. "Does his family know?"

Another nod. "Jackson was with them at the hospital when I went to check in before coming here. I made sure I told them how Caleb saved my life, and how I would always live to honor that sacrifice."

"Oh, Hank. I can't even imagine what it was like to do that."

"I told them if they ever needed anything, I'd be available to help them out. And do you know what Mrs. Davis said?"

"What?"

"She said she just needed her son." He rubbed his hand over his face and let it linger on the roughness of his grown-in stubble. "The way Mrs. Davis looked at me, the pain in seeing me standing there instead of Caleb, I'll never forget it."

"What can I do?" she asked, gently raising her hand to his face. She cupped his cheek, and he immediately leaned into the soft warmth that came from her. Pulling his face towards her, she looked into his eyes and asked again, "What can I do, Hank?"

"I'm not sure why I'm here, sunshine. I shouldn't have interrupted your night. I know you're still upset with me and I shouldn't have come out here and asked for comfort from you. I should go back to the station. I just needed..." he took a deep breath. "I just needed to see you. I needed to remember that there is good in the world, that there is happiness."

"Being with me helps you remember that?" she asked, eyes wide.

"Of course it does, Daisy. It's hard to not want to be by your side every minute of the damn day, because you feel so good to be around."

Daisy blushed and ran her hand across Hank's back. She laid her head down on his shoulder. "Yeah, well, it's hard not wanting to be around you, too."

He smiled at her, softly kissing the top of her head before standing.

"I should get back to the station. There'll be lots of paperwork to fill out, and I need to check in on everyone."

"Of course. You'll let me know if there's anything I can do, right?"

"Yes."

"Hank?"

"Yeah, sunshine?"

"Why don't you come back out here when you are done with taking care of everything?"

"I'm not sure when that will be."

"I'll wait. Just come back to me, okay?"

"Okay."

TWENTY-FIVE

Daisy thought about trying to go back to sleep, but the overwhelming need to help in some way made her give up on that notion almost immediately. First, she went to the kitchen. She'd whip up some breakfast things for the guys at the firehouse. They'd all be exhausted and working through their grief. She was sure the last thing they'd be thinking about would be getting something nutritious into their bodies.

Two hours later, she had muffins, pancakes, fresh egg scramble, bacon, and breakfast sausage all cooked up and packaged, ready to go into town. Daisy saw Jackson's younger brother Jordan turn into her driveway and walked to the porch to meet him.

"Hey, Jordan. Everything okay?"

"Hey, Daisy. Did you hear what happened last night?"

Her heart could not possibly ache more than it did at that moment. So many people loved Caleb. It felt like an impossible task to continue on in his absence.

"I did. I still can't believe it. I feel numb about it, almost like someone is going to come tell me it was just a mistake, and he was actually off with Jackson enjoying some fishing down at the lake."

"I know. Caleb was just at my parent's house a week ago for family dinner. He's been like another older brother to me since he moved here."

Daisy placed her hand on Jordan's shoulder.

"I'm so sorry. If there's anything that I can do for your family, if Jackson needs anything, please let me know."

"Thanks. I will."

"So, uh, not that I'm not happy to see you, but what are you doing out here?"

"Oh, Hank didn't tell you?"

"No, I haven't talked to Hank since before dawn."

Jordan nodded. "I ran into him at the firehouse. I was heading out after checking on Jackson, and Hank asked if I could stop out and see if you needed help with the morning chores. He mentioned that your shoulder might be bothering you again."

"That really is so sweet, but I'll manage."

"Are you sure? I could use the distraction. I think I'd rather just be with Maisie and Minnie. And Hank mentioned writing me a letter for my college applications in the fall for helping."

"Well, how could I say no to that? It if helps, you can head out there now. But when you're done, could I ask another favor?"

"Sure. Just name it."

"I couldn't sleep after hearing the news. I sort of made a bunch of food for the guys at the firehouse. Would you be willing to drop it off for me on your way back through?"

"Yeah, that's no problem."

———

Daisy was still in her pajamas and robe when Jordan left with the food. Although she would have loved to deliver it herself, she didn't know when Hank would be done with work and she had to be there no matter when he showed up. There was nothing more to do inside but sit and wait, and Daisy needed a distraction. The garden had been harvested just a few days before in anticipation of the farmer's market, but she could head out there and spend a few minutes looking for anything that might have turned ripe since then.

An hour later, once she'd placed her random harvests into the kitchen to be cleaned, Daisy stripped off her pajamas. She'd worked up more of a sweat than she thought possible under an unusually warm rising sun.

With water dripping off of her as she stepped out of the shower, the familiar sound of tires on the gravel in front of her house drifted in her open window. She couldn't stop from muttering under her breath. Of course, it would work out that way, that she would be sopping wet and disheveled when he arrived back home. Out of breath, more so at the realization that he had kept his word and returned to her than the feverish pace at which she was trying to get dried off, she threw her dress on over her head and dashed out of her bedroom.

Stumbling down the stairs, she opened the door just as Hank was parking his truck. Daisy watched as he slowly got out, the dirt and dust from the night settling into the lines of his face and fading into the uniform he wore. Hair dripping down her body, she made her way off the porch and bounded towards him.

A small smile grew on his face, and her heart slammed inside her chest as she launched herself into his arms.

"You came back to me." She buried her face into the scruff of his neck.

"Hey, I'll always keep my promises." He looked into her eyes, a hunger there she recognized reflected her own desires.

"What does this mean, Hank?"

He didn't answer. Instead, a crease appeared between his eyebrows and his eyes squeezed on the edges, as if he was trying to understand what she was asking.

"What does coming back out here this morning mean for us?" When he didn't reply again, she continued. "Because I want this to mean that you are trusting me to take care of you. That you are choosing me to walk through this horrible moment with you, like you've done for me so many times over the past few weeks."

He swallowed roughly. "It does."

Her heart ached in the best way. She needed to keep going. Her soul was bursting to finally say what she wanted and what she needed.

"I want it to mean that you are choosing me. All of me. So that I can finally have all of you. The good parts, and the bad." Her voice was small, but she knew he'd heard every word.

"I'm trying to protect you, Daisy. I'm broken, and I don't want to hurt you."

"Are you even listening to me? I want it all, Hank. I want the parts that are easy, and the parts that you're afraid will hurt me. I'm broken too, but did you ever stop to think that maybe we're both broken in exactly the way the other person needs? Our broken pieces fit together. I'm stronger when I'm with you."

His eyes roamed over her face, and she could see the storm raging inside him. He would decide in that moment, and she would either allow herself to fall in love with him or be shattered into a million pieces.

"Hank." Her throat was suddenly dry and burning.

"Sunshine," he replied, waiting in the searing anticipation that was building between them.

She reached up and placed her hands on his scruffy cheeks, ever so slightly guiding his face down towards her own. Was she really going to take the initiative again? Hadn't she promised herself she would make him prove he wanted her? Or had he already done that by coming back that morning?

On her tiptoes, she leaned towards him, her lips buzzing with the wanting of a million nerve-endings. Biting the smallest corner of her bottom lip, she heard Hank grumble and couldn't help but smile.

"Daisy. I choose you." Breathless, and clearly not interested in waiting for her to respond, Hank dipped his head towards hers, deepening their embrace. Her body erupted, and she melted into his arms. As he pulled away, Daisy pushed closer to him, feeling every inch of his hard body press into the soft curves of hers. She was well aware of just how much this kiss was charging his body, and a giggle erupted from her throat.

"Was that kiss funny to you?"

"No, not funny. Nothing about this is funny."

"I should probably go back to my house—"

"No," she snapped.

"No?"

"You just said that you chose me. So stay. Every time you've been here before, it's been for me. I want to take care of you."

He stilled.

"Unless you want to be alone."

"The last thing I want is to be alone."

His lips came crashing down onto hers again. Her hand roamed across his chest, over his shoulders and down his arms, until she took his hand in hers.

"Good. Come get your breakfast then. I'll make your favorite."

"Your brownies?"

She laughed. "I don't think my brownies count as a breakfast food. I've got steak and eggs." Her eyes twinkled. "And brownies for a little treat afterwards."

She turned to walk into the house, but Hank's firm grip on her hand stopped her from moving. He pulled Daisy into another hug, and she buried her face in the crook of his neck. His beard tickled her forehead, and she raised her hand to run her fingers along his jawline and down into the scruff. When he lifted her chin so that she was looking directly at him, a little sigh escaped from her mouth as she took in the fire burning behind his melted chocolate eyes. In a blink, he was kissing her, and it took every ounce of restraint she had to not wrap her legs around his body and ask him to carry her up to bed.

"Hank, if you keep doing that, I don't think we'll make it to breakfast."

"Mmmm, I'm sure we can leave it in the fridge for later."

"No," she sighed as she pushed away from his chest. "You need to eat. I have a feeling we're going to need the energy after you sleep. And I actually do mean sleep."

They walked towards her dining room, Hank stopping to take his shoes off near the door.

"Sit. I'll be right back." He sat in the chair like the weight of the world was on his shoulders, looking more weary than the charged up man she had been looking at outside just a moment before.

Daisy grabbed the steak from the refrigerator and set it out on the counter while she started heating her grandmother's favorite cast iron pan. Twenty minutes later, Daisy put the finishing touches on the tray and poured a large cup of coffee for Hank. Walking back into the dining room, she couldn't help but feel a tug at her heart when she saw Hank, fast asleep in his chair.

"Hank," she whispered.

He jumped awake, concern filling his features until he met Daisy's eyes.

"Well, hey there, Sheriff. You want to just go up to bed? I know it's been a long night."

"Sorry," he yawned. "Breakfast looks so good. I'm okay." Daisy nodded, handing him his plate and coffee. His hand softly caught her wrist, and before she knew it, she was being pulled onto his lap. Twisting, she pressed her face into his chest as he held her, breathing in his scent. It was an intoxicating mix of his normal body wash, sweat, dirt, and rain. The gravity of what he had been through, what the community had lost that night, slammed into her.

As hard as she had been trying to push all of her emotions away in order to help Hank, she lost control as he held her. Tears fell from her eyes and threatened to never stop.

Hank ran his hand in calming circles around her back and she felt so safe there.

"I-I'm sorry." She lifted her head to look into his eyes. A little hiccup escaped as she wiped the tears from his glistening eyes. "I'm supposed to be supporting you and here you are, comforting me."

"You are supporting me, Daisy. This...you letting me hold you in my arms...is exactly what I needed."

Placing a hand on his cheek, she asked, "What else can I do?"

He shut his eyes, and Daisy felt his chest still.

"I need to shower. But then, will you lay down with me?"

She already knew there would never be a time when she'd refuse that request.

"Of course I will." Wiggling free, Hank stopped her by tightening his embrace. Understanding that this was part of what he needed, she snuggled down tightly to his chest.

"Sunshine. Don't leave my arms."

How could she not melt into him with a request like that?

Her heart pounded as she let Hank carry her up the stairs and into the room he'd stayed in before.

"We could sleep in my room, you know?"

"I think the memories from the other night would have me doing everything but sleeping, Daisy." She knew a heavy blush painted across her face at the thought of what the two of them had shared just two days earlier. "Besides, I've fallen in love with this space. What can I say?"

"Just the space?" Daisy teased, nibbling on her bottom lip as he set her down on the bed. She wasn't sure how he could love a room she'd last decorated when she was sixteen. The boy band posters and hot pink bedding were making her flush in embarrassment. She'd stayed in that room for months after moving back to Bell Ridge and always meant to redecorate, but eventually convinced herself that her grandparents would want her to move into the master bedroom. Renovating that room had taken her attention away from fixing the guest rooms, which she was regretting.

"Maybe it's how the room is filled with sunshine." The corners of his eyes turned up as he smiled. He wasn't referring to the light given off by the star at the center of the solar system. He was referring to her.

Her fingers reached out and began undoing the buttons on the shirt of his uniform. Once she had successfully removed both that and the cotton t-shirt he was wearing underneath, she raked her fingernails down his chest and abs. The groan he stifled as she unbuckled his belt and popped the button on his pants had her smiling. It would always be amazing to her that she could have such an effect on him. When he was nothing more than a gorgeous man standing in front of her in his boxers, she kissed him one last time and sent him on his way for a shower.

Ten minutes later, Hank walked back into the room with a towel slung low across his hips. Daisy pulled the covers back and motioned for him to crawl under the comforter. He rolled to face the middle of the bed, and she did the same as she laid down. God, he was so warm, and she fit so perfectly right into his arms. Resting her head on his chest, her breathing matched the rhythm of his. Safe in each other's arms, they both fell asleep.

TWENTY-SIX

Daisy looked up from the book she was reading on the couch as Hank walked out of his bedroom. Over the last two weeks, they'd spent nearly all of their time together at her house, but he'd asked her over with a sly look in his eye earlier that morning, and she happily agreed. Her breath sped up as her eyes roamed over his body, looking absolutely delicious in a pair of fitted jeans and a dark shirt that was just tight enough to pull across his chest and arms.

"Where are you going looking so handsome?"

"The question you should ask is not where am *I'm* going, but where are *we* going?"

"We?"

"Yes. I'm taking you out tonight."

"What? Why?"

"It's the Bell Ridge block party tonight. As sheriff, I have to go. As my girlfriend, so do you."

His girlfriend?

Things had been really great between the two of them since he'd shown up on her porch in the middle of the night, but was she ready to fully give her heart over to him? The tentative smile on his face told her he was waiting for her reaction to his use of the word.

"Daisy?" His voice calling her name pulled her out of her spiral.

"Oh, uh, yes. I think your girlfriend can swing that tonight."

Placing the bookmark forcefully into the open page of the book, her legs carried her over to Hank, where she stood on her tiptoes and planted a sweet kiss on his cheek.

"I really like the sound of that, you know?" he growled.

"What's that?"

"You calling yourself my girlfriend."

"I really enjoyed saying it. Now, is my boyfriend going to drive me out to my house so I can change, or does he want me to go dressed in this?" Her fingers ran across his shirt, tracing the muscles thinly veiled by the fabric. The heat in his eyes fanned over her body. Of course, he wouldn't want her to go anywhere dressed only in his t-shirt and a skimpy pair of lace panties. After the fun afternoon they'd had together in Hank's bed, she hadn't felt like getting dressed in anything else.

"If you keep doing that while wearing my shirt, we'll never get out of this house. I won't be able to stop myself from keeping you occupied for the entire night," he groaned.

"That doesn't sound so bad to me." Her hand traced the line between his abs.

Grabbing her waist, Hank hoisted Daisy over his shoulder and patted her ass gently as he walked into his bedroom. She giggled as his fingers teasingly dug into her sides, tickling her. He set her down on the bed with a scorching kiss and chuckled as he walked into his closet.

"We don't need to head out to the farm," his voice called out from the closet. "I picked up something for you to wear tonight."

"You bought me clothes?"

"I saw this and immediately thought of you. I know you'll look amazing in it." Hank walked out holding a navy blue dress covered in small daisies.

"I love it so much, Hank. Thank you!" She stood up from the bed and took the dress into her hands, holding it against her body and twirling. "And thank you for not getting me flowers with daisies in them. A dress with them is perfect though."

Hank looked at her with his brows furrowed. "You don't like the actual flowers?"

"I love them. I think they are beautiful, but unfortunately I'm allergic to them. I had an anaphylactic episode when I was seven." She watched the shock wash across his face. "My grandparents wanted to make my birthday really special. It was the first one I was living with them for, and they bought me a big arrangement of daisies. I almost died."

"That's terrifying."

"It's something I've just gotten used to. Honestly, I keep medication in my purse and in the upper cupboard by the sink in the kitchen. If I'm ever exposed to them, I just inject myself and I'll hopefully be good to go."

"I can't believe how calm you are talking about this. It's terrifying."

"I've had eighteen years to come to terms with it. You've had eighteen seconds." The worry on his face made her feel bad. "It really is okay."

"You aren't allergic to just the image of daisies, right? That's not a thing, is it? I'll feel really terrible if I have to stab you in your perfect ass with a giant needle."

Daisy laughed. "I think we are okay on that front. And it'd be my thigh, not my ass." She got on her tiptoes and kissed Hank. "Thank you, Hank. The dress is perfect."

———

"Does this count as our first date?" Daisy asked, slipping her hand into Hank's.

His brows knit together, as if he were thoughtfully planning a response to her question. "I guess it does. I should have planned something before this. In my defense, this hasn't been the most conventional relationship."

"No, I guess it hasn't, especially when we spent a week living together after practically not talking at all for an entire year."

"I'll never be happy you were hurt, but I'm happy I wised up and stepped in to help."

"Not that I'll ever admit I needed the help, but I'm thankful for your persistence."

He squeezed her fingers gently as they made their way closer to the food trucks at the entrance of the block party.

"Hungry?" he asked.

"Starving!"

"You go pick out a table to sit at and I'll grab us some drinks. Then we can solidify our plan of attack for the food."

"Perfect." She leaned up and planted a kiss on his lips.

It took a few minutes, but Daisy finally found an open table in view of the town square. Bell Ridge was a really charming town no matter when you visited, but it came to life during the town's block parties. Her eyes wandered from the twinkling lights that were hanging between all the lamp posts down the street, to the center of town that had a local band playing in the large, white gazebo where she'd stood a decade before taking pictures for her prom.

Emma's diner sat behind the gazebo on the other side of the town square. Daisy selfishly hoped to see her at the block party, but from how busy it looked from where she was standing, there was probably a slim chance that Emma could get away. Pulling out her cell to see if Emma had replied to her earlier texts about meeting up, Daisy sighed at the sight of no new messages. She'd just have to convince Hank to head over to the diner later for a slice of Emma's pie of the day.

"Why is your head buried in your phone when we've got all this amazing people-watching out here for free?" The familiar voice had her smiling.

"Hey, Jake. You're totally right." She turned off her phone and slipped it into her pocket. "I was just trying to see if Emma sent me a text back. I didn't know if she was planning on coming here tonight, but the diner looks super busy, so I'm probably out of luck. I will say, though, I'm surprised to see you. The hospital actually let you have a night off?"

"Crazy, right? I agreed to pick up four shifts over the next month for Dr. Monroe just to cover tonight, but I love the block party, so it's worth it."

"Hey, babe." Hank slid up next to Daisy, handing her a white wine slushy before sliding his hand over the back of her chair possessively. The move made her skin feel like it was on fire, and she took a large sip of her slushy to cool her down.

"Oh, what's this? No 'hey babe' for me?" Jake joked, and Daisy nearly choked on her drink.

"I don't think our friendship will ever consist of me calling you babe. Sorry, man."

"No hard feelings." Jake's eyes bounced between Hank and Daisy. "I'm glad you two figured everything out."

"Me too." Daisy looked up into Hank's eyes and smiled as he dipped his head towards her for a little kiss.

Jake cleared his throat as their small kiss turned into Hank tasting the inside of her mouth. "As much as I love seeing you guys together, I think maybe a few members of our charming community might have been scandalized by that display." Heat flooded Daisy's cheeks. "They probably need a distraction to calm down. May I have this dance?" Jake held his hand out to Daisy. Smiling, she turned to Hank and winked.

"Of course. Let's go." A laugh rose in her chest when Hank let out a low grumble as they walked away.

"So, how's the shoulder feeling?"

"It's good. Hank was very strict with me about getting plenty of rest."

"Thank you, Daisy."

"For what?"

"For letting Hank in. For letting him help you. For forgiving him for being the biggest idiot ever." He rolled his eyes, which pulled a laugh from her. "I've never seen him so happy, and I know that's because of you."

"Well, I don't know about all that."

"No, it's true. I've been worried about him. Worried he wouldn't ever pull himself out of the funk of having Anna leave him. But then you came along, speeding right into his heart, and although it took him long enough, I'm glad he finally has you."

Daisy smiled and forced down the lump in her throat.

"How did you know about the speeding?"

It was Jake's turn to burst out laughing. "Daisy, I'm sorry, but if I have to hear the story of the first time he met you one more time, I might move to Canada."

"He really talked about me that much?"

"I'd never say Hank is big on talking, especially about anything personal, but he has a funny habit of mentioning you."

"I'm truly the lucky one out of the two of us. It's so nice to have someone so fiercely, and stubbornly, protect me. I'm not used to it, and I've certainly fought against it enough."

"Did you know, after your accident, he sent me at least fifty questions a day that week, making sure you were okay?"

"What? No." She was sure her face correctly displayed how absolutely mortified she was at the idea of Hank bothering Jake over all the little things she experienced.

"Yes. He was driving me crazy, but that's when I knew he had it bad. You were never just someone he felt obligated to help."

"What did he ask you?"

"Oh, everything from if you were sleeping enough to if he should be worried about how you refused to take your pain medication. He even asked me if you'd spent too much time out in the sun one day, and if he needed to watch out for dehydration. The man is a goner. When the two of you have kids, I'll be disconnecting my phone for sure."

When they had kids.

Daisy's heart flooded with warmth as she thought about a future with Hank. It meant everything to her to have someone she could count on by her side.

If she wasn't careful, her emotions would overwhelm her senses, and she'd be in a puddle on the dance floor. The familiar burn of holding everything back was already swelling in her throat. A tear made its way onto her cheek and she quickly batted it away, just as a warm hand slid across her lower back.

"You're not making my woman cry right now, are you, Jake?"

"Shit, yeah, I might have. You okay, Daisy?"

"Yes, I'm fine. They aren't bad tears." She giggled, heat flushing her entire body at the way Hank claimed her.

"Well, you're definitely off dance duty. May I?" Hank reached his hand out and pulled her into his chest. Jake mumbled something about heading off to find some food, but Daisy couldn't pay attention to anything other than Hank's hand, which was drifting lower and lower on her back.

"It took everything in me to let you walk over here and dance with him."

"Oh, were you a little jealous?"

"A little? Sunshine, I almost just ended the longest friendship I have here in Bell Ridge."

"Hank!"

"Don't distract me. Why were you crying?"

"I wasn't crying. It was just a little tear."

"Okay, why was there even a single tear on your face?"

She rested her head on his chest. "I just realized how thankful I am for you."

"I'm thankful for you too, Daisy." He placed a kiss on the top of her head, and they swayed back and forth to the music. Although there were dozens of other couples dancing in the square with them, they might as well have been the only ones there.

"I didn't know if you were going to ask me to dance."

"And let you think I didn't remember our conversation about your grandparents loving this part of the block party? Please."

"I can almost feel them here. It's like their spirits are dancing next to us."

"I bet in some parallel universe they are."

"So much for no more tears," she whispered and pulled her hand away from Hank's to wipe her eyes. His firm hands stopped her though, and it was the warmth of his fingers that she felt on the delicate skin beneath her eye, as he swept away the tears.

A cool breeze made its way through the square, and Daisy shivered. Her skin tingled, and the hair on her neck stood up. The same uneasy feeling settled in her stomach as the night she was chased through the fairgrounds.

"Hank..."

He met her eyes and frowned.

"What is it?"

"I feel like someone is watching us."

"Of course they are sunshine. You're beautiful. I'm sure every man here is staring in jealousy."

Daisy felt the blush grow across her chest and up into her cheeks. It had been such a sweet comment, but she couldn't shake the pit growing in her stomach.

"No, that's not what I mean. I think someone is watching us." She took a small half step back from him, swinging her head around the crowd.

People had gathered in the far field for the town's bonfire, although a few were still in line at the food trucks. Nothing seemed out of sorts, but she still felt unwanted eyes on her.

Scanning the edge of the field, her breath hitched. A shadowed figure was standing just in front of the tree line, and she'd caught their eyes watching her.

"Hank," she hissed. "Over at the trees. Who is that?"

Hank's head swiveled, his eyes locking on the person.

"I see them." They watched the shadow retreat into the crowd. Hank grabbed Daisy's hand and brought her over to the table where Jake had set out a whole platter of different treats.

"Hey guys. I didn't know what everyone would want, so I just grabbed a bunch of things to share." Looking at Hank's expression, Jake frowned. "Everything okay?"

"I need you to stay with Daisy. Right here. Don't leave her side, got it?"

"Yeah, absolutely. You okay?" he asked, turning to Daisy. She felt like she had lost all the love-flushed color in her cheeks.

"Mhmm." It wasn't a great answer, but it was all she could get out as she sat in the chair next to Jake, watching Hank head off towards the trees.

"What was that all about?"

"I felt like I was being watched. We noticed someone over by the trees staring and when we both turned towards them, they took off."

Jake sat up straight. "Do you think it's the guy who's been giving you trouble?"

"I don't know." A shiver made its way down Daisy's body. Jake must have noticed, because he quickly took her hand in his and gave it a reassuring squeeze.

Daisy and Jake sat silently, waiting for Hank's return. When he finally made it back to the two of them, Daisy's heart sank at the look on his face. He sat down, pulling her chair closer to his. With his arm wrapped around her back, she sank into his chest.

"You didn't find the person?"

"No. And even if I had, it's not illegal to be watching people at a public event."

"Do you think it was Dale?"

"Maybe. I think the person was taller than Dale though, but it was hard to tell with them standing in the shadows."

"How much longer do we need to stay?" she asked.

"You want to go?"

"I'm sorry. We were having such a nice time, it's just that... I just don't feel...I don't know. I don't want to be looking over my shoulder all night."

Hank stood. "Then let's get you home."

"Thanks for the dance tonight, Jake. Sorry we have to leave early."

"Don't worry about it for a second. I'd rather know you were safe. Besides, I've had my heart set on a slice of Emma's pie of the day since this morning when I heard it was key lime. I'll see you both later."

Even heading back to Hank's truck, Daisy still had the lingering feeling of being watched. She stood, arms wrapped around herself, as Hank opened the passenger side door.

"You okay, sunshine?"

"Is this ever going to end, Hank? I don't want to live with this feeling for the rest of my life."

"I know, Daisy. I don't want this to go on any longer than it already has. We just don't have any solid leads right now. It makes me so damn mad, but I promise you I'll do whatever it takes to make sure you are safe and that they never hurt you again." He pulled her into an embrace and kissed the top of her head. It was one of those moves that instantly made her feel safe, and at the same time, weak in the knees.

"Come on, let's get you home. I'll check on Maisie and Minnie and then we'll figure out how to make sure our first official date gets a happy ending." The mischievous twinkle in his eye had her laughing.

"Oh, I think I know exactly how to make sure this date leaves us both smiling and wanting more." When his eyes shot up to his hairline, Daisy laughed again and continued, "With freshly baked brownies, of course!"

"I seem to remember really enjoying your brownie batter..." Hank playfully spanked her as she jumped into the truck.

"Play your cards right, and I just might let you lick the spatula."

"I promise there's somewhere else I'd love to lick if you're giving me choices."

"Hank!"

His hand reached around the back of her neck and pulled her in for a kiss. As Hank climbed into the driver's seat a few seconds later, Daisy's mind was thoroughly distracted from the fear that had been consuming her just moments before. Her hand moved to rest on his thigh as they made their way towards the farm.

"That smile on your face makes me think you're feeling better," he said.

"Feeling lots of things right now, Sheriff. I suggest you really step on the gas so we can get those brownies...um, baking." Although the cab of the truck was dark, she was certain he could see the blazing flush that had just flooded her face.

"If you don't stop nibbling on your bottom lip, I'll have to pull the truck over and make good on my promise, sunshine." Her whole body tingled at the thought.

When they finally pulled up to her house, Daisy was a melted ocean of anticipation and desire. She waited for Hank to open her door, shrieking when he scooped her up in his arms and carried her up to the porch, the air between them electrified.

"Let's go make those brownies, Daisy."

TWENTY-SEVEN

"You really think sunflowers are a good idea?" Daisy sounded uncertain, but he knew she was just pushing to make sure he really believed the idea would be successful, not just because he wanted to support her. And he did. Her business plan was rock solid and really seemed like exactly what Bell Ridge needed to draw in more visitors.

"Yes! If you want people to come out to the farm, I think we plant sunflowers in the field behind the barn. That way, they can come out and take their own cuttings as a fun outing."

"And if no one comes out, I can still use them for the cuttings I offer at the farmer's market."

"Exactly."

They strolled hand in hand down through the town square.

"I really would love to have a little farm stand out by the road, too. Like a little self-serve station where I can set out eggs from the hens and little flower arrangements. Maybe even some of my brownies." She winked at him.

He stopped, gasping dramatically with his hand over his

heart. "Nope, huh-uh. I'll build you a farm stand. Sure, no problem. But those brownies are all mine."

Her laughter filled the air. He could listen to that sound forever, relishing the grip it had on his heart. Daisy hopped up onto her tiptoes, planting a gentle kiss on his cheek.

"I'm all yours, Sheriff, but we need to learn to share the brownies."

"Hank." A sharp voice interrupted their conversation.

Turning to where he heard his name, his mouth fell open in shock when he saw who was standing before them.

"Anna..."

"Wait, Anna as in...your ex-fiancee, Anna?" Daisy whispered.

"Yes." Hank said through his grinding teeth.

"Hank. Do you have a minute to talk?"

"No."

Not only no, but hell no. Not now, especially with Daisy standing next to him. He could see her eyes change, no longer filled with laughter as she looked at Anna. Something flashed in the cerulean blue. Was it worry? Whatever it was, Hank wanted to get her away from Anna.

"I know I don't deserve it."

"What are you even doing here? After all this time?"

Daisy squeezed his hand. "I'm going to give you two a moment. I'll just be over on the benches by the pharmacy when you're done."

"No, sunshine. Stay." He squeezed her hand tighter as he felt her pull away.

"Hank. You need to speak with her on your own. This is between the two of you. I'll just be right over there." He watched her point to a bench halfway down the block.

Daisy gave Anna a cool smile and Hank felt her hand run across his back before she walked to the bench in front of the pharmacy.

"Didn't realize you were mentoring Girl Scouts." Hank's blood pressure surged at her dig against Daisy's age.

"Anna, I don't really care about anything you have to say. Do you have any idea what the past five years have been like for me? You just left. No chance for a discussion, no chance for me to figure out what was wrong and to make it right. All those years and you just left like I wasn't good enough."

"I know it was wrong, Hank, but I didn't know how to tell you I was unhappy. Your job came first, and I was afraid it always would. I could not continue living in that fear."

"Is that all you have to say to me?"

"I guess so. Except, I didn't really say it yet, but I'm sorry. I've spent the past five years thinking about you, and praying you were okay."

"Right."

"I'm telling you the truth. Listen, I'm in town visiting my folks for the next three days. I know you don't owe me anything, but I'd love to sit down and just talk about things."

Rubbing his hand over his face, he didn't know what to say. Sure, closure would be nice. But hadn't he already moved on from those hurt feelings? Wasn't he whole now that he was with Daisy?

"No. I have a busy weekend with Daisy and won't be available. I guess I should say thank you. If you hadn't left, I'd be stuck in a loveless marriage with you, staying just to do the right thing. But now, I get to have a beautiful life with Daisy. Safe trip home, Anna, wherever that is now."

"Hank. Please. Just coffee this afternoon. Please."

He had nothing left to say to her. But there was something that was keeping him from feeling complete closure from the situation. He would be a better man for Daisy if he could finally close the door on the hurt that Anna caused.

"Fine. Meet me at Emma's at three."

Not waiting to hear her response, he walked to find Daisy.

———

Hank sat in his usual booth, keeping a keen eye out for Anna's arrival. He wasn't happy to be here, but Daisy had backed up his decision, even agreeing that it would be good for Hank to hear Anna apologize and accept the closure. The diner's bell rang out, and he watched her walk in, a confident smile on her face that reminded him of how she'd been their entire relationship. So sure of herself. One thing he was sure of, he never wanted to see her again after this.

"How could I sign my whole life away without knowing what was out there in the world?" There he was two minutes later, sitting across from Anna, listening to her explain how easy it was to leave him.

"Sign your life away? It was a life we'd spent building together! You don't think you could have clued me in at any point during our relationship that you wanted to leave?"

"I don't have a good excuse, Hank. Things just became too overwhelming and that day I packed up and left... I just couldn't face you. I needed space."

Hank tried to settle the anger surging in his veins as he took a deep breath.

"And what did you find when you got that space?"

"That no one out there compared to you."

Her hand reached across the table, and she touched his hand. Hank jumped back like someone had doused him with acid. Both his hands fell into his lap.

"Anna. That's bullshit, and you and I both know it. You weren't happy with me, you were just going through the motions. And over the last five years, I've learned that the same was true for me."

"Hank, I mean it. I was stupid to run away, but I never wanted to hurt you. I just needed a moment of freedom. I needed to get away from the pressure of this small town."

"A moment? You think five years is a moment? I haven't heard a peep from you since your goodbye letter."

"I've wanted to call. I've wanted to hear your voice. I just, I've been weak."

"I would have gone with you. All you had to do was say the words and I would have given you the world."

"I know you would have, but I didn't know who I was, and I needed to figure that out on my own."

Hank sighed, staring into his coffee.

"Look, I'm not sure if you knew this or not, but I kept tabs on you while I was away," she said. "I know that you never dated after me. I know you buried yourself into your work and I thought that maybe, well, maybe that meant you were waiting for me to come back."

"No, it certainly did not mean that," he growled. He hadn't been waiting for Anna. No. He didn't know it during all those years of isolating himself away from relationships, but he was waiting for Daisy. She was everything he wanted.

"Well, this thing, whatever you have going on with...what did you say her name was? Daisy? It can't be that serious. She's what? Ten years younger than you? What could she possibly offer to someone in your stage of life?"

"Stop."

"What you have is new. I'm sure it's even fun and exciting to be with someone so much younger, Hank. But you and I have history. We have a foundation."

"A foundation! Of what? Running away when things got tough? No. There is only history between you and me, and not good history."

"She won't be able to give you what you need."

"And you would?" His voice was deep, red hot anger pouring through his vocal cords as his hands slammed onto the table. "In between me tiptoeing around wondering what you'd leave me over next? No, thank you. You asked what she could offer? Warmth. Love. Acceptance of who I am and unwavering support of my goals. Kindness and sunshine and every good thing in this world is wrapped up in that woman and you don't even come close to her. I love her, Anna. And you coming back to speak to me won't change that."

"Hank, that was uncalled for," she said as she placed her hand over his.

He looked at their hands, together as they had been so many times over the years they dated, and he felt nothing other than the overwhelming desire to recoil from her touch.

Pulling his hand back to his lap, he sighed.

"I came here for closure, Anna. I got that. I don't think we have anything further to discuss. I'm with Daisy. I choose her in this moment, and I'll choose her in the next, and every single moment that comes after. Have a safe trip home, wherever that may be now." Standing up, he pulled his wallet from his back pocket and paid for his coffee.

Leaving the diner, Hank wrenched open the door to his truck. He was more than ready to see Daisy. For only a moment, he turned back towards the diner, watching Aaron Callum slide into the booth with Anna. They were a weird combination, but Hank didn't care. Let him have her. He had Daisy, and his heart squeezed inside his chest, thinking about how much he loved her. With a breath, Hank turned away from the woman who he once loved and marched towards his future.

———

Wiping the tears from her eyes as quickly as they were falling was quite the task, and Daisy had all but given up after a few minutes. The weather was beautiful, a cool breeze blowing across the front porch where she sat, but she felt chilled to the bone.

Daisy had supported Hank's decision to go speak with Anna. To hear what she wanted to say to him all this time. But she knew exactly what the woman would say to him, just by the fiery look in her eyes that morning. She wanted him back. They had history. Big history. And Daisy knew this was just going to be another time where she was left behind. What was so wrong with her that the people she loved found it so easy to leave?

She let out a strangled laugh as she thought about seeing Anna earlier. There was nothing special about Daisy, but Anna was like a runway model. Tall, thin, beautifully put together. Here Daisy was in her ripped and tattered overalls, hair pulled up into a messy bun and not a speck of makeup on her face. She was short and squishy and downright frumpy.

Her heart jumped in her chest as she saw Hank's truck making its way towards the house. She did her best to dry her tears and took a big drink of the tea to soothe her burning throat.

"Daisy?" Hank gently spoke her name, frozen in place on the porch steps. She could see him searching her face, watching the tears fall with confusion. "Hey, what's wrong?"

"She's really beautiful, Hank. I can see why you would be with her."

"Okay..."

"I won't stand in the way, you know. I won't cause a scene when you go back to her."

"When I go back to her?"

"I mean it, Hank. She broke your heart and now she's here. To what? Tell you she's ready to fix it. Go. Have that chance. It's okay." She wanted to sound so strong in her resolve, but the tears flowing down her face gave away how she was truly feeling.

Hank made his way onto the porch and sat down beside her, pulling her over onto his lap and wrapping his strong, warm arms around her body. Daisy didn't want to, but her body responded automatically to the safety she felt in his arms, and she buried her face in his chest.

"Sunshine, you can't honestly think that just because she came to talk to me, it would mean we'd be getting back together. I haven't seen her in five years. I don't have any feelings for her, except maybe contempt. And she may have broken my heart all those years ago, but it's whole now, thanks to you."

"But she's so beautiful, Hank. Tall and thin and done up like she's about to walk in a Parisian fashion show. I can't compete with that. I'm wearing ripped overalls and a shirt I've had for ten years now. My thighs jiggle when I walk and I'm pretty sure there is dirt on my face from the garden this morning."

"You are the most beautiful woman I have ever seen in my entire life." Hank lifted her face towards his with his warm hand, sweeping away her tears. "I love your overalls, I love your earth covered freckles, and I especially love the way your thighs jiggle when you walk. You have nothing to worry about. No woman will ever compare to you."

His thumb rested on her cheek and swept away a tear. "Now that we have that all settled. I have something for you."

"You do?"

"Give me one minute to grab it."

She eagerly watched as he walked to his truck, taking a small package out from the passenger's side.

"I saw this at the farmer's market a while ago and immediately thought of you. It's been riding around in the glove compartment of my truck since then, reminding me of the hope I had that maybe things would all work out." Hank handed the small package to Daisy and stepped back, sitting on the porch swing a few feet away from her.

"Go ahead, open it." She tore at the wrapping paper before opening a small black box.

"Oh, Hank. It's beautiful. I love it." She quickly held up the necklace, a gorgeous sunflower pendant falling into place as the chain dangled from her hand.

"Sunflowers always make me think of you. They move to face the sun every day and that's just like you and me. I'm always moving to get more of you, because you are my sunshine."

Tears filled Daisy's eyes. She stood up from her chair, walking over to him, necklace in hand. Hank reached out and pulled her onto his lap.

"Here, let me." Daisy smiled and swept her hair away from her neck. "Beautiful, just like the woman wearing it."

She leaned in, pressing her lips to his. Heat burst through her body. Her tongue pushed through his lips, exploring his mouth over and over. A relentless hunt to taste him, the man she loved.

Twenty-Eight

"I've got it," Daisy yelled as she walked to answer the knock that came from her front door. Peeking out the window, an unmarked delivery van sat parked in her driveway. She hesitated for a moment before opening the door.

"Hello, can I help you?" Her hand automatically drifted to the sunflower pendant laying at the base of her neck. She'd found herself playing with it in the days since Hank gave it to her, a sense of calm washing over her whenever she did.

"Are you Daisy Hughes?" Her smile lit up at the young worker, a kid maybe sixteen or seventeen years old. Probably working his first job. She loved seeing how hard working the kids in her town were.

"Yes, I am."

"This is for you."

The teen picked up a vase from behind him and before Daisy could react, a bouquet was being shoved into her face.

"Oh, my..." she took the vase from the delivery person, a cough starting in her chest at the fragrant scent. The coughing continued as she shut the door. Her face began to feel funny. Itchy, even.

Moving the vase away from her face, her lungs strained trying to pull in air. It didn't feel like any was making it into her body. Spots danced in her eyes, which were now burning and painful.

The floral arrangement was beautiful, but her heart immediately went into overdrive when she got a glimpse of what was hidden at the center: daisies. She looked for the delivery person to signal that she needed help, but he had already made it back to his vehicle, reversing out of her driveway at a record pace.

Her lungs wheezed, as she tried to force her chest to accept the air she was desperately pulling in. Who would have sent her these? Nearly everyone knows she has a terrible allergy. She needed to get her legs to move from the spot they were currently glued to!

Her medicine was all the way in the kitchen with Hank. And she needed it fast. But, lord, everything in her body was on fire. She dropped the vase and heard it shatter into a million little pieces. Stumbling, she willed her legs to move.

A strangled sound escaped her tight throat as her head hit the floor and darkness pulled her under.

———

Hank busied himself with cleaning up the daily garden harvest while Daisy was in the living room. She looked so adorable in her overalls, bent over in the garden, pulling her harvest this morning. And he was more than happy to help. After all, the view had been glorious.

Was that a knock at the door? Quickly wiping the tomato juice off his hands, still smiling about his memories from the morning, he made his way towards the door.

"I've got it," Daisy called from the living room.

Something pulled in the pit of his stomach. Maybe he should have been the one to get the door. He wanted her to know that he trusted her instincts, especially after she'd expressed how his protectiveness could sometimes make her feel like he thought less of her.

No, Hank would let her answer the door, knowing that she wouldn't put herself at risk and open it if she didn't know the person who knocked. Not thinking anything more about it, he turned back to the vegetables scattered about the counter. Was she planning on preserving all this stuff? She'd definitely need more jars soon. He made a mental note to pick some up for her when he went back into town. After all, they'd nearly used up her stash making jam for the market a few weeks ago.

A sudden, loud crash pulled him from his thoughts.

"Daisy?" He waited for a response. Nothing. That pit in his stomach started aching again as he walked towards the living room.

"Daisy?"

His eyes focused on her body, laying on the floor, flowers and broken glass all around her.

"Hey! What happened?" He flew to the side of her, lifting her head into his lap and taking her face into his hands. Seeing her blue-tinged lips and her swollen face, Hank's hands shook as he pulled out the phone in his pocket and called for an ambulance.

"9-1-1, what's your emergency?"

"This is Sheriff Hank Porter. I'm at 618 Mayfair Road. I have a twenty-five-year-old woman who is having a reaction to something. She's struggling to breathe and turning blue."

"Okay, Sheriff. I have emergency services dispatched to you. Was she exposed to any chemicals or is it possible she was exposed to something she could be allergic to?"

Hank barely heard the question over the hard pull of Daisy's lungs, fighting to allow any air in. Looking at the flowers scattered among the broken glass and water, he saw the culprit. Someone had sent her an arrangement with daisies in it! He needed to get her out of the house, into the fresh air, and he needed to do it right then.

"She's allergic to daisies. Someone sent her some in an arrangement. Oh, shit!"

"Sheriff?" The emergency operator was trying to get his attention, but Hank already knew what he needed to do.

He gently placed Daisy's head back onto the floor and ran to the kitchen for her emergency epinephrine injector. Panic swept through him as he tried to remember where she'd shown him it was, but after nearly ripping three cupboard doors off their hinges, he found the spot.

Running back to the living room, Hank swept Daisy up into his arms, falling into the soft grass beside the driveway. His eyes met hers and he watched as the light slowly drained.

"No, no, no, Daisy! Come on, sunshine. You stay right here with me. Stay awake. Where the HELL is that ambulance?"

Even though the sirens were growing louder, Hank understood the situation was too dire. He wasted no more time before injecting the medication into her leg. Slowly, while massaging the spot the large needle had just injected the medication into, he watched Daisy gain some color back in her complexion. He felt her body relax into him and her rattled, constricted breathing became less labored.

"Oh, lord. Daisy, you scared the hell out of me."

"Hank..." her voice was weak.

"Shhhh sweetheart, don't say anything. I can hear the ambulance coming now. They'll make sure everything is okay."

He held her tightly as the ambulance showed up, willing

his mind to shove down his anxieties by watching her chest rise and fall with each breath.

"Hey, Sheriff, you doing okay?" one of the paramedics asked after they had Daisy loaded onto the gurney.

"I'm fine. You just take care of her."

Hank gently kissed Daisy on the forehead, relief flooding through him when she gave a little smile in response.

"I'll be right behind the ambulance. I just need to speak with Heath quickly before I go."

As the ambulance pulled away, Hank met his deputy, Heath Williams, near the front porch.

"I'm going to follow her to the hospital. I need you to bag whatever evidence we can use, then clean up the flowers for me, okay? Make sure there isn't a single trace of them here when I come back. She's allergic to the daisies."

"That's the ultimate irony."

"Yeah, tell me about it."

"Alright, get out of here and go take care of your woman. I'll make sure everything here is covered. Send me an update about how she's doing and I'll let you know when I've got everything finished."

His woman. God, that felt amazing to hear.

"Thanks, Heath. There's just one thing I need to see first. I want to be able to tell her who sent them."

"You think it'll say?" Deputy Williams asked as they watched the ambulance leave.

"There's only one way to find out." Hank took the front stairs two at a time.

"You think someone sent them to her knowing about her allergy?" Hank gave the deputy a knowing look.

"With everything that's been going on here lately, I can't just chalk this up to a coincidence."

"If they were sent with malicious intent, I doubt they signed the card."

Deputy Williams was likely right, but Hank had to see for himself before he left.

Entering the house, glass crunched under each step they took. Hank bent down to retrieve the card, nausea filling his throat as he read the signature.

"You okay, boss? Who sent the flowers?" Deputy Williams asked.

"Apparently, I did."

"I'm feeling perfectly fine. There's no reason to keep me any longer, Dr. Winters."

Daisy winced at the raw feeling in her throat. If she hadn't already known what happened, she could almost convince herself it was painful because she'd eaten sandpaper for lunch.

"Daisy, you had an anaphylactic reaction. You need to stay for observations. It's likely you could have a secondary attack or have symptoms arise and I'd rather you be here where we can take care of you." A pang of sadness filled Daisy's chest. She wished Jake was on shift. It certainly would be useful to have a friendly face around to help calm Hank down. Dr. Winters was nice, but all that talk of secondary attacks and adverse symptoms wouldn't work in her favor.

Speaking of Hank, that man was so busy stomping across the floor at the foot of her bed, she wondered if a nurse was going to need to take his blood pressure soon to make sure he didn't have some sort of episode. His whole body was radiating anger, but it made little sense. Was he angry at her for the flowers that someone sent? Was he mad that the day had been disrupted with yet another trip to the hospital?

"Hank. Please. You're making me nervous, clomping around like that."

She watched his attention switch to her as he found his

way to the seat beside her bed. His hand quickly scooped hers up and, without another thought, Daisy felt her body relax as his thumb traced tiny circles onto the back of her hand.

"If you leave now, I'm afraid it will be against medical advice, Daisy."

"She's not going anywhere. We'll wait until you feel confident it's safe for her to go home."

"Good." Dr. Winters smiled at Hank, looking one thousand percent like a cat that ate a canary. "Like I said, just a few hours and then I'll re-evaluate your request to get out of here. Okay?"

"Okay. Thank you, Dr. Winters." Daisy resigned, as she laid her head back and closed her eyes.

Once the doctor had left the room, she sat back up, watching Hank stare at her for a moment. It was almost as though he was trying to memorize how she looked. Maybe he felt angry because he saw how severe her allergy was and it triggered a fear in him?

"Hank—"

Before she could continue, his mouth brushed over hers. It was a whisper of a kiss, but she felt how it overflowed with tentative love. A kiss that was meant to move her heart closer to his. And it did just that.

"Daisy, do you have any idea how close I thought I was to losing you?"

Her hand found its way to his cheek.

"I'm fine. I promise. Random things like that are why I keep my prescription up to date and in the house."

Grasping her hand from his face, he sat down on the edge of her bed. Their thighs touched, and a spark rushed through Daisy as she thought back to the feather-light kiss they'd shared just seconds before. It really had nearly shattered her.

"I don't think it was random." She knew he hadn't meant to say that out loud, but it didn't matter. He had.

"What do you mean? Someone sent me flowers, they just didn't know about my allergy. It's okay. I'm sure it was an honest mistake."

"It wasn't. I'm sure of it."

"Was there a card with it? Maybe it was from my old office friends? Everyone knows the anniversary of my grandparents' accident is coming up. If someone from there sent them, they might not know."

"It wasn't someone with pure intentions, Daisy."

"And how can you be so sure?"

"The note said the flowers were from me." Her heart felt like it stopped. Silence lingered between them for only a millisecond, but it felt like a lifetime.

"You sent me flowers? Why didn't you have pure intentions?" Her voice was shaky, unsure if he was making a confession or what he had actually meant.

"No, I didn't send them. I wish I had, because I would have made sure they never even came close to a daisy, let alone contained enough to kill you ten times over."

"Why would someone send me flowers and then say they were from you?"

"To hide their identity. To make it come back on me if they could..." he shuddered and raised her hand to his lips, and she knew he couldn't finish that thought. Clearing his throat, he continued. "I've got my deputies trying to figure out who sent them. We know the florist they came from. We can hopefully trace things back to the real sender."

Just then, a knock came from the hallway. Aaron stepped into the room.

"Daisy! Are you okay?"

She felt Hank go stiff beside her.

"Hey, Aaron. Yeah, I'm fine. Just an allergic reaction. How did you know I was here?"

"Oh, mom saw the ambulance at your place. She took a

tumble down the front steps, trying to make sure everything was okay. Broke her wrist and got a nasty cut on her forehead. She'll be fine, though, just getting stitched up now. As soon as I knew mom was okay, I asked a nurse for your room number and came to check on you."

"Oh, my goodness. You let her know I'm thinking of her and if either of you needs anything while she's recovering, don't hesitate to call. I can stop over whenever!"

"Thanks, Daisy. I'll let her know."

Hank cleared his throat, staring straight at Aaron.

"Uh, well, I'll let you get some rest. You feel better fast, okay?"

"Of course. Thanks for checking on me, and please let your mom know I'm thinking of her." Daisy smiled as Aaron gave a quick nod.

"Sheriff." Aaron slowly moved his eyes away from Daisy and down to their joined hands. Daisy could have sworn his smile tightened ever so slightly, but by the time Hank acknowledged him, Aaron had fully recovered.

"That's too bad about Mrs. Callum," Daisy said once Aaron had left.

"Yeah. But just so you know, you'll not be going anywhere if they ask for help."

"What do you mean?"

"Daisy, someone just tried to kill you. The only thing you're going to be doing is staying right where I can protect you."

"You could come with me."

"And walk into what?"

"You really think Mrs. Callum is trying to kill me? She's one of the sweetest women I've ever met."

"No, I don't think it's Mrs. Callum. But the way Aaron looks at you, I don't like it."

"Hank. It's no secret he's been interested in me. But he's

never acted in any way that was inappropriate. He's a part of my friend group. I can't stop living my life, stop offering to help people, stop being who I am down in my core."

Hank stood up and moved back from her bed.

"Why aren't you taking this threat more seriously?"

"What do you want me to do, Hank? Agree to let you put me in a jail cell and throw away the key to protect me? I don't want to live like that."

"If that's what it takes for you to be safe and stay alive until we figure out and stop who is behind all this, then yes! I want to lock you away."

———

"Are you doing okay over there?" he asked as they drove towards Daisy's house. The doctor had cleared her from observation after a few hours, but tell that to his nerves. He wasn't sure he'd ever recover from watching the woman he loved turn the most terrifying shade of gray as she struggled to breathe.

"I'm fine. I promise."

"I think almost dying from anaphylaxis is pretty bad, Daisy."

"It's not the first time, Hank, and I don't think it will be the last. Unfortunately, having a severe allergy means accidents like that can happen."

He sighed and removed one of his hands from the steering wheel, taking a minute to rake it through his disheveled hair.

"It wasn't an accident, Daisy. And I need you to take that fact more seriously. Someone is escalating their attacks against you. We need to talk about the changes you need to make to keep yourself safe."

"Just great. Like I really need the man that I love thinking so damn little of me. That I don't know when I'm in danger and I don't know how to keep myself safe." Her grumbles would have made him laugh had his heart not stopped at her admission of loving him.

"You love me?" Hank knew his mouth was slightly ajar, and he probably looked ridiculous as he stared at Daisy, but that didn't matter. She loved him.

"What?" The look of complete confusion written across her face made him laugh. She'd obviously not meant for him to know that, but those words were like a balm for his worried heart.

"You just said I'm the man you love."

"I most certainly did not."

"No, you did." He pointed his finger at her. "And don't think you can gaslight me like you did when you yelled out my name while you were in the bathtub a few weeks ago. I know, Daisy."

Her cheeks turned the most amazing shade of pink.

"Well, I can tell you one thing. Right now, you certainly are the man I find most aggravating in this whole wide world."

Daisy shot him a fiery look, and he shrank in his seat.

"Why are you so mad at me, sunshine?"

"Why? Why, Hank? You honestly can't figure it out? I do love you, you jerk. Not that this is how I imagined ever telling you. So, guess what? Your opinion of me matters. You are grumpy and stubborn and constantly confuse me with your need to protect me and your utter lack of confidence that I can protect myself. Lord help me though, because when you smile at me, when you take my face in your hands and you kiss me, when you hold me as I cry, my heart feels like it's going to explode. I mean it when I say that I won't do anything reckless, and I want you to trust me. It's not just because I'm worried about myself. I don't want to lose you."

"You're afraid of that?"

"Of course I am. We only just stopped dancing around our feelings for each other, and I'm too invested in making us work. So don't think you're the only person here afraid. I'm not only terrified that you'll be injured or killed doing your job, but it makes me physically sick to know that there is a possibility you could die trying to protect me. I can't even think about that..." a fat tear rolled down her cheek as her voice broke. She cleared her throat, pain flashing across her face before she concealed it. "I don't want to deal with it all right now, Hank, so just hush and focus on driving."

"Hmm," Hank mumbled, flipping on his turn signal and maneuvering the truck over on the side of the road.

"'Hmm' what? What are you doing?"

His hand rubbed over his jaw before his piercing eyes connected with hers.

"I saw you there, Daisy."

"Where?"

"At the accident where Caleb was killed. In the seconds where I thought my life was going to end. I didn't have a flash-back to my childhood, or even a flash of memories from recent years. I saw you. In the future. I was coming home to you and our family. You were standing on the porch at the farm, yelling after the most adorable little girl in a sunflower dress who had your blonde hair. The both of you were lit up by the sun, looking like angels who just arrived from Heaven. Your belly was round with another child we were expecting. I felt such happiness in that moment, Daisy."

"You can't say that to me, Hank."

"Why? I want that future, Daisy. I love you."

"You really love me too?" He watched as a smile stretched across her face.

"Of course I do. I've been hung up on you since the very first night I kissed you. I love how you're always thinking of how you can help people in the community. I love how your entire face lights up when you talk about flowers and vegeta-bles and berries, or when you talk about Maisie and Minnie, and how much you love your mean chickens. I love how you stand on your tiptoes when you want a kiss from me. I love the way your nose is always covered in a dusting of dirt when you've been out in the garden. I love the way your body fits perfectly in my arms when we fall asleep together. I love the way you lean into me when you cry, like I'm the only thing keeping you anchored to the ground, and although I wish you never had a reason to cry, I love the way your eyes sparkle when you've finally released all that you've been holding in."

He touched her cheek, wiping away the tears that were falling, before sweeping his hand over her shoulder and intertwining her fingers with his.

"The future I want with you, the future I saw, I can't breathe knowing that it might never happen because I didn't protect you," he admitted.

"I want that future too, Hank. I know you'll always protect me. I just need you to trust that I love you enough to keep myself safe, too."

"I just…"

"Have a little faith in me."

———

"What are you doing?" Hank asked as she unbuckled her seat belt.

"What I've been wanting to do since we got inside from bringing in the vegetables from the garden this morning. I'm going to kiss you, Hank Porter. And then we're going to practice making a baby together." She watched the desire flair in his eyes as she moved in for her kiss.

Hank's hands landed softly on her back, running up and down the fabric of her dress as his tongue explored her mouth. Daisy shifted, climbing onto his lap. She used her own hands to lift her dress over her legs and bottom. His fingers gripped her hips as she moved them in tiny circles in his lap. He rewarded her with the sweetest groan of desire that radiated through his chest and warmed something deep inside herself.

He laughed and continued to pepper her neck with kisses. "You need to stop doing that, or I can't be held responsible for what happens next."

"Being responsible right now doesn't sound all that fun." Her teeth nipped at his earlobe while her hands reached down to his belt and worked to undo the clasp. Once he was free from his pants, Daisy grasped him, savoring the feeling as his cock grew rock hard in her hand. She was enjoying watching him lose control at her touch. When her own throbbing ache became too much to ignore, Hank plunged inside her and the sound of her moans filled the truck.

"Oh God, Hank. I love you." Her hips rocked back and forth, controlling the tempo as she moved up and down, until he filled her so completely she felt as though she may burst. His grunts of pleasure drove her wild, increasing her pace to a feverish level while she chased the growing fire in her core.

"I love you so much, Daisy." His fingers left her hips, traveling up her stomach and landing under her bra. He cupped her breasts, quickly rubbing his thumbs over her taut nipples. The sensation was overwhelming.

"Fuck, you're perfect sunshine. This is all I need. Just you and me."

"You and me," she repeated breathlessly as her orgasm raced towards her. "Forever."

"Forever."

Hearing him say those words drove her crazy, the height of her pleasure crashing down around her as her climax rolled through her body.

———

"Hey, I thought maybe you could use a cup of tea." Hank walked out onto the front porch and Daisy gently closed the book she had been reading.

"Thank you. Are you going to join me out here? I'd love to have someone to snuggle with."

Hank hesitated.

"If you don't want to, I can always ask Maisie to join me up here, but I think she might break the swing and, honestly, I'm not up for having to fix it right now."

That got a smile from him.

"As much as I would love to see you try to get a cow up onto the swing with you, I think I need to be holding you as much as you need a cuddle right now."

The swing momentarily stopped as Hank's weight settled on the seat, and Daisy tipped so that she was resting solidly against his chest. They sat, drinking their tea as Hank moved the swing back and forth. Before breaking the silence, she felt his grip on her arm squeeze tightly.

"We need to have a serious discussion."

She knew this was coming. Her episode that morning had been terrifying, but it was one she had been able to mentally prepare for. Daisy had a clear memory of the first time it happened as a child, and since that day, she'd been almost in a state of waiting for the next time. Hank had known about her allergy, but he'd never experienced her having a reaction. There was no doubt that the horrible possibilities of how the day might have turned out were swirling in his mind.

"Can we wait? I almost died today." She tried to tease him into relaxing a bit, but not a single muscle in his body gave way.

"That's not funny."

"Hank, I'm okay. I don't want you to be sitting there thinking you could have done anything differently or feeling any guilt."

"I should have answered the door. We know there is a threat out there, and I didn't even think to stop you. I just can't stop thinking about the what ifs. What if you hadn't dropped the vase and alerted me to the problem? What if I hadn't gotten your medicine to you in time? What if you had died?" Raw emotions strained his voice, and she snuggled into him.

"Hank."

"It would have been all my fault, Daisy. And I can't live knowing that."

Tears swelled in her eyes as she ran her fingers over the pattern on his shirt.

"Are you trying to break up with me?"

"God, no! That's not what I want at all." Hank ran his hand through his beard. "I just think we need to look at this from a different angle. If we say this person who sent you the flowers is the same person who's been behind all the other things that have happened recently, then most likely they are also the person who sent you the notes telling you to leave. It seems like all this might stop if you were to go away."

Her stomach dropped, a queasy feeling lingering as his words swirled around her mind. "But I don't want to go away. I love it here. My life is here. You're here."

"I think you seriously need to think about leaving Bell Ridge."

"Where would I even go, Hank?"

"What about staying in Miami with your cousin?"

"And if I'm in Miami with Grace, who is going to look after the farm? What would I do with Maisie and her calf? What about the chickens and all my crops?"

"I'd be able to look after things for you."

Daisy stared at him, lips slightly parted, while tears filled her eyes.

"If you don't want me looking after them, you could ask Sam or even Aaron."

She didn't say anything. What was there to say? She wasn't going to leave.

"Why aren't you saying anything, sunshine?"

Her eyes focused back on him.

"What am I supposed to say, Hank? I don't want to leave you, and you clearly want me to go."

"What? Damn it. I'm not doing a good job of explaining this." His body shifted, lifting Daisy from his chest. He grabbed her hand and interlaced his fingers with hers. "Don't you think that it's killing me to know you have to leave because I haven't made it safe for you to be here? I haven't had a single lead to follow. Every time something happens, and we think that maybe this person who's after you has slipped up, it just leads us to another dead end. I never want to be away from you, but if I don't stay, how can I make sure we catch whoever is behind all of this? You almost died today, Daisy. You need to be somewhere safe, and that isn't here with me."

Daisy tried to stand, but Hank held on to her.

"Let me go, Hank." The secure pressure from his arms released, and she jumped up from the swing. She wanted to run into the house and slam the door in his face. Over and over, she'd told him how important it was to not leave. And now he just expected her to leave him when things got really tough? No. Absolutely not. She wouldn't give up her home, her income, her relationship, so that some psychopath could win.

Twenty-Nine

"Who were you just talking to?" Daisy's voice cracked, thick with sleep. She yawned and sat up, trying to figure out why Hank had been whispering into his phone.

"Shit, sorry. I didn't want to wake you. That was Heath. I need to go handle some things in town."

"What time is it?"

"Just after five. I already checked in on Maisie, Minnie, and the hens. I'm going to have a deputy come out and sit at the house today while I'm gone, okay?"

"I don't think—"

"I'm not taking any chances. There will be someone out there any time I'm not here. No arguments. Now, go back to sleep and rest."

"Okay." She rolled over to watch him walk out of the bedroom. "Hey, Sheriff? I think you're forgetting something."

Wiggling her eyebrows got a laugh from Hank.

"Sorry, sunshine. How could I forget?" The edge of the bed dipped as he sat, pressing a kiss to her forehead.

"You missed."

"And here I thought forehead kisses were like kryptonite to women."

"Oh, they are," she sighed. "I'm just greedy. I want a forehead kiss for my heart, and a kiss on the lips for my body."

"What do you need for your soul?" he asked.

"You'll just have to come home quickly so you can find out."

"How can I refuse that?"

"You can't." Hank landed a kiss on her lips. "Thank you, Sheriff. Now, hurry along before I realize that kiss won't hold me over for very long, and I convince you to take off your uniform and crawl back into bed with me."

A groan left Hank's throat. She basked in the fact that a little flirting from her could affect him so completely.

———

Just as she finished rinsing and placing the last dish on the mat to dry, a knock sounded at her front door. She nearly let out a groan as she saw who was standing there. Kicking herself for needing to be neighborly, Daisy plastered a smile on her face as she opened the door.

"Hey, Daisy."

"Aaron. What are you doing here?"

"Mom wanted me to check in and see how you were feeling after everything that's happened. She sent me over with some tea to make sure you were doing okay." He held up a small bag of tea leaves and pressed it towards her.

"That's really sweet. Please tell your mom thank you for me."

"I definitely will." His gaze traveled down her body and back to her eyes. "How are you feeling?"

Normally, Aaron was harmless. He'd been a part of her friend group since moving back to Bell Ridge, and even though it was clear he'd wanted more from Daisy than friendship in the past, he'd never pushed things or made her feel uncomfortable. So why did his gaze bother her so much now?

"Almost back to one hundred percent. How's your mom doing?"

"Oh yeah, she's good. A little sore and slow moving around today, but on the mend." He looked behind her, into the house. "Listen, do you have a minute to talk?"

No. She didn't. But her good manners won out once again. Waving to the deputy parked in her driveway, Daisy stepped aside from the doorway.

"Sure. Why don't you come on in? Can I interest you in some tea?"

She held the bag he'd just gifted her up.

"Oh no, I'm not a fan of chamomile. Please make some for yourself, though."

Daisy rearmed the alarm, dropped the dry tea on her kitchen counter, and made her way to the living room.

"No tea?" He asked when she returned to the room empty-handed.

"Not right now. I really appreciate you bringing it over, though."

She sat on the opposite end of the couch from Aaron, her hands placed in her lap. He stared at her, appearing frozen in thought, until she cleared her throat and caught his attention.

"Is everything okay, Daisy?"

"Why wouldn't it be?"

"I just mean, well, I overheard someone in town talking about how Hank was the one to send you those flowers. And I know he's been spending a lot of time out here after your accident. I just wanted to make sure you're safe. You know I'd be over here in a heartbeat if you needed help. You can always call."

People in town were gossiping about Hank? She immediately felt defensive.

"What? No! I don't know who would have said that, but I am not in any danger from Hank, I swear. It's really sweet of you to come check on me, though. You and your mom are great neighbors, but I promise, Hank is not the one behind all the weird things that have been happening."

"Okay, well, does he have any leads?"

"Not that I know of. It's been really unsettling, but I'm sure we'll get it figured out soon enough."

"Yeah, I just can't believe all the weird things that have been going on. I'm wondering if Bell Ridge is still a safe place to live. Have you thought about leaving?"

Her discussion with Hank from the night before bounced into her mind. There, of course, had been a time right after her grandparents died where she thought it would be too much for her to take on. All the memories, all the upkeep, all the expectations. But the thought of another family living there, tending to the land that her grandparents had poured their hopes and dreams into, it just broke her heart.

"I think if this had happened last year, when I first got here, then yeah, I might have thought about it. But I love it here. I'm not about to abandon everything my grandparents worked so hard to build just because someone decided they had a problem with me and didn't want to come talk it out like an adult."

"Things could get worse though, Daisy. What if you get hurt...or worse? Is this all really worth it?"

"Aaron, I appreciate the concern, but I will not run from whoever is doing all this. It's just not who I am."

"You know, my cousin is back in town and I just worry about her safety. If someone can get away with doing this to you, is Bell Ridge really safe for anyone?"

"I didn't realize you had extended family in the area."

"Yeah. I just worry. About you, about her. I don't want anything bad to happen."

"Aaron, that's really, really sweet and I am so thankful I have friends like you to have my back. I promise, Hank is a really good guy, and he's keeping me safe."

———

"Are you coming home soon?" Daisy's hand grasped on to her cell phone, uncertainty churning in her stomach.

"Things are taking longer here than I thought. I'm sorry." Hank paused, probably waiting for her response, but she just stayed silent. "Everything okay, sunshine? You sound upset."

"Aaron was here. He dropped off some tea from his mom. Apparently, he just wanted to check in and make sure I was doing okay."

"Did he hurt you?"

"No, Hank. It's nothing like that. I've told you before, he's my friend. I just...he said I should leave town for a bit and it just made me think about our conversation last night. Maybe I am putting too many people at risk being here."

"Have you changed your mind? Do you want to leave?"

"No. I don't. And I don't want to rehash everything we already talked about last night. It's just the fact that he said other people might not be safe here because of me. I couldn't live with myself if something happened to anyone else." Her voice pitched higher than normal, and she cleared her throat.

"Take a breath, Daisy. No one is saying you have to. Your safety is just as important as any other person. You deserve to be safe. Not to protect others, but for yourself. And I've been thinking. I know it made you upset last night when I said it, but I still want you to go." He paused, and she bit the inside of her cheek. "And while I feel responsible for finding who is doing this and making sure they can never hurt you again, I also realize that it's important to keep you safe wherever you decide to go. So, if you decide you want to leave Bell Ridge, I'll go with you. I'll take a leave of absence and we'll go somewhere together."

"You'd do that? You'd leave and go with me?"

"Of course I would, sunshine. There's no way I'm letting the woman I love leave town without me tagging along."

She sniffled.

"Daisy, are you crying?"

More sniffling. "No, it's just allergies."

"That's not even funny."

"Yeah, probably still too soon, huh?"

"Definitely."

"I love you, Hank. In case I haven't made that abundantly clear. I do."

"I love you too, Daisy. Let me know what you decide, okay? You can pack right now and when I get back, we can figure out where to go."

"You're the best. Be safe and make it home to me in one piece."

"Always."

THIRTY

At the back of her closet, Daisy pulled on the handle of her luggage. Was she really about to pack and leave? It didn't feel right to tuck tail and run, but she was tired of the constant fear that nagged in the back of her mind. Hank was right, and she was finally feeling ready to admit it. Unfortunately, it just wasn't safe to stay. Hopefully, this nightmare would all be over before she had to think of leaving permanently.

As horrible as it was to be leaving the farm, Daisy couldn't help but feel a bit of lightness in her heart, knowing that Hank was going to be with her. She knew if he hadn't offered, she would have stayed. The past year had been the hardest year of her life, and now that she had Hank, there was no way she was letting him go.

She needed to call Sam, to see if he could take on caring for Maisie, and Minnie, and her hens, too. If not, she would reach out to Aaron. Hank might not like it, but he was her friend, and she knew she could count on him too, if needed. And she'd need to reach out to Grace. As much as she didn't want to bother her cousin, a trip to the beaches of Miami with Hank did sound pretty great.

Lost in her mind making lists of things she needed to pack, Daisy almost didn't hear the knock at her door. Almost. Peeking down the stairs, her jaw dropped when she saw the last person she'd ever expect to be standing on her front porch. Swinging the front door open, she took a sharp breath and tried to calm her anger.

"Anna? What are you doing here?"

"Hello, Daisy. This is quite a lovely place you have."

Daisy's heart was in her throat. She never wanted to see this woman again out in town, let alone standing on her front porch.

"Thank you. It belonged to my grandparents." They stood in silence for a moment. Daisy didn't care, though. That had been all the conversation she could muster for the woman.

"Listen, I know you probably don't want to see me ever again, but I feel like we got off on the wrong foot before."

"Oh, you mean when you told Hank you wanted to be back with him, even though he and I are together and in love?" She saw Anna physically recoil at hearing Daisy say she was in love with Hank.

"I just...well," tears fell from her eyes. "I just wanted to apologize. I'm not that type of woman. I don't know what came over me, but I just needed to tell you I'm so sorry. I'm sure Hank told you the awful things I said, and I wish I could take them back."

Daisy watched as remorse filled Anna's face. She hated seeing someone hurt, and if she could patch things over with Anna, that might make things less awkward in the future if they bumped into her while she visited her parents in Bell Ridge.

"Why don't you come in for a minute? I'm all for making amends."

"That's so kind of you," she sniffled. "I'd love to."

Daisy pointed to the dining room table as she rearmed the security panel. "Here, have a seat. Would you like something to drink?"

"Would it be too much of a bother for me to ask for a cup of tea?"

"No, that's no problem. Do you have a preference?"

"Chamomile? I could use something to calm my nerves."

"Of course. I actually was just given some from a friend this morning. I'll make it for both of us."

"Perfect."

Daisy kept a close eye on Anna as she boiled water in the kitchen. Aside from glaring around the room and typing a message on her phone, the woman sat at her dining room table in silence.

"So..." Daisy prompted, sipping her tea slowly. She was astonished that Anna had drained her cup almost the instant that Daisy set it in front of her.

"I'm sorry, Daisy. I should have just walked away when I saw Hank with you. There was a part of me that was hoping I would come back to Bell Ridge and he would be the same Hank I'd left five years ago. Still in love with me. Still willing to give me a second chance. And when I saw him with you, I just sort of lost all sense of myself. I'm not normally like that, and I could instantly see how much you mean to him. I shouldn't have asked him to meet me for coffee, and I shouldn't have been so forward with him."

"Forward how?"

"I assumed he told you. He was probably just trying to spare me the embarrassment."

That familiar, painful pit was back in her stomach.

"Forward how?"

"I kissed him. And then I asked him to leave you, and to be with me."

"I see." She smoothed her hands against her shirt, trying to calm the anger building within her. The smirk on Anna's face did not help the situation.

"Please don't be mad at him. This was honestly just me losing my mind a bit, knowing he was no longer available."

"I think, yeah, I think it's time for you to go." Daisy stood, gesturing with her arm at the front door.

When Anna stood, the color drained from her face as she turned to Daisy.

"Oh, I-I don't feel so well."

"Anna?"

Anna swayed, holding her head in her hand until she collapsed to the ground. Daisy felt her own head swimming suspiciously, as nausea rose in her belly, and her skin went clammy. That's when she saw someone walking up her driveway, dressed in all black with a mask covering their face. Darkness threatened to take over her vision. She needed help. She needed Hank.

———

"Heath, are you available to pick up the shift this weekend for Roger?" This wasn't even his problem to fix, and yet, there he was, a headache incoming, trying to wrangle coverage and make sure the next few days were taken care of.

"Yeah, Hank, I can take that. It's no problem."

"Thanks man, I really appreciate it. I know Roger does too."

The phone in his pocket vibrated. A flutter of excitement burst through his chest as his favorite picture of Daisy jumped up on the screen. He was more than ready to get back out to the farm and hold her in his arms for the rest of the day.

"I gotta take this. Thanks again, man." Turning from his

deputy, Hank accepted the call. "Well, hey there, sunshine. Missing me already?"

"Hank…" the panic in her voice ripped at his chest. His stomach clenched.

"Honey, what's going on? Are you okay?"

"A-Anna stopped by. She wanted to talk." She sounded weak, and Hank held his breath as she explained. "I made some tea, and we talked. S-she collapsed. I-I don't feel right. Everything is blurry and my heart is racing."

Hank grabbed his keys as he jumped out of the chair.

"Do you need me to call an ambulance?"

"Hank. Someone is outside the house. I d-don't think…"

"Are they still there?"

"Oh, God."

"What?"

"They just came in. I heard them disarm the security system."

What the fuck? There was a deputy stationed at the house. Hank had checked in with him just a few hours ago. How was this happening?

"Where's Deputy Forsyth? He's the person I had stationed at the house today."

"His vehicle is there, but I couldn't get out front for help."

"He would stop anyone from going in —"

"Hank…" she interrupted.

"What?"

"I don't think it's the deputy. I can hear their footsteps."

Those last words sent chills straight to his bones.

"I'm coming, Daisy. Get somewhere fast and hide."

"I'm in my closet, but I can hear them coming upstairs, Hank. I don't think you're going to make it."

Hank ran through the station, yelling instructions to his deputies as quickly as possible before he made it out to his truck.

"I'm going to make it, baby. Try not to panic. Do you have the mace Kara gave you?"

"I d-didn't have time to grab it. They're outside the room. My head, Hank. It feels like it's going to explode." Her voice was a whisper.

"Don't talk anymore, sunshine. Just stay quiet. I'm coming."

"I love you, Hank."

A heartbeat passed and Hank heard the most gut wrenching sound he'd ever heard as the sheriff. Daisy's scream, piercing as the intruder took hold of her, seared into his brain before the line went dead. It ripped his soul to shreds and punched him so hard he was struggling to breathe.

"Daisy? Daisy!" Hank frantically called out her name, but it was pointless. He was still fifteen minutes away from the farm.

He prayed harder than he ever had before, begging and bartering. He'd give anything, he'd give his own life, for her to be okay. She just needed to be okay.

Over the radio, Hank heard the dispatch order for all available deputies to route to her address. His fear speared him in the heart. He never wanted to leave Daisy alone, but he had. Against his better judgment, he'd gotten comfortable with the safety measures in place and messed up the only job that really mattered. He'd failed at keeping the woman he loved safe.

Fuck! If she wasn't at the farm when he got there, he'd never stop looking for her. He'd tear apart every square inch of land in Clarence County to find her, and then he'd move on to all of Texas, and the whole damn world if he had to.

He dialed the deputy assigned to watch Daisy's house, but the line went immediately to voicemail. When he finally arrived at the farm, he saw the sheriff's department vehicle parked exactly where he'd expect it to be. Rushing over, Hank found the driver's side window rolled down, with Deputy

Forsyth slumped over in his seat. The man was unconscious, but had a steady heartbeat and his breathing was normal. Had someone drugged him? Was the assailant someone he'd known and rolled down his window to chat with? Hank's stomach clenched as he called dispatch.

Arriving at the house, weapon drawn, he would not wait for the sirens he could hear in the distance to catch up with him. The front door was wide open, swinging sickly in the breeze. There was no sound except the beating of his own heart, and he had to stop and take a breath to calm the noise before entering. Emotions didn't matter right now. No matter how terrified he was of losing Daisy, her safety, and finding her, had to come first. He flipped the switch in his mind, turning off his emotions. The roaring thoughts stopped and only his training and pure muscle memory guided him inside.

Walking steadily, gripping onto his weapon, he moved through the house without making a sound. She wasn't there. He could feel it in his bones. Whoever entered the house uninvited had taken her away. Hank knew no matter how many rooms he searched through, he wouldn't find her there.

Running up the stairs, his anger nearly ripped him apart as he got to Daisy's bedroom. She had put up a fight, and there was evidence of that all over the room where, just that morning, she had been safe in his arms. The carpet that laid in front of her bed was askew, threatening to trip up anyone who walked across it. The closet doors where she had sought shelter were open, with clothes scattered across the floor. There was no blood, no sign that her assailant had injured her. At least not here at her house. He held onto that thought, even though it was barely enough to keep his legs from collapsing underneath him.

Walking back downstairs, determined to continue his search around the property for any clues, his heart clenched in his chest. There was Anna, brunette hair splayed out all around her, lying on the dining room floor.

"Anna? Hey, can you hear me?"

Her eyelids fluttered at the recognition of his voice.

"Hank? What happened?"

"Take it easy," he said as he helped her sit up. "You lost consciousness."

"I-I did? Oh, my head is pounding. Is Daisy okay?"

"She's not here. Did you see who took her?"

"No. I mean, the l-last thing I remember was her telling me to leave. When I got up, oh ow." She lifted her hand to her head before continuing, "I was so lightheaded. I must have passed out."

"Just sit here for a minute and get your bearings. An ambulance will be here shortly."

"Where are you going?" she asked as he walked away.

"I have to find Daisy."

"Won't you just stay here with me for a minute? I'm scared Hank."

"Anna, just sit tight. I can hear my deputies coming. Just listen to the sirens getting louder and breathe. They'll come help you." And with that, he ran out of the house.

"But, I wanted you..." he heard Anna say, but it didn't matter. The only thing he cared about was finding Daisy.

THIRTY-ONE

Daisy's entire body felt heavy and cold. So cold. She gave her best effort to open her eyes, but every inch of her body felt disconnected from her mind. If she could just get her eyes to open, maybe things would make sense.

Dizziness overwhelmed her when she was finally able to see. It was cold, dark, and musty, wherever she was. As her eyes adjusted to the dim light, a cabin materialized around her. A very rustic one at that. She began taking inventory of her body. Her arms and legs could barely move. Whatever drugs she'd been given had really wiped out her strength. A shudder ripped through her body at the realization that whoever had her there removed all of her clothes except for her bra and panties.

"Well hello, sleeping beauty. I was wondering when you'd finally come around. It's damn near midnight." The familiar voice put her mind at ease, but her gut clenched with unease.

"Aaron? You found me. C-can you help me get back home?"

"I really am sorry this happened."

"I-it's okay." She winced at a sharp pain in her head. "I'm just so happy you stopped whoever came after me. Where are we?"

"My family's cabin on the west side of Clarence County."

"I didn't know you guys had property out here. H-how did you find me? Who took me?"

His shoulders sagged, and the nervousness that had originally waned when she'd heard his voice returned with a vengeance.

"Like I said, Daisy, I really am sorry it came to all this. It really was your own stubbornness that led me to take such extreme measures."

He turned towards her, and the look in his eyes made her bones shake and her mouth run dry.

"What's going on?"

"If only you'd listened to my warnings. Those notes should have been enough to get you to leave. But you don't know how to quit when you're ahead. And because you are so dimwitted and stubborn, I've had to take drastic actions to get what I want."

Shit. Hank had been right. He didn't trust Aaron, and she, like a fool, had defended him.

"No, please. Help me, Aaron. Please, just help me get out of here."

"Now, why would I do that when I worked so damn hard to get you here?"

"W-what do you mean?"

"You should have just gone out with me. My mom tried to put us together more than once, and that would have just solved everything. Then I wouldn't have had to do all of this. I mean, I almost had to kill you in front of the damn sheriff! Like that wouldn't have gotten me into some hot shit."

She heard the words coming out of his mouth, but her brain refused to help make sense of it. There was no way this man, her friend who she'd known most of her life, someone who supported her this last year, was the person behind trying to hurt her. It didn't make sense.

"I don't understand."

"You don't see it. Your truck's brake lines being cut? Your house being broken into? Stalking you through the fair? Delivering flowers you are deathly allergic to?"

"T-that was all you?"

"I even hired Dale to turn you into his little plaything. He almost ruined everything for me when he wasn't able to finish our deal."

"Why? Because I wasn't interested in you? Because I just wanted to be friends?"

"No Daisy, don't flatter yourself. I've never really been into stupid, fat, blonde bitches."

"Then why?" Her tone was defiant, anger surging through her veins at his harsh words.

"I never thought you'd stay."

"Stay where?"

"I never thought you'd claim their farm as your own." Daisy's eyes narrowed in on Aaron, focused on hearing his explanation. "Your grandparents were taking forever to kick off, and that land should have been mine." Aaron rolled his eyes as a gasp escaped at the mention of her grandparents. "Oh, for fuck's sake, Daisy. My mother made an agreement with them years ago. That land was meant to be mine. But along you came, and they left it up to you to decide what you wanted to do with it." He pulled a blade from the back pocket of his dirty ripped jeans and began twirling it between his fingers.

Daisy took a sharp breath and tried to piece together what he was telling her. Everything was still so foggy, and her brain just wasn't keeping up.

"Aaron, why didn't you come to me? Why didn't you tell me this before now? It didn't have to go this far."

"So you'll do the right thing? You'll give me the land that is rightfully mine?"

Daisy hesitated, knowing she should just tell him what he wanted to hear, but not wanting to. The farmhouse was her happy place, her connection to the only family that had ever loved her unconditionally. It's where she fell in love with Hank.

"Just what I thought," he responded, fire blazing in the depths of his black eyes. Aaron took a step towards her, running the blade lightly over the skin on her face, down her neck and over her shoulder. Then, he pressed it into the flesh over her heart, drawing blood in a thick line up to her clavicle. Tears pressed out from the corners of her eyes as the pain registered.

"A-Aaron. Stop, please. Y-you need help. You're sick. Please don't hurt me. Let me go and I'll make sure Hank knows you didn't mean to hurt me."

"There's no one coming for you, Daisy. Not even Hank. He's too busy caring for Anna, who I left in a heap on your dining room floor. As soon as you are out of the picture, and I will make sure that happens, he'll go back to her."

A knock came at the door and Daisy didn't think. She screamed as loud as she could, pushing all the oxygen from her body out into the world. Aaron's face turned bright red, veins in his neck bulging with anger. He didn't hesitate before landing a blow to her jaw, and when that only left her stunned, he followed up with a forceful fist to her temple. Crying out in pain, darkness filled her field of vision.

Time passed, but Daisy had no idea how much. Her vision was blurry, and each time she tried to open her eyes, the pain behind them consumed her, pulling her back into darkness. Finally, there came a time when she woke and the pain wasn't so all-consuming. Slightly opening her eyes, she surveyed her surroundings. She couldn't see anyone, but heard voices. Voices? Yes. Someone had joined Aaron, and the voice was light and quiet. It was also...feminine. The knock at the door. Had it been from his mom? She loved Mrs. Callum like she had loved her grandparents, and her stomach rolled, thinking she could have any part in this.

"I left the note for Hank. He didn't even care that they had to take me to the hospital. He didn't visit, he was just too busy looking for her."

The venom in the woman's voice made nausea claw at Daisy's throat, and she immediately knew that Mrs. Callum was not in the cabin with them. No, in fact, it had been Anna's voice who filled the space just a moment ago.

"Did they question you?"

"Of course they did. I didn't tell them anything, though. I didn't see you take her, so I wasn't lying."

Gasping as the pain in her head overwhelmed her, she shifted in the bed.

"Well, look who finally decided to join the conversation. You really look awful. Good."

"Anna? I don't understand."

"You wouldn't sweetheart, you seem a bit daft, if I'm being honest."

"Please, just tell me what's going on so I can understand. I didn't know you two knew each other." Daisy actually didn't care at all what the two of them had to say, other than to find out what their end goal was. She just needed a few minutes to plot an attack they wouldn't see coming. To look for a weapon. To figure out how to trap them inside while she got away.

"Remember the conversation we had yesterday? About the cousin I was so worried about? Daisy, meet my cousin, Anna."

The shock must have been written across her face, because Aaron's laughter filled the cabin. "We're not first cousins. There's at least a branch or two of the family tree in between us, but that doesn't mean she's not family. When I realized you and Hank were officially a couple, I needed to revamp my plan. I would have you taken care of, and Anna would make sure that Hank remained distracted."

"I want him back. I'll make sure I'm around to console him after they find your body. He'll realize we were always meant for each other and we'll grow close again as I help him heal from his loss."

Just perfect. Not only did she need to deal with one psychopath, apparently she would have to figure out a way to survive them both. She tried to focus her eyes. It was so dark in the cabin, the only light source now coming from the fireplace. There had to be a way out of this. Maybe if there was something heavy around, she could use it as a weapon.

"Don't you think, Daisy?"

Dread pooled in her stomach as the woman's gaze hit hers.

"Sorry. Head injury over here. You'll have to repeat that last part for me."

Anna scoffed.

"I was saying that Hank and I are much more suited for one another. I mean, what could he possibly see in you, other than an easy lay? I know my aunt thought you'd be a good match for my cousin here, but he has some standards. No one likes a fat bitch, babe."

Fire flowed into Daisy's veins, her blood pressure rising enough that her heartbeat painfully pounded in her skull. No. She wouldn't give this monster the satisfaction of a fighting response.

"Yeah. Exactly. I'm not right for Hank. I tried telling him to go back to you today, but he wouldn't listen to me."

Daisy watched something flick across Anna's face. Maybe

if she could placate Anna, there would be a way out of all of this. No way in hell would she ever give Hank to this woman, and she knew he'd never take her back, but Daisy had to try anything that seems like it could even remotely work to get her out of this situation. "I told him I was going to leave. To visit my cousin in Miami, and that I didn't want him to go with me."

"He's mine. He waited for me, all this time, never dating. I just had things to figure out. If you hadn't tricked him, if you hadn't flashed your doe eyes and faked needing help every two seconds, he still would have been waiting for me. Thankfully, Aaron called me when you lured Hank in with your sad, scared Bambi act."

Lord, this woman was absolutely deranged. Aaron's sick actions were the reason she had been scared in the first place!

"I know, Anna. And look, I'm so sorry. Woman to woman, I will back off and leave him alone. I'll tell Hank that what we had is over, and that he needs to return to you. Let me go, and I'll make it right. I'll go to Miami, and I won't come back."

Anna stared at her. The look in her eyes made Daisy want to vomit. "What else can I do? How do I walk away from this alive?"

Aaron walked over to the table and picked up a stack of papers. He tossed them at Daisy.

"Sadly, for you, I don't think there is a scenario where that happens."

"I understand Anna's play here, but how do you think you'll get the land? There isn't a legal document that says you get the land if I die."

"No, there isn't. But since you haven't set up anything legally, you're going to sign these papers that say the house and land are to go up for auction in the case of your death. Luckily, both Anna and I have explored your house when you weren't there and discovered the cabinet where you keep all your important papers. After your tragic and heart wrenching death, I'll help uncover your last wishes. And guess who owns the only land auction house within a hundred miles?"

Daisy didn't have to wait long for the answer.

"That would be my daddy and his business partners. They'll see that Aaron gets the land," Anna announced.

It was clear to Daisy now. She died, and both Aaron and Anna got what they wanted.

"You've really thought of everything." She was going to die at the hand of a man she'd grown up playing with. Someone who'd lived right next door to her practically her whole life. Someone she considered a friend.

"Aaron, you know me. We grew up together. How can you think about doing this to me? Hurting me? Killing me?"

"You know, I feel like in another time, another place, I really could have had so much fun with you. Unfortunately, we're running out of time. And I'm losing my patience." Aaron pulled a gun from the back of his jeans and handed it to Anna. Daisy's stomach flipped.

"Tare care of her, Anna. Prove yourself. Earn Hank."

Anna raised the gun and pointed it directly at Daisy's face. Time stopped. Her lungs froze, painfully refusing to draw breath into her body. And then Daisy saw Anna's resolve falter. The gun lowered slightly and a sliver of hope bloomed in her heart.

"Aaron. Maybe she's more agreeable to what we want than we thought. If she left, we could both have what we wanted without having to dispose of her. It could be a lot less complicated than you're making it."

Something about the way Anna said that brought Daisy out of her despair. She wouldn't leave Hank without giving every ounce of energy she had to stay alive. She couldn't just lay down and let something like that happen because she was scared. The speech she gave him about trusting her to protect herself rang out in her mind. She was about to live up to what she said.

A dark shadow moved across Aaron's face, a horrific mask of deranged expression now in place. He pulled the gun from Anna's hands and scowled at her.

Daisy would need to incapacitate Aaron first. He had the gun now. There were a few decorations that caught her eye as she looked around the room, but nothing with any weight or sharp edges. She could see a porcelain pitcher on the kitchen counter, but that was too far away. If she tried to make it that far, she would be caught before she made it out of the room.

Her eyes traveled back to the flames, dancing wildly in the rustic fireplace. And that's when she saw it, a perfect weapon. The fire poker. Sharp on one end, long handle, which would be good for swinging. It was her only option. Moving her attention back to Aaron and Anna, she waited for her opportunity.

"There's no backing down now, Anna. You'd be a fool to think that she's just going to give us both what we want and leave. The second we let her out of here, she's running right to Hank, and there will be a manhunt for us. We'll spend our lives on the run or in jail."

"I don't know. I don't know if I can go through with it, Aaron. Being here, seeing her like that. I just don't have the stomach for it. I want to be with Hank. I want you to get your land, but I don't want to do it this way." Anna moved towards the door. "You should just take care of her if you need to do it that way. You know I'd never tell, but it's just not—"

In that second, Aaron raised his arm and pointed the gun at his cousin. Daisy heard a loud bang, its echo ringing in her ears, followed by a scream that pierced the air.

Anna's body slumped to the floor, crimson blood flowing from the gunshot wound to her head.

"Such a pity she couldn't earn her reward. Oh well, one down, one to go." Aaron turned the gun on Daisy.

She closed her eyes and waited. One heartbeat. The beautiful memory of Hank talking about the life he saw for the two of them filled her mind. Two heartbeats. The desire to make it back to him and make his vision a reality filled every cell in her body with determination. A third heartbeat. No loud bang, no indescribable pain.

His hot breath scorched her skin as he leaned into her neck and whispered. Nausea settled in the back of her throat as her body fought through the onslaught of adrenaline and shock.

"Not yet, Daisy. I think I'm going to have some fun with you, after all."

He walked calmly over to the door and took off his boots. Daisy watched as he looked at Anna, a shadow of annoyance dancing across his features.

"What does that mean?" Her voice held steady, even if her eyes couldn't help but flick from Aaron to the gun he was still holding on to.

"Well, since there's been a very drastic change of plans, I need some time to figure out how to frame this all on Anna. I need a release. Something to help get my adrenaline settled so I can think clearly about all of this." As he licked his lips and stared at her chest, Daisy knew exactly how he planned to settle himself.

When he moved to grab the rope from an armchair in the corner of the room, she knew she needed to make her move or she would never have a chance of getting out of that cabin. He couldn't tie her up. There wasn't a single scenario in which she would allow his disgusting fingers to touch her skin.

Tensing the muscles in her arms and legs as a quick test, excitement flooded her system when she realized she could control their movements and could put her plan in motion. Whatever sedative Aaron had dosed her with was likely finally making its way out of her system. As for the blows he landed on her earlier, she was dizzy, but nothing so bad as to stop her from trying to escape.

Daisy took off. There was weakness in her legs and for a split second, she feared she was more likely to smash her face off the ground than to ever make it to the fireplace. But step after step, she got her footing.

The rapid drumming of her pounding heart was the only sound in the room. She had no time to think about Aaron lunging for her after the initial surprise waned from his face. The poker was easy enough to pull from the holder by the fireplace, and she gripped it in her hands. One look at where he was in relation to her own body and she swung with all the force her body could give.

A loud crack sizzled through the air in the cabin and Daisy watched as the fire poker contacted Aaron's side. She'd been aiming for his head, but damn if her arms weren't still weak from the sedative and subsequent beating. Her muscles struggled to keep her upright, and swinging the poker had nearly taken her down along with Aaron. Luckily, the hit caused some injury to him, and Aaron bent over, gasping for breath.

She didn't waste any time, not even one second, to see how badly he was injured. Daisy took off towards the door and prayed she would recognize the area once she was outside of the cabin.

An inch away from opening the door, her leg was caught in a vise of fingers before she was thrown to the floor. Aaron climbed up her body as she tried to recover from having the wind knocked out of her. A hit to her temple had her seeing stars, nausea rolling up from the depths of her stomach.

The pressure of his body on hers was unbearable, and her lungs became painfully constricted under his weight. She scratched at his face with her unrestricted arm. There must have been some level of contact as Aaron let out a hiss in pain.

Blood dripped down his gaunt features, and it made him look a hundred times more deranged than when Daisy had first woken up there.

"A-Aaron." Her voice shook with the strain of his body crushing hers. "Please."

"Fuck you, bitch. This is where I take everything from you. This is where I finally win." She saw the anger in his eyes, and as his hands closed around her throat, she knew these would be her last moments if she didn't fight back. Even if she did, her chances of survival were bleak.

With his arms pressing down on her throat, she tried to use her now free arms to break his hold. She scratched at him again, drawing more blood from his face, neck, and arms. She tried to use her legs to kick him, to turn him off of her body, but they were solidly pinned down. As darkness crept in from the corners of her vision, she flailed her arms out in one last ditch effort to find anything she could use as a weapon. Her eyes widened as her hand touched the edge of something cold and hard.

Aaron's gun was lying on the floor, just a fingertip lengths away from her. Stretching her arm and her fingers out as far as they could reach, Daisy grabbed at her last chance for survival.

Darkness swarmed her vision. Aaron was now holding her throat so tightly that no air was filling her lungs. As death marched closer to her, she brought the gun up off the floor, pressed it into his side and pulled the trigger.

Daisy watched his eyes go wide, shock filling them as his hands loosened their grip from her throat. Air pulled into her lungs in painful spasms, the light returning to her vision. Slowly, the room focused, and she rolled to her hands and knees.

Her legs were weak, shaking beneath the weight of her body, but her brain was screaming at her to run. Stepping over Anna's body, she pulled the cabin door open and ran.

The cool, wet grass slipped beneath her feet. She stopped for a moment to take in her surroundings. Should she head into the woods? Or maybe she needed to follow the overgrown path of a driveway down to the road? Aaron was still alive. Could he gain enough strength to follow her if she went to the road?

A shot rang out and Daisy screamed.

"Y-you fucking bitch! Don't move."

Daisy looked back at the cabin, and tears flooded her vision. She wasn't going to get away. Aaron was there, holding something over his side as blood seeped through, pointing his gun directly at her.

His hand shook as he walked down the steps and across the grass towards her.

"I'm going to make this hurt. I'm going to make you wish you'd just went back to your life in Dallas right after I killed your grandparents. You're going to beg for your life and I'm going to think about it with joy every single day when I wake up on my land."

If he thought he was taking the fight out of her, he was wrong. Every word just further drove her desire to get away. She would see Hank again. She would be back on her farm. They would get married, and have a little girl with her blonde hair, and a little boy with Hank's chocolate eyes, and they'd swing on the front porch with their arms wrapped around each other thankful for the life they'd been able to create. Locking those thoughts tight in her heart, Daisy sprang into action.

While his own ongoing rant distracted Aaron, Daisy slammed her knee as hard as she could into the sensitive flesh between his legs. That worked instantly, a winded groan cutting off his ramblings as he fell to his knees.

Her hand flew out, trying to pull the gun from Aaron while the pain incapacitated him. Daisy winced as her head was pulled violently backwards. The gun came up and smashed into her eyebrow, stars dancing in and out of vision as she tried to focus.

Aaron pushed her down into the grass, his arm laying across her throat. Daisy forced her arm up towards his body, raking her fingers down his body until she found the bullet wound. With every ounce of built up rage, Daisy shoved her finger into his ripped open flesh, pressing as hard as she could.

The scream that ripped through the air helped Daisy realize she'd done exactly what she wanted to. It only took a few seconds for the color to drain from his face. Then, his body swayed, and his eyes rolled into the back of his head. She was almost free.

His unconscious body flopped down on top of hers. The weight of his arm on her throat was tough to breathe through, but it was nothing compared to having the full weight of his body fall on her chest. She was exhausted. All she wanted to do was find Hank and wrap up in his arms while she slept for a week.

Determined to make that a reality, Daisy wiggled her body around while pushing against Aaron until she was free from his weight. The sky was still dark, no signs of sunrise to be seen, and as she looked around at her options once more, the gun caught her eye. She wouldn't make the same mistake twice. After grabbing it and engaging the safety, Daisy moved away from the house as quickly as she could manage.

The gravel driveway to the cabin was rough and over-grown, but she needed to get to a road. Stones cut at her feet, and her head throbbed with each step. The blow to her head must have resulted in a cut, because Daisy could feel blood running down her face. But none of that mattered. Not the ache in her head, not the stones in her feet, not the darkness threatening to shut her body down. She could crumble after she was safe.

Lord, the driveway was long. If her ability to judge distance was still functioning after the blows she took to her head, it was at least a quarter mile. When she finally came to the road, her heart skipped a beat. It was quiet and remote. Just like she feared.

Stop. Listen. Pick a path. Run. She needed to get moving.

After a short time, her poor attempt at running turned into walking, and then into stumbles as her body struggled through her fatigue. She was so damn thirsty, and she just wanted to sleep. Could she sit on the side of the road and wait for someone to drive by? Would it be safe?

In the distance, almost like a mirage, flashing lights started getting brighter. The sound of an engine came rumbling towards her and the familiar sting of tears gathered in the back of her eyes.

Please, stop and help me.

Waving her hands in front of her, she stepped out into the middle of the road. The darkness swallowed her field of vision, even as the lights got closer. As the car slowed in front of her, Daisy felt peace wash over her, and complete silence filled her mind as she fell to the road.

THIRTY-TWO

So many avenues searched, and not one damn result! Hank wanted answers, and he wanted them ten hours ago, when Daisy was first taken. But now, the hours moved faster than he thought possible, and dragged on forever at the same time.

Parking his truck in Daisy's driveway, his hand ran through his hair and over the stubble on his chin. A light breeze flitted through the fields outside the farmhouse as his feet hit the dirt. All at once, the gravity of everything slammed into him and he fell to his knees. With tears in his eyes, he prayed.

Lord, please let me find her. Please don't take this beautiful, kind soul away from me. I need her. My heart needs her.

He felt the strangest pull to look up. Moving his eyes from the dirt in front of him, he searched across his field of vision. Nothing seemed out of the ordinary as he looked over the barn, and the fields, the hens, and the small garden by the house. But when he got to the porch, he noticed a paper in the door's window pane that was not there a few hours before.

Jumping to his feet, he sprinted to the door, pulling the note away.

You should have chosen me, Hank. Now I'll make the choice for you.

Daisy's sunflower necklace laid broken on the floorboards of the porch.

Anna.

The investigators had already collected the small amount of evidence from Daisy's house, and everyone had cleared out from the property. Pulling the phone from his pocket, Hank called Deputy Williams, who he knew was still at the station. He'd made Heath officially in charge of finding Daisy, even though everything would still be run through him. When Daisy was found, he wouldn't give the bastard who took her a chance at having their case thrown out because he had a conflict of interest.

"Anna Hines has something to do with Daisy's disappearance." He held up the note that was left for him, even though no one was there to see it.

There was a deafening pause before Heath cleared his throat. "Your ex?"

"Yes."

"I thought you were going home to get some rest, Hank. Maybe you need to sleep for a bit, because what you just said makes no sense."

"Does any of this make sense, Heath? Does Daisy being threatened and then taken make any sense? I will not sleep until she's found, and I don't expect anyone else will either!"

"You're right, Hank. I'm sorry. Why are we pivoting to Anna?"

"I just got to Daisy's. There was a note stuck in her front door for me. There wasn't a name, but I know it was from Anna. We need to question her."

"We still haven't been able to locate Aaron. His mother was pretty adamant that he's been gone helping a friend, but that's a pretty weak alibi if you ask me. I didn't mention why I was looking for him, but I don't think she was lying. Do you want us to keep looking for him?"

"Of course we keep looking for him. He was the last person to see her other than Anna. I just don't know how they fit together. Could Aaron be working with Anna?"

"I mean, there has to be some connection. Nothing is making sense. But your relationship with Daisy could have motivated Anna to do something drastic. If there was jealousy, or if she wanted to get back together with you."

He was right. How did Anna and Aaron fit together? It wasn't just a coincidence that both people had visited Daisy that morning and now she was gone. Sure, Anna had been left in Daisy's dining room, but Hank knew there was something off about how she was acting. It was almost as if she had been wanting him to dote over her, instead of leaving to look for Daisy.

Then it hit him.

"I completely forgot, but I saw Anna and Aaron together a few days ago. I thought it was strange that they looked so cozy. Could they have been planning this together? What are the odds that they both show up to see Daisy on the same day?"

"Shit, Hank. Maybe you are onto something here."

"You know Daisy said she felt weird after having some tea." Hank walked into the house and headed straight to the kitchen. The tea was nowhere to be found. He shook his head, remembering he'd already shared this information hours ago, and the lab had taken the tea to run an analysis on it. "Did we get the analysis back on that yet?"

"Not yet. Where was Anna staying while in town? With her parents?" Deputy Williams asked.

"I'm sure, but there's no way she'd take Daisy there." Hank ran through all the possibilities.

"Is there anywhere you can think they'd take her then? Does the Callum family have property somewhere?"

"Not that I know of. We'll need to run a search. But, you know, Anna's family does have a small hunting cabin in Granger. We went up there a lot when we were engaged."

"I'll call up to the Granger Police Department and have them head out to the cabin, just to be safe."

"It just doesn't feel right to me. I don't think they'd try to take her far. She'd want to be close by."

"Let's run the Callums through the search engine and see if we pick up anything while Granger PD checks out the cabin."

"I'm heading over to see if Aaron's gone home. I want eyes on him at all times if we find him. And someone needs to locate Anna. Bring her in for questioning."

It took him all of three minutes to drive from Daisy's farm to the Callum house, and another twenty seconds to walk up to the front door. Time was of the essence, and Hank was keeping track so he could apologize to Daisy for each and every one of the seconds she'd been gone.

Hank banged on the door. It was nearly three in the morning and he was sure Mrs. Callum wouldn't appreciate being woken up so abruptly, but he prayed she had some answers. Mainly, where Aaron was.

A light on the front porch illuminated, temporarily blinding Hank. Blinking rapidly to force his eyes to adjust faster, he heard the deadbolt lock flip and the door slowly opened.

"Sheriff Porter. What in the world is going on? Is everything okay?"

"Mrs. Callum, is Aaron home right now? I need to speak with him urgently."

"Oh, no. I'm sorry, Hank. He's not home right now." The elderly woman looked scared, the bruises from her fall now varying degrees of deep purple.

"Would it be okay for me to come in for a moment? I just have a few questions I need to ask you and I know you've been recovering the past few days from a spill. I think it would be better if we chatted somewhere you'd be comfortable."

"Of course. Come on in." Mrs. Callum slowly walked towards the couch and then gestured for Hank to sit. "Can I get you anything to drink?"

"No, Ma'am. Thank you, though."

"So, what questions do you have for me?"

"I don't want to keep you, and I understand I've woken you in the middle of the night, but I promise this is very important. Do you have any idea where he may have gone?"

"As I told that deputy before, Aaron told me he was heading out to help a friend in Colcet County, and that reception would be spotty on his ranch."

"So, you didn't send him to check in on Daisy yesterday with some loose leaf tea?"

"What? No. I would have loved to, but no. He was already on his way to his friend's place. How is Daisy doing, by the way? Aaron told me it was a terrible allergic reaction, the poor dear. Is she doing alright?"

"She's actually the reason I'm here, Mrs. Callum. Daisy was abducted from her home yesterday. I was on the phone with her when it happened."

Mrs. Callum inhaled sharply, her pale skin draining of all color.

"Oh, my lord. Do you think someone took Aaron as well? Is that why you're trying to find him?"

"No ma'am. I am sorry to say this, but I think your son had something to do with her disappearance."

Mrs. Callum let out a surprised gasp. "Why would you think that? He always seemed so smitten with her."

"That's the piece I'm missing. That tea I asked about earlier? Aaron gave some to Daisy, saying you sent it over to help calm her nerves. I believe he laced it with something that knocked her out. I was on the phone with her when she started experiencing symptoms and she told me she had just finished drinking the tea. So you can see why I have some suspicions about Aaron." The poor woman put her hand to her chest in clear emotional distress over his accusations. He didn't care, he had to press on. "Can you think of any reason he would do this? Or any place he would have taken her to if he wasn't being truthful about seeing a friend?"

"I can't think of a single thing. Pat and Joe were always such wonderful neighbors to us. Did you know they promised me Aaron would have priority on purchasing the land if Daisy didn't want it? They were going to give my baby a chance at having his own farm."

"What?"

"Well, yes. A few years before they passed, I was speaking to them about how Daniel, as my oldest, was going to inherit this place. I don't completely agree, but my husband had wanted it that way, and so I want to make sure his wishes are met. That meant Aaron wouldn't have a place for himself. Pat and Joe understood how hard Aaron had worked to keep our family legacy going and told me if Daisy sold the farm, they would make sure that she knew my Aaron had to be considered for the purchase of the land and house before anyone else."

There it was. The motive Hank had been struggling to understand. When Daisy came back and stayed on her family's farm, she stopped Aaron from being able to purchase it. What sort of psychopath hurts a twenty-five-year-old woman for that decision? He needed to figure out where Aaron had taken Daisy, and fast.

"Does your family have property anywhere else, Mrs. Callum?"

"Well, my husband had an old hunting cabin on the west end of Clarence County, but Aaron wouldn't be interested in inheriting that. It's very remote and isn't cleared for farming."

"I'm going to need the address, Mrs. Callum. As fast as you can."

Three minutes later, Hank raced to his truck. Siren and flashing lights went on and he pressed the gas pedal to the floor. It was late. He doubted too many people would be out on the roads he was about to travel on anyway, but if they were, the siren and lights would alert them to his speed.

Hold on Daisy, please. I'm so close, sunshine. He prayed she could feel him getting closer, that somehow she knew he was coming for her.

The road that led to the Callum's property was winding and deserted. He hadn't seen a cabin or house for at least five miles. When he was just a few short miles away, Hank turned through one particularly steep curve and slammed on his brakes.

Fuck. What was he seeing? Was she really standing right there in the middle of the road?

Throwing the truck into park, Hank pushed open the door. Before he could even reach her, he watched as she crumbled to the pavement.

"Daisy?" His heart slammed in his chest as he scooped her up from the ground. "Sunshine, can you hear me? Open those beautiful blue eyes for me." The headlights from his vehicle illuminated her body, grotesquely highlighting how hard she'd fought to survive. Blood congealed on her face, surrounded by an angry blue and purple bruise at her temple. Her skin was freezing cold, entirely exposed except for her bra and under-wear, and her feet were dirty and cut.

He needed to decide whether to call in for an ambulance or take her into the hospital himself, but Hank knew that waiting on an ambulance meant more time exposed where Aaron or Anna could find them. In that moment, he knew what his decision had to be.

Pulling Daisy closer to his chest, he stood, bringing her to the truck. He laid her in the passenger seat, wishing he could hold her close. Instead, he ran around the front and buckled in, driving just as fast as he had to find her, now heading towards the hospital.

"Hank, what's going on? Any update on Daisy?" Jake answered his phone on the second ring.

"I've got her, Jake. I found her, but she's unconscious and injured. She feels hypothermic to me, and I'm driving as fast as I can to get her to the hospital." He heard the tears in his own voice and tried to push down the fear that she wouldn't wake up.

"Hank, breathe. You've got her and I'm already running around getting ready to head in. I'll be there in ten minutes, fifteen tops."

"Thank you, Jake."

"Of course. Get there safely and we'll take care of her."

The next fifteen minutes went by in a blur. Hank pulled up to the emergency room entrance, barely slowing down before he fully stopped. Scooping Daisy up out of the seat, he ran into the hospital yelling for help. Jake appeared from a room and immediately directed Hank to set Daisy down on the bed.

Hank stepped back, but not completely out of the room as Jake started evaluating her. At some point, a nurse tried to usher him from the room, but he'd nearly bit her head off at the suggestion and Jake had forced him to sit down in the corner. He should probably apologize to the nurse, but his focus was solely on Daisy and why she hadn't woken.

Nurses drew vials of blood and started an IV. They draped blankets over her still form as they cleaned her cuts. All the while, Hank prayed for her to wake.

"Hank, you can come sit closer now." Jake clasped his hand on Hank's shoulder.

"Is she going to be okay?"

"Right now, I'm mainly concerned about the extent of the bruising around her throat and the hit she clearly took to her head. Since she had a concussion recently, the likelihood of a recurrent concussion causing an issue is something we need to take into consideration. Sit with her. Let her know she's safe, and that you found her."

"You didn't answer my question."

"Daisy is tough. I mean, she puts up with you, so she has to be. I'll have more answers soon."

"I know. Thanks for everything, buddy. I appreciate you being here."

Jake left the room as Hank picked up Daisy's hand, willing the warmth from his touch to weave its way into her heart and wake her. She looked so small, so fragile laying there. She needed him to keep her safe, and he had failed. How would he ever live knowing they hurt her because he failed her so completely?

His phone vibrated in his pocket for what seemed like the millionth time. As much as he didn't want to take his eyes off of Daisy, he knew the people who loved her as much as he did deserved to know what was going on. He sent off a group text with a quick update and turned his phone to silent.

Laying his head against her hip, Hank closed his eyes, welcoming the relief that flooded his body, knowing she was there beside him.

Thirty-Three

Slowly, Daisy drifted out of the darkest fog. There was a noise, rhythmic and sharp, but she couldn't place it. Why did her body feel like it was being swallowed up by quicksand? She couldn't move if she wanted to.

The rhythm of the beeping, yes, what she was hearing was beeping, picked up as her panic swelled. Was she hooked up to some sort of machine? Was she at the hospital?

Memories from the last twenty-four hours rushed into her mind as she fought to wake up. Feeling sick and disoriented before someone came into her house and pulled her from her hiding spot. Waking up in Aaron's cabin. Watching him shoot Anna. Fighting with every ounce of strength she had to make it back to Hank. Hank!

As if summoned by her thoughts, a warm hand slid over hers. "Daisy, you're safe. It's over, sunshine. Just rest."

She felt the sting of hot tears slipping down her swollen and tender face. "Don't cry, sweetheart. I'm here. You're going to be okay. Try to go back to sleep. You need to rest."

"Hank?" A small, hoarse voice pulled him from his guilt laced dreams as the sharp sunbeams of midday trickled into the hospital room. His eyes flew to hers. The relief of being met with her beautiful blue eyes sparkling back at him was overwhelming.

"Shhh, Daisy. You're okay. Don't talk." He placed his hand on her head and pushed her hair back. She smiled and leaned into the warmth, and his heart shattered with the love he felt for this woman.

"How did you find me?" She licked her dry lips, and Hank immediately brought a small cup of water to her mouth.

"Drink. Just a little."

She winced as she swallowed, the sight immediately twisting Hank's stomach.

"My throat."

"I know sunshine. I'm so sorry. There's a lot of swelling and bruising, so try not to talk. The doctor doesn't think there will be any permanent damage to your vocal cords, which is good news."

She gently nodded.

As he placed the cup back on the side table, Hank set out to answer her questions.

"I had a hunch about Aaron. Mrs. Callum told me about her husband's hunting cabin and I drove out there. You were standing in the middle of the road and then you collapsed." A tear rolled down his cheek as he remembered the sight of her and the relief of knowing he'd been able to find her. "I didn't figure it out fast enough, Daisy. I'm so sorry."

"Did I kill him?" Tears fell from her eyes.

"Shhh. No, he isn't dead, as much as I wish he was. My deputies got to the cabin and arrested him. He was in surgery the last time I heard an update, but he'll never be able to hurt you again. If he lives, which the doctor said is likely, he'll be in jail for a very long time."

"Anna—"

"Please, Daisy. Rest. You don't have to tell me about it right now. There's plenty of time. Just rest."

Daisy held her hand to her throat, then moved her body to one side of the bed. Her large, moon shaped eyes begged him to slide into bed as she patted the space next to her.

"I'm not sure that's smart. You're pretty banged up. I don't want to hurt you more."

"Please," her raw voice begged. "I need you. To feel safe."

How could he deny her that? As gently as he could, and once he'd kicked off his shoes, he settled his body next to hers. His arms lay stiff next to his body. Should he reach out for her? Would she be in pain if he wrapped her up in his arms?

Luckily, he didn't have to overthink things for long. As soon as he was still, Daisy rolled onto his chest, her arm draped across his stomach. He heard her breath him in as she relaxed into his side. A few moments later, she was back asleep.

———

"Hank." A soft hand fell on his shoulder and shook him awake. "Hank."

"Kara? What are you doing here?" He looked down at Daisy, still asleep in his arms.

"I came as soon as I got your text message. There are a bunch of people out in the waiting room for her, too."

"You didn't have to come. I would have called to let you know how everything was going."

"She's family, Hank. You love her, so I love her too."

A lump formed in Hank's throat.

"I do love her. I was so scared, Kara. But she fought like hell to get back to me. I'll never leave her side again."

"I know." Kara grabbed Hank's hand and squeezed. "How are you holding up? Do you need anything?"

"I'm fine. As long as she's here in my arms, and I can feel her breathing, nothing else matters."

He wasn't fine. He didn't know how to calm the raging anger that was boiling inside of him. All he could think about was the fact that he'd almost lost her. It didn't help that Aaron was in the hospital, just two floors below them. Hank had been clear when he spoke with Heath that two deputies were to be assigned to Aaron's room at all times until he was healthy enough to be transferred to the jail. He wouldn't take any chances that Daisy would have to see him before they released her.

And the anger wasn't just for Aaron. He was fucking outraged at his failure. And that's what it had been, a failure. He didn't keep her safe. Her body would heal, and for that he felt relief, but what about her spirit? She'd already been through so much. Would she have room in her heart to forgive him for not being there when she needed him the most? The fear that she wouldn't want to be with him after all she'd been through shot a searing pain around his chest.

"I can see you aren't okay."

"How am I supposed to be? I should have been there. If I hadn't gone in to work to deal with stuff that I could have delegated, none of this would have happened." He spoke barely above a whisper.

"Hank. He would have just been waiting for the next time you left."

"We were going to go away. Let things settle and see if the investigation could find new leads. Daisy was packing to leave when Anna stopped over and all this started. Would she even have suffered as much if Anna wasn't involved? I'm to blame for the cuts and bruises just as much as anyone else."

Tears choked him, and his emotions wouldn't settle. He forced himself to breathe, but it barely helped with the ache in his chest.

"I can't believe that bitch was helping him. She was almost family. How could she not know that what she was doing would destroy any connection you two ever had? I don't like to speak ill of the dead, but I'm glad she's gone. And I wish Aaron was six feet under, too."

"Her parents told one of my deputies she'd been struggling lately. Apparently, she had some reckless behavior that bled back into her job. They fired her a month ago. Her parents didn't know where she was until about ten days ago, when she showed up at their house in a manic state. They tried to help her. I can't help but feel for them."

"You are the most honorable man I know, and I'm not just saying that because you are my brother. You've taken care of Daisy, helped her so much over these past few weeks. I know you love her, but Hank, this is not your fault, and you shouldn't take on all that guilt."

Her words were nice, but they didn't register in his mind. Instead, he held on to his pain.

"Has anyone said how long she'll have to stay?" Kara's question pulled him from his thoughts. "Emma is trying to get in here to see her, but I said she'd probably be out of it for a day or two and we should let her rest."

"Thank you for that, Kara. They want to monitor her for at least another day, but she's doing really well, considering. When I get her home, I swear I'm going to bubble wrap her and make her stay in bed for a month."

"I'd rather be naked and wrapped in your arms." Daisy shifted and groaned, and his brain had to force his heart not to read too much into her words. She was still groggy from the pain medicine, not fully aware of what she was saying.

"Oh man, Hank. You are going to have your hands full with this one. I love it." Kara laughed.

"Hi, Kara."

"Hey, girl. You look like you've been through hell."

"Kara!" Hank bellowed, shrinking back when he felt Daisy flinch.

Daisy just smiled, or rather, gave her best attempt with all the swelling and bruising on her face. He felt her pressing harder into his chest and tightened his arms slightly to remind her she was safe.

"Yeah, but I gave them hell, too." Her voice was still raw, and he reached for the plastic cup of water to offer her a drink.

"That-a-girl," Kara winked. "I'll leave you two alone and let everyone know that she's doing well, but not up for visitors right now." Hank nodded in approval of his sister's assessment. "Daisy, honestly, I'm so happy you are okay. You just call or text anytime you need help keeping my brother in line. I'll be over in a heartbeat to kick his ass if he steps out of line."

There was a moment of silence as they waited for Kara to leave. When the door shut, and they were back to being alone, Hank closed his eyes and gently pulled Daisy closer. He felt the warmth of her hand on his face, his eyes springing open in surprise. Their eyes met, and she moved her head up to kiss him. He couldn't let that happen. Not until he'd apologized and begged for her forgiveness.

"Hank?" He didn't miss the edge of emotion in it as she questioned why he pulled back from her.

"I need to say something, Daisy. I need to say it now before I realize I'm too weak of a man and give myself an out."

"Whatever it is, it's nothing we can't get through together."

"I need to apologize."

She didn't say anything. Instead, she let her eyes close, breathed in deeply, and shook her head.

"Please don't say anything. I need to get this off my chest before you decide if you want me to stay or if it would be better for me to go." He cleared his throat, already trying to push away any emotion that might bubble over and stop him from continuing. "I wasn't there to keep you safe. I wasn't there to stop them from taking you, and I wasn't there to stop them from hurting you. I wasn't even there to rescue you from them. You had to go through all of that by yourself and I'll understand if you can never look at me the same as you did before. I'll understand if you don't want to be with me anymore."

"Hank -"

"I mean it, Daisy. I failed you. I've never been more ashamed of anything before. And watching you here, in this hospital bed, when I should have been able to stop it all, I'll never forgive myself for the things you've had to endure."

"Hank-"

"I'm the fucking sheriff for crying out loud. I should have been able to figure out who it was before they got their hands on you. Daisy..." His hands rested on both sides of her face. "I understand if you never want to see me again. It will kill me, but I'll make sure you never have to be around me again, if that's what you need."

Daisy's hands reached up and gently moved Hank's from her face.

"Is that everything you wanted to say?"

He searched her eyes, trying to see some sign of how she was feeling after he laid everything on the table.

"Yes. That's all I wanted to say."

"Good. So now, I'm going to say something, and I want you to listen to me."

She waited, and he slowly gave her a nod.

"I don't want to spend a single second away from you. Not one. I don't blame you for any of this. It's Aaron and Anna who I blame."

She licked her lips, squeezing his hand tight in hers. "I love you, Hank. You're stuck with me. Now, kiss me and help me start my recovery."

Daisy had been in the hospital for three days. She was finally being released, and it wasn't a moment too soon. Sure, she was sore. She would be for a few more weeks. And the headaches would continue during that time too, maybe even longer. But there would be no complaints from her.

"Are you sure you're ready to go? You are looking a little flushed. Maybe we should stay another night, just to be sure everything's okay."

"Hank, I love you so much, but I need to get out of here. I'm ready." She reached out for his hand, smiling as he walked over and laced his fingers with hers. "And besides, I know Jake told you to call if you had any concerns. Poor guy will not get any rest if I know you."

Hank's laugh filled the room.

"You're probably right. But I'll try to control myself."

He kissed the top of her head and released her hand, ready to pack up the last of her items. He'd already taken out the flowers and balloons that had been dropped off over the last few days from all their friends.

A shiver ran through her as thoughts about returning home flooded her mind. Sam had been over to the farm watching after Maisie, Minnie, and her chickens. He assured her everything was going fine, and he promised he'd continue to check in on them while she recovered, so Hank could mainly focus on her. Emma mentioned stopping out there to clean and put everything back in order when she'd stopped in to visit. Her friends were still stunned by Aaron's actions, but everyone had come together to make her return home as smooth as possible.

As hard as she tried, she just couldn't hide the fact that she was feeling apprehensive about seeing the farm. Her hands rubbed together as the anxiety took hold. Hank crouched down, gently pulling her hands apart.

"It's okay to be nervous. And it's okay if you don't feel ready to go back there right now. We can always spend some time at my house if you're not ready."

"I appreciate that, but I won't let him win. I'm ready to go make that vision you had of me, barefoot and pregnant on the front porch, a reality."

A growl hummed in his chest, and she had to work hard to suppress a laugh. Hank sank into the bed next to her, wrapping his arms around her back.

"Don't tempt me, sunshine," he whispered. "You need to rest. Everything else will come when it's meant to."

"Including me?" She wiggled her eyebrows as best as she could. His laugh was a balm for her nerves.

"Yes. Including you, honey."

"God, I can't wait."

"What do you say? Are you ready to head out and enjoy the rest of forever together?"

THIRTY-FOUR

"Good morning, beautiful." Hank's scratchy morning voice stirred Daisy from her twilight sleep. She had been having the sweetest dream about her upcoming wedding day. Looking down at the ring on her finger, her heart fluttered with all the possibilities her future held.

It had been two weeks since they had released her from the hospital. And two weeks since Hank had proposed to her on the front porch before they'd even walked inside. He'd clearly had some help with the setup. Dozens of vases filled with sunflowers covered the porch and took her breath away before she even saw him down on one knee.

It was the easiest decision of her life to say yes. And the most perfect moment for him to ask, too. When she walked into the house, she didn't see the table where she'd had the tainted tea, or the stairs where she'd been dragged down by a masked figure. No. She saw the living room where she would dance with Hank after stressful days. And the kitchen where she would cook all their family meals. She saw the bedroom where Hank stayed all those weeks ago, that they would turn into a nursery for their babies in the future.

She had physical scars that would always remind her of everything that had happened there, but she wouldn't let the mental scars stop her from loving the house that was her family's forever home.

"Mmm. Good morning."

"You were smiling in your sleep."

"That's because I was dreaming of you. Or maybe I'm still dreaming now. If that's the case, don't you dare wake me up."

"I think this is real life, sunshine. Wait, let me check." He quickly pinched Daisy's bottom, eliciting a little small yip from her and a quick swat of his hand.

"Well, I'm definitely awake," she giggled. "I need to call Grace. I've been putting it off, but she deserves to know what happened to our grandparents, and I've been wanting to tell her our exciting news." Daisy stretched in the morning sunlight. In the time since Aaron and Anna had taken her, her body had mostly healed. Just her headaches and the occasional bout of dizziness lingered, but Hank hadn't left her alone for a single minute, and she felt so safe wrapped up in his arms.

Hank reached his arm around her and pulled her close to his chest.

"Sounds like a great thing to do after breakfast."

"Oh, and what is on the menu this morning, Sheriff?"

"You." A smirk grew across his face as he buried a kiss into Daisy's neck.

"Hank!" She laughed as his beard tickled her skin. "Now, now, handsome, good things come to those who wait." Daisy quickly slipped out of his embrace and grabbed her phone off the nightstand beside her. Giving Hank a quick wink, she slipped out of the bedroom, closing the door behind her.

Her hands shook nervously as she held the phone. Daisy

had always looked up to her cousin, and she was anxious about sharing all the details of what she'd gone through.

"Hello?" A quiet, small voice came onto the line. For a moment, it confused her. Grace was no shy wallflower. In fact, she had always been so lively, vibrant...and loud.

"Grace? Hi, it's Daisy. I hope I'm not calling at a bad time?"

"Oh, no...it's fine. I'm just in the bathroom and don't want to wake up my boyfriend."

Heat flushed Daisy's face.

"Sorry, I guess I forget fancy Miami people probably don't wake up at the crack of dawn like farmers do."

"It's fine. We just had a...busy night. I can't talk for long, Daisy. I don't want Carter to wake up and see that I'm not there."

Was that fear in her voice?

"Oh, I understand. I won't take up much time. I just wanted to call and let you know I learned something about Grandma Pat and Grandpa Joe's accident. You deserve to know."

"Okay."

"It wasn't just an accident. Someone planned out the whole thing. Someone took their lives on purpose."

"Oh, Daisy. Do they know who did it?"

She pushed down the emotions that were rising in her throat, strangling her breath, and cutting out her voice.

"Do you remember the Callums? They own the property next to Grandma and Grandpa's land."

"The name sounds familiar. Wasn't one of their boys around my age? Adam?"

"Aaron. Yes. He's the one who did it."

Daisy heard Grace inhale sharply.

"Grace? Are you okay?"

"I'm just shocked, Daisy. Did he say why he did it?"

"He...well, he wanted their land. Apparently, when I moved off to college and then stayed in the city, Grandma and Grandpa didn't think I'd be coming back. They promised Mrs. Callum that if the land went up for sale after they passed one day, that they would make sure Aaron was given the chance to buy it first. Aaron thought it was taking too long for him to get his land."

"But they left the land to you in their will."

"Yes, but they did so I could sell it and split the money between you and me. When I called you and we talked it over, and I stayed, that threw a major wrench into Aaron's plans. He pretended to be my friend for this whole time, Grace. And he wasn't. Not even close." Daisy shuddered, not wanting to relive everything she'd been through. She'd tell her cousin one day, but that day was not today. Besides, she really just wanted to share the happy news of her engagement. To focus on the good instead of the fear that followed her now.

"Are you okay?"

"I'm fine. It's all good now. But there's still a lot more to the story."

"Daisy, I can hear Carter getting up. I need to go. Thank you for calling me. I love you."

Before Daisy could tell her cousin about her engagement or even say she loved her too, the line went dead.

Walking back to the room at the end of the hall, Daisy couldn't help but laugh at the sight of Hank still in bed, smiling back at her.

"How'd the call go?"

He held out his hand, urging her to rejoin him in bed.

"Good. She sounded off, though, not her usual spunky self. And she hung up the call really abruptly. I just hope everything's okay."

"I'm sure it is. You can always try giving her another call later. It is still pretty early for the rest of the world."

"Meanwhile, I feel lazy lounging in bed."

"Well, get used to it. Because I plan to keep you here all day...and night."

Daisy laughed as she snuggled closer to Hank.

"I love you, Sheriff."

"I love you too, sunshine."

———

"Who was that on the phone?" Carter asked as Grace walked back into the room.

Fear shot through Grace, her legs immediately feeling weak beneath her.

"Sorry. I thought it might be the doctor's office calling with some of my test results from last week. It ended up being just a telemarketer. I didn't want to wake you."

Grace watched the shadows creep into his eyes.

"You know you are not allowed to answer the phone when I'm not present. Hand it over."

When Grace hesitated, Carter lunged from his spot on their bed and gripped her wrist tightly.

"Ow, that hurts."

"Like I give a shit, Grace. Give it to me, now. Or don't you want me to see who you were really talking to? The person you're sleeping with behind my back? Maybe he's the father of that bastard baby in your belly."

It would have been shocking to Grace to hear those words coming from Carter, but this wasn't the first time he'd expressed those thoughts. In fact, she waited for the hit to her face that would normally accompany the accusations. When it didn't happen, she looked up, realizing she was cowering in fear. She had dropped to her knees, covering her baby, who was now large in her belly, with her arms.

"I-I'm not sleeping with anyone else, Carter. I don't know how many times I have to say it."

"Shut up, Grace. And give me that fucking phone!" His rage was on full display as he yanked the phone from her hands, throwing it to the floor time and time again, until parts were falling from it and the screen was smashed beyond repair.

"And don't think you'll be getting another one anytime soon. You have given me no reason to trust you, Grace. This is on you."

"I'm sorry." The words were thick in her throat, and nausea rolled through her body. "I n-need a way for the doctor's office to reach me, Carter. You know they put me on modified bed rest because of my blood pressure."

"They can contact me with your results. And you can tell the guard here at the penthouse if you need to contact them. They'll call the office for you after checking with me."

He turned to her. "Don't forget that we have the fundraising gala tonight for the survivors of domestic abuse. I'll be expecting you dressed and ready to go by six."

Well, if that wasn't the universe's own perverse brand of irony. In the past, she had been in awe of Carter's philanthropic endeavors, and the domestic abuse fundraiser his real estate development firm sponsored had always been a highlight of that. But now that she herself was part of that statistic, now that she was stuck in an abusive relationship, she wanted to vomit at the thought of people praising Carter at the event.

"I'm on bed rest. I can't leave the apartment. I can't be on my feet all night. Something might happen to the baby."

Carter stomped back across the room, pinning her arms by her sides and pressing her body against the wall. His mouth rested on her ear as his hot breath spewed his final round of venom at her.

"The baby, the baby...it's always about the fucking baby,

isn't it, Grace? Well, guess what? I don't give a fuck about the baby. If it was up to me, you'd have taken care of the problem the same night you told me about it. I don't want to be tied down like that. But you've forced me to play the part of the doting soon-to-be dad, and tonight is another chance for me to show what a powerhouse I actually am to those around me. It's finally time for something to be about me, Grace. You owe this to me. For all the misery you've put me through with this pregnancy. You better not do anything to fuck it up."

As Carter walked from the room, Grace had two thoughts: *Thank God he didn't hit me* and *please let me get back safely to Bell Ridge.*

Curious about how Grace finds her way to Clarence County and the hometown hero she's hoping to have a second chance with? Be sure to read Grace's story in Jackson (Men of Clarence County Book Two).

Also by Tilly H. Colson

MEN OF CLARENCE COUNTY:

Hank

Jackson

Sebastian

Johnathan

Samuel

SILVER SPRINGS SERIES:

Silver Linings

Silver Secrets

Silver Sanctuary

Silver Shadows

Silver Sunrise

SILVER RIDGE RANCH:

Blue Norther

Sudden Summer

Derecho

Firestorm